CORNERED.

Alex was suddenly aware that something had changed. It took him a few seconds to realize what it was and at once he felt the hairs on the back of his neck bristle and stand on end.

What he had taken to be a tiger-skin rug had just stood up.

It was a tiger, alive and angry.

A white Siberian tiger.

The creature stretched itself. Alex saw the perfect muscles rippling behind the thick fur. He tried to move but found he couldn't. He wondered what had happened to him, then realized. He was terrified. Rooted to the spot. He was just ten steps away from an animal that had, for centuries, inspired dread across three continents.

The tiger growled. It was a low, rumbling noise, somehow more terrible than anything Alex had ever heard. He tried to find the strength to move, to put something between the two of them. But there was nothing.

The tiger took a step forward. It was preparing to leap. Its eyes darkened. Its jaw hung open, revealing the two lines of white dagger teeth. It growled a second time, louder, more continuous.

Then it leaped.

>—<

BOOKS BY ANTHONY HOROWITZ

The Devil and His Boy

THE ALEX RIDER ADVENTURES:
Stormbreaker
Point Blank
Skeleton Key
Eagle Strike
Scorpia
Ark Angel

THE DIAMOND BROTHERS MYSTERIES:
Public Enemy Number Two
The Falcon's Malteser
Three of Diamonds
South by Southeast

SCORPIA

AN ALEX RIDER ADVENTURE

ANTHONY HOROWITZ

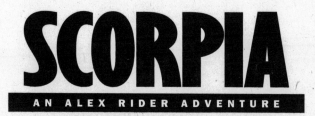

speak

An Imprint of Penguin Group (USA) Inc.

SPEAK

Published by the Penguin Group

Penguin Group (USA) Inc., 345 Hudson Street, New York, New York 10014, U.S.A.

Penguin Group (Canada), 90 Eglinton Avenue East, Suite 700, Toronto, Ontario, Canada M4P 2
(a division of Pearson Penguin Canada Inc.)

Penguin Books Ltd, 80 Strand, London WC2R 0RL, England

Penguin Ireland, 25 St Stephen's Green, Dublin 2, Ireland (a division of Penguin Books Ltd)

Penguin Group (Australia), 250 Camberwell Road, Camberwell, Victoria 3124, Australia
(a division of Pearson Australia Group Pty Ltd)

Penguin Books India Pvt Ltd, 11 Community Centre, Panchsheel Park, New Delhi - 110 017, Ind

Penguin Group (NZ), Cnr Airborne and Rosedale Roads, Albany, Auckland 1310,New Zealand
(a division of Pearson New Zealand Ltd)

Penguin Books (South Africa) (Pty) Ltd, 24 Sturdee Avenue, Rosebank, Johannesburg 2196, South Afr

Registered Offices: Penguin Books Ltd, 80 Strand, London WC2R 0RL, England

First published in the United States of America by Philomel Books,
a division of Penguin Young Readers Group, 2005

Published in Great Britain in 2004 by Walker Books Ltd., London

Published by Speak, an imprint of Penguin Group (USA) Inc., 2006

1 3 5 7 9 10 8 6 4 2

Copyright © Anthony Horowitz, 2004

THE LIBRARY OF CONGRESS HAS CATALOGED THE PHILOMEL EDITION AS FOLLOWS:

Horowitz, Anthony, 1955–
Scorpia / Anthony Horowitz.—1st American ed. p. cm.— (An Alex Rider adventure)
Summary: After being told that his father was an assassin for a criminal organization,
fourteen-year-old Alex goes to Italy to find out more and becomes involved in a plan
to kill thousands of English schoolchildren.
[1. Spies—Fiction. 2. Terrorism—Fiction. 3. Orphans—Fiction. 4. Italy—Fiction.
5. London (England)—Fiction. 6. England—Fiction] I. Title.
PZ7.H7875Sc 2005 [Fic]—dc2 2004009089
ISBN 0-399-24151-5 (hc)

Speak ISBN 0-14-240578-7

Printed in the United States of America

For
MAGGIE NOACH

CONTENTS

1   INVISIBLE SWORD   1

2   SCIPPATORI   16

3   THE WIDOW'S PALACE   26

4   BY INVITATION ONLY   42

5   FLOOD TIDE   60

6   THOUGHTS ON A TRAIN   78

7   CONSANTO   93

8   DESIGNER LABELS   118

9   ALBERT BRIDGE   138

10   HOW TO KILL   157

11   THE BELL TOWER   177

12   "DEAR PRIME MINISTER . . ."   197

13   PIZZA DELIVERY   221

14   COBRA   246

15   REMOTE CONTROL   264

16   DEADLINE   283

17   THE CHURCH OF FORGOTTEN SAINTS   299

18   HIGH RESOLUTION   327

19   DEEP COVER   359

20   A MOTHER'S TOUCH   381

"Go to Venice. Find Scorpia.
And you will find your destiny . . ."

—*Yassen Gregorovich*

1

INVISIBLE SWORD

THE ROOM HAD NO WINDOWS, and that in itself was strange as it was situated in one of the most beautiful cities in the world. If someone had thought to cut through the soundproofed panels, the reinforced steel walls, and the complicated circuitry designed to prevent any form of outside surveillance, they would have found themselves looking at the Grand Canal with the churches and palaces of Venice, Italy, stretching into the distance.

But windows were a security risk—and anyway, the people who met here had no interest in beauty. The room's only door was sealed with a seven-figure security code and two guards, both armed with German-made Heckler and Koch 9mm machine guns, stood impassively in their dark suits, one on either side. A narrow corridor with a plush, gold-colored carpet led to an elevator at the end. It had been a few minutes since the last person—a woman—had appeared behind the sliding doors. She had walked along the corridor past the guards without so much as a glance and they had been careful not to catch her eye. She was wearing X by Clive Christian, one of the most expensive perfumes in the world. The scent had lingered in the air for a moment and then it was gone as the door closed softly behind her.

Julia Charlotte Glennis Rothman had arrived.

She sat at the head of a highly polished conference table—cut from a type of tree that was now extinct—and briefly surveyed the men who had gathered here.

There were eight of them. The oldest, bold and wheezy with sore eyes, was about seventy, wearing a crumpled gray suit. The man next to him was Chinese, while the man opposite, fair-haired with an open-neck shirt, was from Australia. It was clear that the people who had congregated in this place came from many different parts of the world, but they had one thing in common; a stillness, a coldness even, that made the room as cheerful as a morgue. Not one of them greeted Mrs. Rothman as she took her seat. Nor did they bother looking at the time. If she had arrived, it must be exactly one o'clock. That was when the meeting was meant to begin.

"Good afternoon," Mrs. Rothman said.

A few heads nodded, but nobody spoke. Greetings were a waste of words.

The nine people sitting around the table made up the executive board of one of the most ruthless and successful criminal organizations in the world. The old man's name was Max Grendel. The Chinese man was Dr. Three. The Australian had many names but seldom used any of them. They had come to this room without windows to go over the final details of an operation that would, in just a few weeks, make them richer by the sum of one hundred million dollars.

The organization was called Scorpia.

It was a fanciful name, they all knew it, invented by someone who had probably read too much James Bond. But they had to call themselves something and in the end they had chosen a name drawn from their four main fields of activity.

Sabotage. Corruption. Intelligence. Assassination.

Scorpia. A name that worked in a surprising number of languages and that rolled off the tongue of anyone who might wish to employ them. Scorpia. Seven letters that were now on the database of every police force and security agency in the world.

The organization was formed in the early eighties, at the end of the so-called Cold War, the secret war that had been fought for decades between Russia, China, America, and Europe. Every government in the world had its own army of spies and assassins . . . all of them prepared to kill, or to die for their country. What they weren't prepared to do, though, was to find themselves out of work. And with the end of the Cold War, a number of them saw that was exactly what they would soon be. They weren't needed anymore. It was time to go into business for themselves.

They came together one Sunday morning in Paris. Their first meeting took place at the Maison Berthillon, a famous ice cream parlor on the Ile Saint-Louis, not far from Notre Dame. They all knew each other. They had tried to kill each other often enough. But now, in the pretty, wood-paneled room with its antique mirrors and lace curtains, and over twelve dishes of Berthillon's famous wild strawberry ice cream, they discussed how they might work together and make themselves rich. At this meeting, Scorpia was born.

Since then it had flourished. Scorpia was all over the world. It had brought down two governments and arranged for a third to be elected unfairly. It had destroyed dozens of businesses, corrupted politicians and civil servants, engineered several major ecological disasters, and killed anyone who got in its way. It was now responsible for one-tenth of the world's terrorism, which it undertook on a contract basis. Scorpia liked to think of itself as the Microsoft of crime—but in fact, compared to Scorpia, Microsoft was strictly small-time.

There had once been twelve executives. Only nine were left. One had died of cancer. Two had been murdered. But that wasn't a bad record after twenty years of violent crime. There had never been a single leader of Scorpia. All nine were equal partners, but one executive would be assigned to each new project, working in alphabetical order.

The project they were discussing this afternoon had been given a code name: Invisible Sword. Julia Rothman was in command.

"I would like to report to the committee that everything is progressing on schedule," she began.

There was a trace of a Welsh accent in her voice. She had in fact been born in Aberystwyth, Wales. Her parents had been Welsh nationalists, burning down the cottages of English vacationers who had bought them as second homes. Unfortunately, they burned one of these cottages with the English family still inside it, and when Julia was six, she found herself in an institution while her parents began life sentences in jail. This was, in a way, the start of her own criminal career.

"It is now three months," she went on, "since we were approached by our client, a gentleman in the Middle East. To call him rich would be an understatement. He is a multibillionaire. This man has looked at the world, at the balance of power, and he has decided that something has gone seriously wrong. He has asked us to remedy it.

"In a nutshell, our client believes that the West has become too powerful. He looks at Great Britain and the United States. It was the friendship between them that won the Second World War. And it is this same friendship that now allows the West to invade any country that it pleases and to take anything it wants. Our client has asked us to end the Anglo-American alliance once and for all.

"What can I tell you about our client?" Mrs. Rothman smiled sweetly. "Perhaps he is a visionary, interested only in world peace. Perhaps he is completely insane. Either way, it doesn't make any difference to us. He has offered us an enormous sum of money— one hundred million dollars, to be exact—to do what he wants. To humble Britain and the United States and to ensure they cease to work together as a world power. And I am happy to be able to tell you that twenty million dollars, the first installment of that money, arrived in our Swiss bank yesterday. We are now ready to move into phase two."

There was silence in the room. As the men waited for Mrs. Rothman to speak again, the faint hum of an air conditioner could be heard. But no sound came from outside.

"Phase two—the final phase—will take place three weeks from now. I can promise you that very soon the English and the Americans will be at each other's throats. More than that: By the end of the month both countries will be on their knees. The US will be hated throughout the entire world. England will have witnessed a horror beyond anything they could ever have imagined. We will all be a great deal richer. And our client will consider his money well spent."

"Excuse me, Mrs. Rothman. I have a question. . . ."

Dr. Three bowed his head politely. His face seemed to be made of wax and his hair—jet-black— looked twenty years younger than the rest of him. It had to be dyed. He was very small and might have been a retired teacher. He might have been many things, but he was, in fact, the world expert on torture and pain. He had written several books on the subject.

"How many people do you intend to kill?" he asked politely.

Julia Rothman considered. "It's still difficult to be precise, Dr. Three," she replied. "But it will certainly be thousands. Many thousands."

"And they will all be children?"

"Yes. They will mainly be twelve and thirteen years old." She sighed. "It is, it goes without saying, very unfortunate. I adore children even though I'm glad I never had any of my own. But that's the plan. And I have to say, the psychological effect of so many young people dying will, I think, be useful. Does it concern you?"

"Not at all, Mrs. Rothman." Dr. Three shook his head.

"Does anyone else have any objections?"

Nobody spoke, but out of the corner of her eye, Mrs. Rothman noticed Max Grendel shift uncomfortably on his chair at the far end of the table. He was the oldest man in the room, seventy-three, with sagging skin and liver spots on his forehead. He suffered from an eye disease that made him weep constantly. He was dabbing at his eyes now with a tissue. It was hard to believe that he had been a commander in the German secret police and had once personally strangled a foreign spy during a performance of Beethoven's Fifth. But it was not he who spoke.

"Are preparations complete in London?" the Australian asked.

"Construction in the church finished a week ago. The platform, the gas cylinders, and the rest of the machinery will be delivered later today."

"Will Invisible Sword work?" asked another of the men.

It was typical of Levi Kroll to be blunt and to the point. He had joined Scorpia from Mossad, the Israeli secret service, and still thought of himself as a soldier. For twenty years he had slept with an FN 9mm pistol under his pillow. Then, one night, it had gone off. He was a large man with a beard that covered most of his face, concealing the worst of his injuries. A patch covered the empty socket where his left eye had once been.

"Of course it will work." Mrs. Rothman was offended.

"It's been tested?"

"We're testing it right now. But I have to tell you that Professor Liebermann is something of a genius.

A boring little man if you have to spend time with him . . . and heaven knows I've had to do plenty of that. But he's created a brand-new weapon and the beauty of it is that all the experts in the world won't know what it is or how it operates. Of course, they'll work it out in the end, and I've made plans for that eventuality. But by then it will be too late. The streets of London will be littered with corpses. It'll be the worst thing to have happened to children in a city since the Pied Piper."

"And what about Liebermann?" Dr. Three asked.

"I haven't quite decided yet. We'll probably have to kill him too. He may have invented Invisible Sword, but he has no idea how we plan to use it. I expect he'll object. So he'll have to go."

Mrs. Rothman looked around the room. "Is there anything else?" she asked.

"Yes." Max Grendel spread his hands across the surface of the table. Mrs. Rothman wasn't surprised that he had something to say. He was a father and a grandfather. Worse than that, in his old age he had become sentimental.

"I have been with Scorpia from the very beginning," he said. "I remember still our first meeting in Paris. I have earned many millions of dollars working with you and I've enjoyed everything we've done. But this project . . . Invisible Sword. Are we really going to kill so many children? How will we be able to live with ourselves?"

"Rather more comfortably than before," Mrs. Rothman muttered.

"No, no, Julia." Grendel shook his head. A single tear trickled from one of his diseased eyes. "This will come as no surprise to you. We spoke of this the last time we met. But I have decided that enough is enough. I'm an old man. I want to retire to my castle in Vienna. Invisible Sword will be your greatest achievement, I am sure. But I no longer have a heart for it. It is time for me to retire. You must go ahead without me."

"You can't retire!" Levi Kroll snapped.

"Why did you not tell us about this earlier?" another of the men asked angrily. He was black but with Japanese eyes. There was a diamond the size of a pea embedded in one of his front teeth.

"I told Mrs. Rothman," Max Grendel said reasonably. "She's the project leader. I felt there was no need to inform the entire committee."

"We really don't need to argue about this, Mr. Mikato," Julia Rothman said. "Max has been talking about retiring for a long time now and I think we should respect his wishes. It's certainly a shame. But as my late husband used to say—all good things come to an end."

Mrs. Rothman's multimillionaire husband had fallen to his death from a seventeenth-story window. It had happened just two days after his marriage to her.

"It's very sad, Max," she went on. "But I'm sure you're doing the right thing. It's time for you to go."

She went with him down to the jetty, taking the elevator to the ground floor. At last they stood in the bright sunlight with the sounds and smells of real life all around. Max Grendel glanced back at the palazzo—the four-story building from which he had just emerged. It was, he thought, as beautiful as its owner. For when Julia Rothman wasn't at her apartment in New York or her villa at Turtle Bay on the island of Tobago, this was where she lived, right on the edge of the Grand Canal.

Grendel looked for his motorboat. It seemed to have already left, but a gondola was waiting to take him back down the canal. Mrs. Rothman took his arm. "I'll miss you," she said.

"Thank you, Julia." Max Grendel patted her arm. "I'll miss you too."

"I don't know how we'll manage without you."

"Invisible Sword cannot fail. Not with you at the head."

She stopped suddenly. "I almost forgot," she said. "I have something for you." She snapped a finger and a servant ran forward carrying a large box wrapped in pink and blue paper, tied with a silver bow. "It's a present for you," she said.

"A retirement present?"

"Something to remember us by."

Max Grendel had stopped beside the gondola. It was bobbing up and down on the choppy surface. A gondolier stood in the back, dressed in a traditional striped jersey, leaning on his pole. "Thank you, my dear," he said. "And good luck."

"Enjoy yourself, Max. And keep in touch."

She kissed him, her lips lightly touching his withered cheek. Then she helped him into the gondola. He sat down awkwardly, the brightly colored box resting on his knees. At once the gondolier pulled away. Mrs. Rothman raised a hand. The little boat cut swiftly through the gray canal.

Mrs. Rothman turned and went back into the building.

Max Grendel watched her sadly. He knew that life wouldn't be the same without Scorpia. For more than two decades he had devoted all his energies to the organization. It had kept him young, kept him alive. But now there were his grandchildren to consider. He thought of little Hans and Rudi—the twins. They too were twelve years old. The same age as Scorpia's targets in London. He couldn't be part of it. He had made the right decision.

He had almost forgotten the package resting on his thighs. That was typical of Julia. Perhaps it was because she was the only woman on the executive committee, but she had always been the one who was most emotional. He wondered what she had bought him. The parcel was heavy. On an impulse, he pulled the ribbon, then ripped off the paper.

It was an executive briefcase. It was obviously expensive. He could tell from the quality of the leather, the hand-stitching . . . and there was the label. It had been made by Gucci. His initials—MUG—had been engraved in gold just under the handle. With a smile he opened it.

And screamed as the contents spilled over him.

Scorpions. Dozens of them. They were at least four inches long, sand colored, with tiny pincers and fat, swollen bodies. As they tipped into his lap and began to climb his shirt, he recognized them for what they were: hairy thick-tail scorpions from the *Parabuthus* species, the most deadly in the world.

Max Grendel fell backward, shrieking, his eyes bulging, his arms and legs flailing as the hideous creatures found the folds in his clothes and crawled through his shirt into his armpits and down under the waistband of his trousers. The first one stung him on the side of his neck, the next on his chest. Then, suddenly, the scorpions were stinging him everywhere, over and over again, until his screams died unheard in his throat.

His heart gave out long before the neurotoxins killed him. As the gondola floated gently forward, being steered now toward the island cemetery of Venice, the tourists might have noticed him lying still with his hands spread out, gazing with sightless eyes at the bright Venetian sky.

2

SCIPPATORI

FOR THE TWO THIEVES ON the 200cc Vespa scooter, it was a case of the wrong victim, in the wrong place, on the wrong Sunday morning in August.

It seemed that all life had gathered in the Piazza Esmerelda, a few miles outside Venice. Church had just finished and whole families were strolling together in the brilliant sunlight; grandmothers in black, boys and girls in their best suits and Communion dresses. The coffee bars and ice cream shops had opened, spilling their customers onto the sidewalks and out into the street. A huge fountain—all naked gods and serpents—gushed jets of ice-cold water. And there was a market. Stalls had been set up selling kites, dried flowers, old postcards, clockwork birds, and packets of seed for the hundreds of pigeons that strutted and squawked around.

In the middle of all this, two English schoolboys

sat at a table drinking lemon water ice. One was short and dark, with spiky black hair and bright blue eyes. The other was Alex Rider.

It was the beginning of September. A month had passed since Alex's final confrontation with Damian Cray on *Air Force One*—the American presidential plane. It had been the end of an adventure that had taken him to Paris and Amsterdam and finally to the main runway at Heathrow Airport even as a dozen nuclear missiles had been fired at targets all around the world. Alex had managed to destroy the missiles. He had been there when Cray died. And at last he had gone home with the usual collection of bruises and scratches only to find a grim-faced and determined Jack Starbright waiting for him in the main living room. Jack was his housekeeper, but she was also his friend and, as always, she was worried about him.

"You can't keep this up, Alex," she said. "I mean, if you have to go out and save the world now and then, I'm not going to argue with that. But this is getting ridiculous. You come home bruised and battered and completely exhausted. You need a vacation! A week in the sun!"

"You're right." Alex was unusually quiet. Jack had noticed it at once. He had barely said anything about

Cray or what had happened in those last minutes on the runway. "I want to go to Venice," he announced suddenly.

"Venice?"

"Yes."

"All right. I'll get the tickets. If you like, we can visit Florence too—"

"Actually, Jack, I was thinking of going with a friend. Tom Harris. You know . . . he's at Brookland. He's got a brother living in Naples and he's going over to visit him. He said I could come too."

"Yeah. Sure." For a moment Jack was disappointed. But then she brightened up. "That's a great idea, Alex. You ought to spend more time with your own friends. Venice and Naples will be terrific. And the main thing is to make sure you have a real rest."

Alex glanced at Tom now as they sipped their drinks in the Italian square. Tom Harris was his best friend at Brookland. A lot of the other children—and most of the teachers—thought he wasn't too bright. It was certainly true that he was regularly bottom in everything. But the best thing about him was that he didn't care. He always managed to be cheerful and he was always fun to be with. And what Tom lacked in the classroom, he made up for on the sports field. He was captain of the school soccer team and Alex's main rival on sports day, beating him at hurdles, five hundred meters, and the pole vault.

Tom had been talking about this trip to Italy for some time, but it was only recently that Alex had discovered why he was so keen to go. His parents were going through a messy divorce and this summer things had come to a head with moving vans, lawyers' letters, and long, bitter silences. Tom wanted to get as far away from it as he could and the invitation from his older brother couldn't have come at a better time.

"What did you say this was called?" he asked, putting down his spoon.

"It's a *granita*," Alex said. It was what he always ordered when he was in Italy: crushed ice with fresh lemon juice squeezed over it. It was halfway between an ice cream and a drink and there was nothing in the world more refreshing.

"It's good." Tom nodded. He was wearing Diesel light-sensitive sunglasses that he had bought for himself at Heathrow duty-free. They were one size too big for his face and kept slipping down his nose. "Are you going to be at school next term?" he asked suddenly.

Alex shrugged. "Of course."

"You were hardly there last term—or the term before."

"I was ill."

Tom thought for a moment. "You do know that nobody believes that," he said.

"Why not?"

"Because nobody's that ill. It's just not possible." Tom lowered his voice. "Do you know that there's a rumor you're a crook?"

"What?"

"That's why you're away so much. You're in trouble with the police."

"Is that what you think?"

"No. But Miss Bedfordshire asked me about you. She knows we're mates. She said you got into trouble once for stealing a crane or something. She heard about that from someone and she thinks you're in therapy."

"Therapy?" Alex was staggered.

"Yeah. She's quite sorry for you. She thinks that's why you have to go away so much. You know . . . to see a shrink."

Jane Bedfordshire was the school secretary, an attractive woman in her forties who had always had a soft spot for Alex. Alex couldn't believe what Tom was telling him. Did she really believe he was mad?

"You don't think that, do you?" he asked.

"I don't know. You're certainly very strange."

"Thanks!"

A clock struck twelve. Alex and Tom were staying in a youth hostel in the little town of San Lorenzo, just outside Venice itself. Tom's parents had showered him with money—probably out of guilt, he said—but even so, it was cheaper to stay here than in the main city.

"So are you . . . ?" Tom began.

He broke off. It had happened very quickly and both boys had seen it, on the opposite side of the square.

There was an elegantly dressed woman, out with her two children. She had just stepped off the sidewalk and was about to cross the road when a motorbike surged forward. It was a 200cc Vespa Granturismo, almost brand-new, with two men riding it. They were both dressed in jeans and loose, long-sleeved shirts. The passenger had a helmet and visor, as much to hide his identity as to protect him if they crashed. The driver—wearing sunglasses—steered toward the woman, as though he intended to run her over. But at the last moment he veered away.

At the same time, the other man reached out and snatched her handbag. It was done so neatly that Alex knew the two men were professionals . . . *scippatori*, as they were known in Italy. Bag thieves.

Both her children had seen what had happened. One of them was shouting and pointing but there was nothing they could do. The bike was already accelerating away. The driver had his head low. His partner was cradling the leather bag in his lap. They were speeding diagonally across the square, heading toward Alex and Tom. It had seemed that there were people everywhere a few moments before, but suddenly the center of the square was empty and there was nothing to prevent their escape.

Alex got up and ran forward.

"Alex!" Tom called after him.

"Stay back!"

Briefly, Alex considered blocking the path of the Vespa. But it was hopeless. The driver would easily be able to swerve around him—and if he chose not to, Alex really would end up in the hospital. The bike was already doing about forty miles per hour, its single-cylinder, four-stroke engine carrying the two thieves effortlessly toward him. Alex certainly wasn't going to stand in its way.

He looked around him, wondering if there was something he could throw. A net? A bucket of water? But there was no net and the fountain was too far away, although there were buckets. . . .

The bike was less than twenty yards away, accelerating all the time. Alex ran forward and snatched a bucket from the flower stall, emptied it, scattering dried flowers across the sidewalk, and filled it with birdseed from the stall next door. Both the stall owners were shouting at him in Italian, but he ignored them. Without stopping, he swung around and hurled the birdseed at the Vespa just as it was about to go past him. Tom was watching . . . first in amazement, then with disappointment. If Alex had thought the great shower of seed would knock the two men off the bike, it hadn't worked. They were continuing regardless.

But that hadn't been his plan.

There must have been two or three hundred pigeons in the square and all of them had seen the seed shooting out of the bucket. The two riders were covered in it. Seed had lodged in the folds of their clothes, under their collars, and in the sides of their sneakers. There was a small pile of it caught in the driver's crotch. Some had fallen into the woman's bag. Some had become trapped in the driver's hair.

For the pigeons, the bag thieves had suddenly become a meal on wheels. With a soft explosion of gray feathers, they came swooping out of the sky, falling on the two men from all directions. Suddenly the driver had a pigeon clinging to the side of his face with its claws while its beak hammered at his head, tearing the seed out of his hair. There was another pigeon at his throat, a third between his legs, pecking at the most sensitive area of all. His passenger had two pigeons on his neck, another one hanging off his shirt, another half-buried in the stolen bag. And more pigeons were joining in. There must have been at least twenty of them, flapping and batting around them, a twisting cloud of feathers, claws, and—triggered by greed and excitement—flying pellets of white bird droppings.

The driver was blinded, one hand on the handlebars, the other tearing at his face. As Alex watched, the bike performed a 180-degree turn so that now it was coming back, heading straight toward them, moving faster than ever. For a moment he stood poised, waiting to throw himself aside. It looked as though he was going to be run over. But then the bike veered a second time and now it was heading for the fountain, the two men barely visible in a cloud of beating wings.

The front wheel hit the fountain's edge and the bike crumpled. Both men were thrown off. The birds scattered. In the brief second before he hit the water, the man who had grabbed the handbag yelled and let go of it. Almost in slow motion, the bag arced through the air. Alex took two steps forward and caught it.

And then it was all over. The two thieves were a tangled heap, half-submerged in cold water. The Vespa was lying, buckled and broken, on the ground. A pair of Italian policemen, who had arrived when it was almost too late, were hurrying toward them. The stall owners were laughing and applauding. Tom was staring. Alex went over to the woman and gave her the bag.

"I think this is yours," he said.

The woman stared at him in astonishment. Alex turned and walked back to his friend. He sat down at the table.

"Alex . . ." Tom began. "How . . . ?"

Alex smiled. "It was just something I picked up in therapy," he said.

3

THE WIDOW'S PALACE

THAT AFTERNOON, the two boys stood in front of yet another grand palace in the heart of Venice.

"It's called the Contarini del Bovolo," Alex said, consulting his guidebook. "It says here that the staircase is shaped a bit like the shell of a snail. And *bovolo* is the Venetian word for 'snail shell.' "

Tom stifled a yawn. "That's fascinating, Alex," he said. "But if I see one more palace, one more church, or one more canal, I think I'm going to throw myself under a bus."

"There aren't any buses in Venice," Alex reminded him.

"A water bus, then. If it doesn't hit me, maybe I'll get lucky and drown." He sighed. "You know the trouble with this place? The entire city's like a museum. A bloody great museum. I feel like I've been here half my life."

Alex couldn't bring himself to agree. He had never

been anywhere quite like Venice—but then there was nowhere in the world remotely like it with its narrow streets and dark canals twisting around each other in an intricate, amazing knot. Every building seemed to compete with its neighbor to be more ornate and more spectacular. A short walk could take you across four centuries and every corner seemed to lead to another surprise. It might be a canal-side market with great slabs of meat laid out on the tables and fish dripping blood onto the paving stones. Or a church, seemingly floating, surrounded by water on all four sides. A grand hotel or a tiny local restaurant. Even the shops were works of art with windows framing exotic masks, brilliantly colored glass vases, dried pasta, and antiques. It was a museum, maybe, but one that was truly alive.

And yet, part of him felt guilty for dragging Tom here. Tom would have preferred to go straight down to Naples, but Alex had managed to persuade him to spend a few days, first, in Venice. What he hadn't been able to tell his friend was his real reason for coming here.

Scorpia.

He still hadn't forgotten the last words that Yassen Gregorovich had spoken on the plane even as he lay dying. Night after night he had thought about them, turning over in bed, unable to get to sleep. His father—John Rider—had worked with Yassen. He had once saved Yassen's life. But then John Rider had been killed by MI6, the very same people who had forced Alex to work for them three times: lying to him, manipulating him, and finally dumping him when he was no longer needed. It was almost impossible to believe, but Yassen had offered him proof.

"Go to Venice. Find Scorpia. And you will find your destiny . . ."

The trouble was, he had absolutely no idea what Yassen Gregorovich had meant by his last words. Scorpia could be a person. Alex had looked in the telephone book and had found no fewer than fourteen people living in and around Venice with that name. It could be a business. Or it could be a single building. *Scuole* were homes set up for poor people. La Scala was an opera house in Milan. But Scorpia didn't seem to be anything. No signs pointed to it. No streets were named after it.

It was only now that he was here, one day before they were due to leave, that Alex began to see that it had been hopeless from the start. If Yassen had told him the truth, the two men—he and John Rider—had been hired killers. Had they worked for Scorpia? If so, Scorpia would be very carefully concealed . . . perhaps inside one of these old palaces. Alex looked again at the staircase his guidebook had described. How was he to know that the steps themselves didn't lead to Scorpia? Scorpia could be anywhere. Or anyone. And after six days in Venice, Alex was nowhere.

"Where shall we go now?" Tom asked.

"I don't know. What do you want to do?"

"I'd like to see a movie. The trouble is, they're all in Italian. I don't know. We could go down to St. Mark's and feed the pigeons. You seem to like pigeons . . ."

And that was when Alex saw it, a flash of silver as the sun reflected off something on the edge of his vision. He turned his head. There was nothing. A canal leading away. Another canal crossing it. A single motor cruiser sliding underneath a bridge. The usual facade of ancient brown walls dotted with wooden shutters. A church dome rising above the red roof tiles. He had imagined it.

But then the cruiser began to turn and that was when he saw it a second time and knew that it was really there. It was a silver scorpion decorating the side of the boat, pinned to the wooden bow. Alex stared as it swung into the second canal. This wasn't a gondola or a chugging, public *vaporetto*, but a sleek, private motorboat—all polished teak, curtained windows, and leather seats. There were two crew members in immaculate white jackets and shorts, one at the wheel, the other serving a drink to the only passenger. This was a woman, sitting upright, looking straight ahead. Alex only had time to glimpse black hair, an upturned nose, a face with no expression. Then the motorboat completed its turn and disappeared from sight.

A scorpion decorating a motorboat.

Scorpia.

It was only the most slender of connections, but suddenly Alex was determined to find out where the boat was going. It was almost as though the silver scorpion had been sent to guide him to whatever it was he was meant to find. And there was something else. The stillness of the woman sitting in the back. How was it possible to be carried through this amazing city without registering some emotion, without— at least—turning her head from left to right? Alex thought of Yassen Gregorovich. He would have been the same. He and this woman were two of a kind.

Alex turned urgently to Tom. "I'll meet you back at the hostel," he said.

"Why?" Tom began. "Where are you going?"

"I'll tell you later!"

And with that he was gone, ducking between an antique shop and a café, up the narrowest of alleyways, trying to follow the direction of the boat.

But almost at once, he saw that he had a problem. The city of Venice had been originally built on no fewer than a hundred islands. He had read it in his guidebook the first day he'd arrived. In the fifteenth century, the area had been little more than a swamp. That was why there were no roads—just waterways and oddly shaped bits of land connected by bridges. The woman was on the water. Alex was on the land. Following her would be like trying to find his way through an impossible maze in which his path and hers would never meet.

Already he had lost her. The alleyway he had taken should have continued straight ahead. Instead it suddenly turned at an angle, blocked by a tall section of apartments. He ran around the corner, watched by two Italian women, both in black dresses, sitting outside on wooden stools. There was a canal ahead of him, but it was empty. A flight of heavy stone steps led down to the murky water, but there was no way forward . . . unless he wanted to swim.

He craned around to the left and was rewarded

with a glimpse of wood and water churned up by the propellers of the motorboat as it passed a fleet of gondolas that were roped together beside a rotting jetty. There was the woman, sitting in the back, now sipping a glass of wine. The boat continued underneath a bridge so tiny, there was barely room to pass.

There was only one thing he could do. He turned around and retraced his steps, running as fast as he could. The two Italian women saw him again and shook their heads disapprovingly. He hadn't realized how hot it was. The sun seemed to be trapped in the narrow streets, and even in the shadows the heat still lingered. Already sweating, he burst back out on the street where he had begun. There was no sign of Tom. Alex guessed he would already set out for the hostel, happy to get a rest.

Which way?

Suddenly every street and every corner looked the same. Relying on his sense of direction, Alex turned left and ran past a fruit shop, a candle shop, and an open-air restaurant with the waiters already laying the tables for lunch. He came to a turning and there was the bridge—so short, he could cross it in five steps. He stopped in the middle and leaned over the edge, gazing down the canal. The smell of stagnant water

reached up to his nostrils. There was nothing. The
boat was nowhere to be seen.

But he knew which way it had been going. It still
wasn't too late . . . if he could only keep moving. He
darted forward. A Japanese tourist had just been
about to take a photograph of his wife and daughter.
Alex actually heard the camera shutter click as he ran
between him and them. When they got back to Tokyo,
they would have a picture of a slim, athletic boy with
long, fair hair, dressed in a Billabong T-shirt, with
sweat running down his face and determination in his
eyes. Something to remember him by.

A crowd of tourists. A student playing a guitar.
Another café. Waiters with silver trays. Alex plowed
through them all, ignoring the shouts of protest
thrown after him. There was no sign of water anywhere. The street seemed to go on forever. But he
knew there must be a canal somewhere ahead.

He found it. The road fell away suddenly. Gray
water lapped past. He had reached the Grand Canal,
the largest waterway in Venice. And there was the motorboat with the silver scorpion, now fully visible. It
was at least fifty yards away, surrounded by other ves-
sels, and getting farther with every second that passed.

Alex knew that if he lost it now, he wouldn't find

it again. There were too many channels it could take, opening up on both sides. He had come to a wooden platform floating on the water just ahead of him and he realized it was one of the landing docks for the *vaporetti*—the Venice water buses. There was a kiosk selling tickets, a mass of people milling about. A yellow sign gave the name of this point on the canal: *Santa Maria del Giglio*. A large, crowded boat was just pulling out, a number one bus. The school party had taken it from the main railway station the day they arrived and Alex knew that it traveled the full length of the canal. It was moving very slowly but already a couple of yards separated it from the landing dock.

Alex glanced back. There was no way he was going to be able to find his way through the labyrinth of streets in pursuit of the motorboat. The water bus was his only hope. But it was already too far away. He had missed it and there might not be another one for five or ten minutes. A gondola drew past, the gondolier singing in Italian to the grinning family of tourists he was carrying. For a moment Alex thought of stealing the gondola. Then he had a better idea.

The oar was slanting toward him and he reached out, snatching it from the gondolier's hands. Taken by surprise, the gondolier shouted out in Italian, twisted around, and lost his balance. The family looked on in alarm as he plunged backward into the water. Meanwhile, Alex had tested the oar. It was about ten yards long and heavy. The gondolier had been holding it vertically, using the splayed paddle end to guide his boat through the water. Alex ran forward. He stabbed down with the blade, thrusting it into the Grand Canal, hoping the water wouldn't be too deep.

He was lucky. The tide was low and the bottom of the canal was littered with everything from old washing machines to bicycles and wheelbarrows, cheerfully thrown in by the Venetian residents with no thought of pollution. The bottom of the oar hit something solid and Alex was able to use the length of solid wood to propel himself forward. It was exactly the same technique he had used pole-vaulting at Brookland sports day. For a moment he was in the air, leaning backward, suspended over the Grand Canal. Then he swung down, sweeping through the open entrance of the water bus and landing on the deck. He dropped the oar behind him and looked around. The other passengers were staring at him in amazement. But he was on board.

There are very few ticket collectors on the water buses in Venice, which is why most young people in the city somehow "forget" to buy their tickets before they get on board. So there was nobody to challenge Alex about his unorthodox method of arrival or to demand a fare. He leaned over the edge, grateful for the breeze sweeping over the surface of the water. And he hadn't lost the motorboat. It was still ahead of him, traveling away from the main lagoon and back into the heart of the city. A slender wooden bridge stretched out over the canal ahead of him and Alex recognized it at once as the Bridge of the Academy, leading to the biggest art gallery in the city. For a moment he wondered what he was doing. He had just abandoned his friend. He had run the full length of Venice. And why? What did he have to go on? A silver scorpion decorating a private boat. He must be out of his mind.

The vaporetto began to slow down. It had already reached the next landing dock. Alex tensed himself. He knew that if he waited for one load of passengers to get off and another to get on, he would never see the motorboat again. He was on the other side of the canal now. The streets were a little less crowded here. Alex caught his breath. He wondered how much farther he could run.

And then he saw, with a surge of relief, that the motorboat had also arrived at its destination. It was

pulling into a palace a little farther up, stopping behind a series of wooden poles that slanted out of the
water as though, like javelins, they had been thrown
there by chance. As Alex watched, two more uniformed servants appeared. One moored the boat. The
other held out a white-gloved hand. The woman took
the hand and stepped ashore. She was wearing a
tight-fitting cream-colored dress with a jacket cut
short above the waist. A handbag swung from her
arm. She could have been a model stepping off the
front cover of a fashion magazine. She didn't hesitate.
While the servants busied themselves with her suit-
cases, unloading them from the boat, she disappeared
behind a stone column.

The water bus was about to leave again. Quickly,
Alex stepped off and climbed onto the landing dock.
Once again he had to work his way around the buildings that crowded onto the Grand Canal. But this time
he knew what he was looking for. A few minutes later,
he found it.

It was a typical Venetian palace, pink and white,
its narrow windows built into a fantastic embroidery
of pillars, arches, and balustrades . . . like something
out of a production of *Romeo and Juliet*. But what
made the place so unforgettable was its position. It

didn't just face the Grand Canal. It sank right into it, the water lapping against the brickwork. The woman from the boat had gone through some sort of portcullis, as though entering a castle. But it was a castle that was floating. Or sinking. It was impossible to say where the water ended and the palace floor began.

The building did at least have one side that could be reached by land. It backed onto a wide square with trees and bushes growing out of ornamental tubs. There were men—servants—everywhere, setting up rope barriers, positioning oil-burning torches, and unrolling a red carpet. Carpenters were at work, constructing what looked like a small bandstand. More men were carrying in a variety of crates and boxes. Alex saw champagne bottles, fireworks, different sorts of food. They were obviously preparing for a serious party.

Alex stopped one of them. "Excuse me," he said. "Can you tell me who lives here?"

The man spoke no English. He didn't even try to be friendly. Alex tried a second man, with exactly the same result. He recognized the type . . . he had met men like them before. The guards at the Point Blanc Academy. The technicians at Cray Software Technology. These were people who worked for someone who made them nervous. They were paid to do a job and they never stepped out of line. Were they people with something to hide? Perhaps.

Alex left the square and walked around the side. A second canal ran the full length of the building and this time Alex was luckier. There was an elderly woman, a grandmother figure in a black dress with a white apron, sweeping the towpath. He approached her.

"Do you speak English?" he asked. "Can you help me?"

"*Si, con piacere, piccolo amico.*" The woman nodded. She put the broom down. "I spend many year in London. I speak good English. Who can I do?"

Alex pointed at the building. "What is this place?"

"It is the *Ca' Vedova.*" She tried to explain. "*Ca'* . . . you know . . . in Venice we say *Casa*. It means 'palace.' And *Vedova* . . . ?" She searched for the word. "It is the Palace of the Widow. *Ca' Vedova.*"

"What's going on?"

"There is a big party tonight. For a birthday. Masks and costumes. Many important people come."

"Whose birthday?"

The woman hesitated. Alex was asking too many questions and he could see that she was becoming suspicious. But once again age was on his side. He was only fourteen. What did it matter if he was curious? "*Signora* Rothman. She is very rich lady. The owner of the house."

"Rothman? Like the cigarette?"

But the woman's mouth had suddenly closed and there was fear in her eyes. Alex looked around and saw one of the men from the square, standing at the corner, watching him. He realized he had outstayed his welcome . . . and no one had been that pleased to see him in the first place.

He decided to have one last try. "I'm looking for Scorpia," he said.

The old woman stared at him as though she had been slapped in the face. She picked up the broom and at the same time her eyes darted over to the man at the corner. It was lucky he hadn't heard the exchange. He had sensed something was wrong, but he hadn't moved. Even so, Alex knew it was time to go. "It doesn't matter," he said. "Thank you for your help."

He made his way quickly up the canal. There was yet another bridge ahead of him and he crossed it. Although he didn't know exactly why, he was grateful to leave the *Ca' Vedova* behind him.

As soon as he was out of sight, he stopped and considered what he had learned. A boat with a silver scorpion had led him to a palace. It was owned by a beautiful and wealthy woman who didn't smile. The palace was protected by a number of mean-looking men and the moment he had mentioned the name of Scorpia to a cleaning woman, he had suddenly become as welcome as the plague.

It wasn't a lot to go on, but it was enough. There was going to be a masked ball tonight, a birthday party. Important people had been invited. Alex wasn't one of them, but already he had decided. He would be there all the same.

4

BY INVITATION ONLY

THAT NIGHT, THE WIDOW'S Palace slipped back three hundred years in time.

It was an extraordinary sight. The oil-burning torches had been lit and the flames cast orange and black shadows across the square. The servants had changed into eighteenth-century costumes with wigs, tightly fitting stockings, pointed shoes, and waist-coats. A string quartet played in the open air, sitting on the bandstand that Alex had seen being con-structed, underneath the night sky. The stars were out in their thousands and there was even a full moon. It was as though whoever had organized the party had managed to control the weather too.

Guests were arriving by water and on foot. They too were in costume with elaborate hats and richly colored velvet cloaks hanging all the way to the ground. Some carried ebony walking sticks. Others had swords and daggers. But not a single face could be seen among the crowd making its way to the front door. Their faces were hidden behind white masks and gold masks, masks encrusted with jewels and masks surrounded by huge plumes of feathers. It was impossible to know who had been invited to Mrs. Rothman's party—but not just anyone could walk in. The canal entrance to the palace was closed and everyone was being directed up to the main door that Alex had seen earlier that day. Four security guards, themselves wearing the bright red tunics of Venetian courtiers, were positioned there, checking the invitations that the guests had brought with them.

Alex watched all this from the other side of the square. He was crouching behind one of the miniature trees with Tom, the two of them outside the circle of light thrown by the torches. It hadn't been easy to persuade Tom to come. This was meant to be their last night in Venice before they set off for Naples and Tom had been looking forward to a large plate of spaghetti and an early night. Alex had other plans. He had found everything he needed in Venice before he went back to the hostel. But he knew he couldn't do this alone. Tom had to come too.

"Alex, I can't believe you're doing this," Tom whispered now. "Why is this party such a big deal anyway?"

"I can't explain."

"Why not? I don't understand you sometimes. We're meant to be friends, but you never tell me anything."

Alex sighed. He was used to this. When he thought of all the things that had happened to him in the past year, the way he had been dragged into the world of espionage, a world of secrecy and lies, this was the worst part. MI6 had turned him into a spy. And at the same time they had made it impossible for him to be what he wanted . . . an ordinary schoolboy. He had been living two lives, one day saving the world from a nuclear holocaust, the next struggling with his chemistry homework. Two lives, but he had somehow ended up trapped between them. He didn't know where he belonged anymore. There was Tom, there was Jack Starbright, and there was Sabina Pleasure— although she had now moved to America. Apart from them, he had no real friends. It wasn't his choice, but somehow he had ended up alone.

He made up his mind. "All right," he said. "I'll tell you everything. But not now."

"When?"

"Tomorrow. On the train to Naples."

Tom considered. "I'll help you anyway, Alex," he said. "Because that's what friends are for. And I won't make you tell me. Not if you don't want to."

Alex nodded and smiled. "Thanks."

He reached behind him for the sports bag he had brought with him from the hotel. Inside it were the various items he had bought in Venice. Quickly, he stripped off his shorts and T-shirt, then put on a pair of loose-fitting silk trousers and a velvet waistcoat that left his arms and chest bare. Next, he took out a tub of what looked like jelly—except that it was colored gold. Body paint. He scooped some out and rubbed it between his hands, then smeared it over his arms, his neck, and his face. He signaled to Tom, who grimaced and then finished the backs of his shoulders. All his skin was now gold.

Finally, he brought out gold sandals, a white turban with a single mauve feather, and a plain half-mask, just big enough to cover his eyes. He had asked the costume shop to supply him with everything he would need to become a Turkish slave. He hoped the final effect didn't make him look as ridiculous as he felt.

"Are you ready?" he asked.

Tom nodded, wiping his hands on his trousers. "You know . . . you do look a bit sad," he muttered.

"I don't care . . . so long as it works."

"I still think you're completely mad."

Alex watched as more people arrived at the palace. If his plan was going to work, he had to choose the right moment. He also had to wait for the right guests. They were still coming thick and fast, milling around the main entrance while the guards checked their invitations. He glanced over to the Grand Canal. A water taxi had just pulled in and two people were climbing out. Both of them were masked; a man in a frock coat and a woman in a black cloak that trailed behind her. They were perfect. He nodded to Tom. "Now."

"Good luck, Alex." Tom took something out of the sports bag and darted forward, making no attempt to avoid being seen. A moment later, Alex slipped around the other way, keeping to the shadows.

There was a snarl-up at the entrance. A guard was holding an invitation, questioning one of the guests. That was helpful too. Alex needed as much confusion as possible. And Tom must have seen this was the right moment. There was suddenly a loud bang and all heads turned to see a young boy capering in the square, laughing and shouting. He had just let off a firecracker and with everyone watching, he lit another.

"Come sta?" he shouted. How are you? *"Quanto tempo ci vuole per andare a Roma?"* How long does it take to get to Rome? Alex had picked the words out of a guidebook. They were the only Italian Tom had been able to learn.

Tom threw the second firecracker and there was another bang. At the same time, Alex hurried down to the edge of the Grand Canal just as the two guests climbed the steps that would bring them up to the square. His sandals flapped on the paving stones as he ran forward, but nobody noticed him. They were all watching Tom, who was singing "You'll Never Walk Alone" at the top of his voice. Alex reached down and picked up the train of the woman's cloak. As she continued toward the main door, he walked behind her, holding the material above the ground.

It worked exactly as he had hoped. The crowd had quickly tired of the mad English boy who was making a fool of himself. One of the guards had already been sent to deal with him. Out of the corner of his eye, Alex saw Tom turn around and run away. They reached the door and the man in the frock coat handed over his invitation. The guard glanced at the new arrivals and ushered them through. He had assumed that Alex was with the guests. They had brought a Turkish boy with them as part of their disguise. Meanwhile, the guests had assumed that Alex worked in the palace and had been sent to escort them in. Why else would he have appeared?

The three of them passed through the door and into a grand reception hall with white columns, a marble floor, and a domed ceiling covered in mosaic. A pair of double-height glass doors opened into a courtyard with a fountain surrounded by ornamental shrubs and flowers, where at least a hundred guests were chatting, laughing, and drinking champagne from crystal glasses. It was obvious they were all pleased to be there. Servants, identically dressed to the ones outside, circulated with silver trays of food. A man sitting at a harpsichord played Mozart and Vivaldi. In keeping with the atmosphere, all the electric lights had been turned off, but there were beacons mounted on the walls as well as thousands of candles, the flames bowing and dancing in the evening breeze.

Alex had followed his lord and lady into the courtyard, but now he dropped the end of the cloak and slipped to one side. He looked up. The palace rose three floors above him, connected by a spiraling staircase like the one he had seen at the Contarini del Bovolo. The first floor opened onto a gallery with yet more arches and columns, and some of the guests had found their way up here and were strolling slowly together, gazing down on the crowds below. Looking around him, Alex found it hard to believe that this really was the twenty-first century. A perfect illusion had been created within the palace walls.

Now that he was here, he was unsure quite what to do. Had he really found his way to Scorpia? How could he be sure? It occurred to him that if Yassen had been telling the truth and his father really had once worked for these people, they might be happy to meet him. He would ask them what had happened, how his father had died, and they would tell him. He had no need to creep around in disguise.

But suppose he was wrong? He remembered the look of fear on the old woman's face when he had so much as mentioned the name of Scorpia. And then there were the hard-eyed men working outside the palace. They spoke no English and Alex doubted he would be able to explain what he was doing if they caught him. By the time someone had laid their hands on an English dictionary, he might find himself floating facedown in the canal.

No. He had to find out more before he made his approach. Who was this woman—Mrs. Rothman? What was she doing here? It seemed incredible to Alex that a grand masked ball in a Venetian palace could in any way be connected with a murder that had taken place fourteen years ago.

The chimes of the harpsichord rang out. The conversation was getting louder as more and more people arrived. Most of them had taken off their masks—it was impossible otherwise to eat or drink—and Alex saw that this was truly an international gathering. The guests were mainly speaking in Italian, but there were many black and Asian faces among the crowd. He caught sight of a short Chinese man deep in discussion with another man who had a diamond set into his front tooth. A woman he thought he knew crossed the courtyard in front of him and with a start he recognized her as one of the most famous film actresses in the world. Now that he looked around, he saw that the place was packed with Hollywood stars. Why had they been invited? Then he remembered. This was September, the time of the Venice International Film Festival. Well, that told him something about Mrs. Rothman if she had the clout to invite celebrities like these.

Alex knew he couldn't linger too long. He was the only teenager in the palace and it could only be a matter of time before someone noticed him. He was horribly exposed. His arms and his shoulders were bare. The silk trousers were so thin, he could hardly feel them on him. The Turkish disguise might have helped get him in, but it was awkward and unhelpful now that he was actually here. He decided to make a move. There was no sign of Mrs. Rothman on the ground floor. She was the person he most wanted to see. Perhaps he would find her somewhere upstairs.

He made his way through the party-goers and climbed the spiral staircase. He reached the gallery and saw a series of doors opening into the palace itself. It was less crowded here and a few people glanced at him curiously as he proceeded. Alex knew that the important thing was not to stop. If he allowed himself to be challenged, he would soon be thrown out. He went through a door and found himself in an area that was something between a very wide corridor and a room in its own right. A gold-framed mirror hung on one wall above an ornate antique table with a huge vase of flowers. A heavy wardrobe stood opposite. Otherwise, the area was empty.

There was a door at the far end and Alex was about to continue toward it when he heard muffled voices approaching. He looked around for somewhere to hide. There was only the wardrobe. He didn't have time to open it, but he slid against the wall next to it. Like the courtyard, the upper floor was lit only by candles. He hoped the bulk of the wardrobe would throw a big enough shadow to conceal him.

The door had opened. Two people had come out, talking in English; one a man, the other a woman.

"We have received the release certificates and the batch will be on their way the day after tomorrow." It was the man who was speaking. "As I explained to you, Mrs. Rothman, timing is everything."

"The cold chain."

"Exactly. The cold chain cannot be broken. The boxes will be flown to England the same day. After that . . ."

"Thank you, Dr. Liebermann. You have done very well."

The two of them had stopped just out of sight from where Alex was hiding. However, leaning forward, he could see their reflections in the mirror.

Julia Rothman was stunning. There was no other way for Alex to describe her. She was more like a film star than any of the actresses he had seen downstairs, her long black hair falling in waves to her shoulders. She had a mask, but it was in her hand, on the end of a wooden rod, so he was able to see her face, the brilliant, dark eyes, the bloodred lips, the perfect teeth. She was wearing a fantastic dress made of ivory-colored lace and somehow Alex knew that it wasn't a costume but a real antique. A gold necklace set with dark blue sapphires clung to her throat.

The man she was with was the complete opposite of her. He was about fifty years old and, like her, he was in costume—a long, fur-lined cloak with an Elizabethan collar and a peaked hat. He was carrying a wand. Although Alex didn't know it, this was the traditional costume of the medieval plague doctor and it certainly suited the man well. The head that poked out the top was bald and ugly with a large nose and glasses. He was very tall, towering over Julia Rothman. Yet still, somehow, she dwarfed him. Despite the clothes, he looked like a nerd and Alex wondered why he had been invited.

"You do promise me, Mrs. Rothman," he said nervously. "Nobody is going to get hurt."

"Does it really matter?" Mrs. Rothman replied. "You're being paid five million dollars. A small fortune. Think about it, Dr. Liebermann. You're set up for life."

Alex sneaked another look around and saw the woman standing side-on, waiting for the man to speak. Dr. Liebermann was frozen. Caught between greed and fear.

"I don't know," he rasped. "Maybe if you were paying me more—"

"Then maybe we'll have to think about doing just that!" Mrs. Rothman sounded completely relaxed. "But let's not spoil the party by talking about business. I'm coming down to Amalfi in two days' time. I want to be there when the batch leaves and we can talk about money then." She smiled. "Right now, let's go and have a glass of champagne and let me introduce you to some of my famous friends."

They had begun walking again and as they talked, they went past Alex and continued downstairs. For a moment he was tempted to show himself. This was the woman he had come to find. He should approach her before she disappeared back into the crowd. But at the same time he was intrigued. Release certificates and cold chains. He wondered what they had been talking about. Once again, he decided it would be better to find out a little more before he made himself known.

He stepped out into the corridor and went down to the door through which Mrs. Rothman and her friend had just come. He opened it and found himself in a huge room—and one that could truly be called palatial. It must have been at least thirty yards long with a row of floor-to-ceiling windows that gave wonderful views over the Grand Canal. The floor was polished wood, but almost everything else was white. There was a massive fireplace made of white marble with a white tiger-skin rug (Alex winced—he could think of nothing more disgusting) spread out in front of it. White bookshelves lined the far wall, filled with leather-bound books, and, next to a second door, Alex saw a white antique table with what looked like a remote control device for a TV. Opposite the fireplace in front of one of the windows stood a solid walnut desk. Mrs. Rothman's desk? Alex went over to it.

The surface of the desk was empty apart from a white leather blotting pad and a tray with two silver fountain pens. Alex imagined Mrs. Rothman sitting here. It was the sort of desk a judge or a company chairman would have, a desk designed to impress. He looked around quickly, checking there were no security cameras, then tried one of the drawers. It was unlocked but it contained only writing paper and envelopes. He tried the next drawer down. Surprisingly, that one opened too and this time he found himself looking at some sort of brochure with a yellow cover and a name, printed in black:

CONSANTO ENTERPRISES

He opened the cover. The first page showed a picture of a building. It was obviously high-tech, long and angular, with walls made entirely of reflective glass. There was an address underneath the picture: Via Nuova, Amalfi.

Amalfi. That was the place Mrs. Rothman had mentioned a few moments before.

He flicked another page. There were pictures of various men and women in suits and white coats. The staff of Consanto, perhaps? One of them—in the middle of the top row—was Harold Liebermann. His name was printed underneath, but the text was in Italian. Alex wouldn't be able to learn anything from it. He closed the brochure and tried another drawer.

Something moved.

Alex had been sure he was alone. He had been surprised that there was no sign of any security in the
room, particularly if this was Mrs. Rothman's office.
But he was suddenly aware that something had
changed. It took him a few seconds to realize what it
was and at once he felt the hairs on the back of his
neck bristle and stand on end.

What he had taken to be a tiger-skin rug had just
stood up.

It was a tiger, alive and angry.

A white Siberian tiger. How did he know it was
Siberian? The color, of course. And the pale gold-
and-black stripes . . . the fact that it had so few of
them. As the creature turned its eyes on him, weigh-
ing him up, Alex remembered what he knew about this
rarest of species. There were only about five hundred
Siberian tigers left in the wild, with another five hundred in zoos. It was the largest living cat in the world.
And . . . yes! It had five toes on its front paws but only
four on its back. That was a very useful piece of information to consider as the animal prepared to tear
him apart.

Because he had no doubt that that was exactly
what was about to happen. The tiger seemed to have
awoken from a deep sleep, but its yellow eyes were

now fixed on him and he could almost hear the messages being sent to the brain. Food. That was another thing he remembered now. A Siberian tiger could eat seventy pounds of meat at one sitting. By the time this one finished with him, there wouldn't be a great deal left.

Alex's mind was in a whirl. What exactly had he stumbled onto in the Ca' Vedova? What sort of woman didn't bother with locks and security cameras but kept a live tiger beside her desk? The creature stretched itself. Alex saw the perfect muscles rippling behind the thick fur. He tried to move but found that he couldn't. He wondered what had happened to him, then realized. He was terrified. Rooted to the spot. He was just ten steps away from an animal that had, for centuries, inspired dread across three continents. It was almost beyond belief that this tiger should have found itself imprisoned in a Venetian palace. But it was here. That was all that mattered. And whatever the surroundings, the carnage would be the same.

The tiger growled. It was a low, rumbling noise, somehow more terrible than anything Alex had ever heard. He tried to find the strength to move, to put something between the two of them. But there was nothing.

The tiger took a step forward. It was preparing to leap. Its eyes had darkened. Its jaw hung open, revealing the two lines of white dagger teeth. It growled a second time, louder, more continuous.

Then it leaped.

5

FLOOD TIDE

ALEX DID THE ONLY THING he could. Faced with five hundred pounds of snarling tiger leaping toward him, he fell to his knees, at the same time sliding along the wooden floor and disappearing under the desk. The tiger landed above him. He could feel its weight, separated from him only by the surface of the desk— and he could hear its claws gouging into the wood. Two things went through his mind. The first was the sheer improbability of encountering a wild animal, un-chained, in a Venetian palace. The second was the knowledge that if he didn't find a way out of the room fast, this might be the last thought he would ever have.

He had a choice of two doors. The one he had come in through seemed to be the closest. The tiger was half on the floor, half on the desk, momentarily confused. In the jungle it would have found him at once, but this world was totally alien to it. Alex seized his chance and scrambled forward. It was only when

he was out in the open, away from the scant protection of the desk, that he realized he wasn't going to
make it.

The tiger had seen him. Alex had twisted around,
his hands behind him, his legs bent sideways, in the act
of standing up. The tiger had its front paws on the
desk. Neither of them moved. Alex knew that the door
was too far away. There was nowhere else to hide. A
surge of anger washed through him. He should never
have come in here. He should have been more careful.

The tiger roared. Alex had never heard anything
quite like it. A deep, rattling blast of air that made
every nerve stand on end. It was, quite simply, the
sound of terror.

And then the second door opened and a man
came in.

Alex barely registered him. At that moment all his
concentration was fixed on the tiger. But he saw instantly that the man wasn't wearing a costume. He
was dressed in a polo-neck jersey, jeans, and sneakers; the clothes quietly, confidently expensive. And
from the way they clung to him, showing the muscles in his arms and across his chest, Alex could see
he was extremely fit. He was young, in his mid-
twenties. And he was black.

But there was something wrong.

The man turned his head and Alex saw that one side of his face was covered in strange white blotches, as though he had been involved in some sort of chemical accident or perhaps a fire. Then Alex noticed his hands. They, too, were different colors. The man should have been handsome. But in fact he was just a mess.

The man took in what was happening instantly. He saw that the tiger was about to leap down. Without a second thought, he reached out and took the remote control that Alex had noticed on the antique table. He pointed it vaguely in the direction of the tiger and pressed a button.

And then the impossible happened. The tiger climbed off the desk. Alex actually saw its eyes begin to dim. It slumped and lay on the floor. Alex stared. The tiger had turned, in seconds, from a dreadful monster to nothing more than an oversized pussycat. And then it was asleep, its stomach rising and falling, its eyes closed.

How had it worked?

Alex looked back at the man who had just come in. He was still holding the device, whatever it was, in his hand. For a moment Alex wondered if the tiger was even real. Could it possibly be some sort of robot that could be turned on and off by remote control? No. That was ridiculous. He had been close enough to the tiger to see every detail. He had smelled its breath. He could see it now, twitching, as it returned to the jungles it had come from . . . in its dreams. It was a living thing. But somehow it had been turned off as quickly and as easily as a lightbulb. Alex had never felt more out of his depth. He had followed a gondola with a silver scorpion. It had led him into some sort of Italian Wonderland.

"*Chi sei? Cosa fai qui?*"

The man was talking to him. Alex didn't understand the words, but he still got the meaning. Who are you? What are you doing here? He stood up, wishing that he had been able to change out of his costume. He felt half-naked and horribly vulnerable. He wondered if Tom was still waiting for him outside. No. He had told him to go back to the hostel.

The man spoke to him a second time. Alex had no choice.

"I don't speak Italian," he said.

"You're English?" The man switched effortlessly into Alex's language.

"Yes."

"What are you doing in Mrs. Rothman's office?"

"My name is Alex Rider—"

"And my name is Nile. But that's not what I asked you."

"I'm looking for Scorpia."

The man—Nile—smiled, showing perfect teeth. With the tiger neutralized, Alex was able to examine him more closely. If it hadn't been for the discoloration of his skin, he would have been classically handsome. He was clean shaven, elegant, in perfect physical shape. He had black hair, shaved close to the skull, with a pattern—curving lines around the ears. Although he looked relaxed, Alex knew that he was already in a combat stance, poised on the balls of his feet. This was a dangerous man. Alex knew that too. He radiated self-confidence and control. He wasn't alarmed to find a teenager here in the study. He seemed to be amused.

"What do you know about Scorpia?" he asked. His voice was soft and very precise.

Alex said nothing.

"It's a name you overheard downstairs," Nile said. "Or perhaps you found it in the desk. Were you searching the desk? Is that why you're here? Are you a thief?"

"No . . ."

Alex had already decided he'd had enough. Any minute now, someone else would arrive. It was time to go. He turned around and began to move toward the door he had first come in.

"If you take one more step, I'm afraid I'll have to kill you," Nile said.

Alex didn't stop.

He heard the light footfall on the wooden floor behind him and timed it exactly right. At the last moment, he stopped and swiveled around, lashing out with his heel in a back kick that should have driven into the man's abdomen, winding him at the very least and possibly knocking him out. But with a sense of shock he felt his foot meet only empty air. Nile had either anticipated what he was about to do or twisted away with unbelievable speed. Alex turned full circle, trying to follow through with a front jab—the *kizami-zuki*—he had learned at karate. But already it was too late. Nile had moved again and there was a blur of movement as the edge of his hand scythed down. It was like being hit by a block of wood. Alex was almost thrown off his feet. The whole room shuddered and went dark. Desperately he tried to find a defensive position, crossing his arms, keeping his head low. Nile had been expecting it. Alex felt an arm close around his throat. A hand pressed against his head. With a single movement, Nile could now break his neck.

"You shouldn't have done that," Nile said, talking as though to a child. "I did warn you and you didn't listen. So now you're dead."

There was a moment of blinding pain, a flash of white light. Then nothing.

Alex woke up with the feeling that his head had been wrenched off. Even after he had opened his eyes, it took a few seconds for his vision to return. He tried to move a hand and was relieved to see his fingers curl inward. So his neck wasn't broken. He tried to play back what had happened. Nile must have let go of his head at the last moment and used an elbow strike. Alex had been knocked out before, but he had never woken up in as much pain as this. Had Nile meant to kill him? Somehow he doubted it. Even in the short encounter, Alex knew that he had met a master of unarmed combat, someone who knew exactly what he was doing and didn't make mistakes.

He had knocked Alex out and dragged him down here. Where was he? With his head still pounding, Alex looked around him. He didn't like the look of what he saw. He was in a small chamber, somewhere underneath the palace, he guessed. The walls were made of mottled plaster and the way they sloped reminded him of a cellar. The floor had recently flooded. He was standing on a sort of trelliswork of damp and rotting wooden planks. The room was lit by a single bulb behind a dirty glass covering. There were no windows. Alex shivered. It was cold in here, despite the heat of the September evening. And there was something else. He ran a finger along one of the walls and felt a coating of slime. He had thought the cellar was painted a dirty shade of green, but now he realized that the flooding had gone farther than the floor. It had continued all the way up to the ceiling. Even the lightbulb had at some stage been underwater.

As his senses slowly returned to him, Alex recognized the smell of water in the air: the rotting vegetables, mud, and salt of the Venice canal system. He could actually hear it. The waves were lapping, not on the other side of the wall but somewhere underneath him. He knelt down and examined the floor. One of the boards was loose and he was able to swivel it around enough to make a narrow opening. He stretched a hand through and touched water. There was no way out. He turned around. A short flight of wooden steps led up to a solid-looking door. He went up to it and pressed his weight against it. The door was covered in slime too. There was no give in it at all.

What now?

Alex was still dressed in the silk trousers and waistcoat that had been his costume. There was nothing to protect him against the night chill. He thought briefly about Tom, and that at least gave him a little comfort. If Alex hadn't returned to the hostel by the morning, Tom would raise the alarm. Daybreak couldn't be far away. Alex had no idea how long he'd been unconscious and, although he regretted it now, he had taken off his watch when he put on his disguise. There was no sound on the other side of the door. It seemed he had little choice but to wait.

He crouched in a corner, closing his arms around himself. Most of the gold paint had come off. He looked ragged and dirty. He wondered what Scorpia was going to do with him. Surely someone—Nile or Mrs. Rothman—would come down, if only to find out why he had bothered to break in.

He was suddenly exhausted. It was as though the speed of events, from the first sighting of the boat with the silver scorpion to the fight with Nile, had overtaken him. He didn't mean to sleep. He would have thought it impossible. But the next thing he knew, he was jerking awake with a crick in his neck and a cold numbness that had spread through his entire body. Despite everything, he had nodded off, and some sort of siren had just woken him up. He could hear it howling—not inside the palace but far away. At the same time he was aware that something in the room had changed. He looked down and saw water spreading across the surface of the floor.

For a moment he was puzzled. Had a pipe burst? Where was the water coming from? Then his thoughts came together and he understood his fate. Scorpia wasn't interested in him. Nile had told him he was going to die and he had meant what he said.

The sirens were warning that there was going to be a flood. Venice has an alarm system in place all year round. The city stands at sea level and because of the wind and the atmospheric pressure, there are frequent "storm surges." These cause water from the Atlantic to pour into the Venice lagoon with the result that the canals break their banks and whole streets and squares simply disappear for several hours. Cold, black water was bubbling up into the room even now. How high would it go? Alex didn't need to ask. The stains on the walls went all the way up to the ceiling.

The water would rise over him and he would strug-
gle helplessly, unable to stop himself, until he
drowned. Eventually the level would fall again and
they would clear out his body, perhaps dumping him
in the lagoon.

He got to his feet and ran to the door, slamming
his hands against it. He was shouting too, although he
knew it was hopeless. Nobody came. Nobody cared.
He surely wasn't the first to end up locked in here.
Ask too many questions, go into rooms where you had
no right to be—this would be the result.

The water was rising steadily. There must have
been two inches already. The floor had disappeared.
There were no windows. The door was rock solid.
There was only one possible way out of here and Alex
was almost too afraid to try it. But one of the planks
was loose. Maybe there was some sort of well or large
pipe underneath. After all, he reasoned, there had to
be some way for the water to come in.

And it was gushing in now, more quickly than
ever. Alex hurried back down the stairs and found the
water level well over his ankles, almost reaching his
knees. He made a quick calculation. At this rate, the
room would be completely submerged in about ten
minutes. He ripped off the waistcoat and threw it

aside. He wouldn't need that now. He waded forward, searching with the soles of his feet for the loose plank. He remembered that it was somewhere in the middle and soon found it, stubbing his toe against one side of the opening. He knelt down, the water now circling his waist. He wasn't even sure he could squeeze through. And if he did, what would he find on the other side?

He tried to feel with his hands. There was an upsurge of water right underneath him. This was the source of the inflow. The water was coming directly up from some sort of opening. So this was the way out. The only question was—could he do it? He would have to force himself, headfirst through the triangular gap, find the opening, and swim into it. If he got stuck, he would drown upside down. If the passage was blocked—perhaps by a metal grille—he would never make it back again. He was kneeling in front of the worst death imaginable. And the water was traveling up his spine, pitiless and cold.

Sick anger shivered through him. Was this the destiny that Yassen Gregorovich had promised him? Had he come to Venice simply for this? The sirens were still howling. The water had covered the first of the steps and was already lapping at the second. Alex cursed, then took several deep breaths, hyperventilating. When he had forced as much air into his lungs as he thought they could take, he toppled forward and plunged, headfirst, down.

The gap was barely big enough to allow him through. He felt the edge of the wooden floorboards bite into his shoulders, but then he was able to use his hands to push himself forward. He was utterly blind. Even if he had opened his eyes, the water would have been black. He could feel it, pressing against his nostrils and lips. It was ice cold and stinking. God! What a way to die! His stomach had passed through the opening but his hips were stuck. Alex twisted like a snake and felt the lower part of his body come free.

He was already running out of air. He wanted to turn around and go back, but now fresh panic gripped him as he realized that he was trapped inside some sort of tube with no room to go any way except down. His shoulders banged against solid brick. He kicked out with one leg and was rewarded with a stab of pain as his foot hit the wall that now enclosed him. He felt the current swirling around his face and neck . . . ropes of water that wanted to tie him down forever in this black death. He was only aware of the full horror of his situation now that there was no escape from it. No adult would have been able to get this far. It was only because he was smaller that he had been able to make his way into this well shaft or whatever it was. But he had no room to maneuver. The walls were already touching him on every side. If the tube became even a few inches narrower, he would be stuck fast.

He forced himself down. Forward and down, his hands groping ahead of him, dreading the metal bars that would tell him Nile had been laughing at him from the start. His lungs were straining. The pressure was hammering at his chest. He tried not to panic, knowing it would only use up his air more quickly, but already his brain was screaming at him to stop, to breathe in, to give up and accept his fate. Forward and down. He could hold his breath for three minutes. Anyone could. And it couldn't have been more than a minute since he had taken the plunge. Don't give in! Just keep moving . . .

By now he must be ten or fifteen yards under the cellar floor. He reached out and whimpered as his knuckles struck brick. A few precious bubbles of air escaped from between his lips and chased up his body, past his flailing legs. At first he thought he had come to a dead end. For a moment he opened his eyes. It made no difference at all. Open or closed, there was nothing to see. He was in total, utter darkness. His heart seemed to stop beating. In that moment, Alex actually experienced what it was like to die.

But then his other hand felt the bend of the wall and he realized that at last the well shaft was bending. He had reached the bottom of an elongated letter J and somehow he had to get around the curve. Perhaps this was where it finally opened into the canal. As it turned, it tightened. As though the swirling water wasn't enough, Alex felt the brickwork close in on him, scratching his legs and chest. He knew he had very little air left. His lungs were straining and there was a giddy emptiness in his head. He was about to slide into unconsciousness. Well, that would come as a blessing. Maybe he would never feel the water rushing into his mouth and down his throat. Maybe he would be asleep before the end.

He turned the corner. His hands found something—bars of some sort—and he was able to pull his legs around. Only then did he know that his worst fears had been realized. He had come to the end of the well shaft but there was a metal barrier, a circular gate. He was actually holding on to it. There was no way out.

Perhaps it was the sense of having come so far, of being cheated at the end, that gave him strength. Alex pushed and the metal hinges, covered with the rust of three hundred years, shattered. The gate opened. Alex swam forward. His shoulders came clear and he knew that there was nothing above him except water. He kicked out and felt the broken edge of the gate gash into his thigh. But there was no pain. Just a surge of desperation, a need for this to be over.

He was facing up. He could see nothing, but he trusted his natural buoyancy to take him the right way. He felt bubbles hitting his cheeks and eyelids and knew that, without wanting to, he was releasing the last of his breath. How far down had he gone? Did he have enough air left to reach the surface? He kicked as hard as he could, scrabbling with his hands; doing the crawl, only vertically. Once again, he opened his eyes, hoping to see light . . . moonlight, lanterns . . . anything. And maybe there was a glimmer, a white ribbon flickering across his vision.

Alex screamed. Bubbles exploded from his lips. And then the scream itself erupted as he broke through the surface and into the morning light. For a moment his arms and shoulders were clear of the water and he took a huge gasp of air, then fell back. Water splashed all around him. Lying on his back, cushioned by the water, he breathed again. Rivulets of water streamed down the side of his face. Alex knew they were mixed with tears.

He looked around him.

It was about five o'clock in the morning. The sirens were still sounding but there was nobody about. And that was just as well. Alex was floating in the middle of the Grand Canal. He could see the bridge of the Academy, a vague shape in the half-light. The moon was still in the sky, but the sun was already stealing up behind the silent churches and palaces, casting its light across the lagoon.

Alex was so cold that he could no longer feel anything. He was aware only of the deathly grip of the canal, trying to drag him down. With the last of his strength, he swam across to a flight of uneven stone steps. It was on the far side of the Grand Canal, away from the Ca' Vedova. Whatever happened, he never wanted to go near that place again.

He was naked from the waist up. He had lost his

sandals and his trousers were in tatters. Blood was running down one leg, mingling with the filthy canal water. He was soaked. He had no money and his hostel was a train ride away, outside Venice. But Alex didn't care. He was alive.

He took one look back. There was the palace, dark and silent. The party had long ago come to an end.

Slowly, he limped away.

6

THOUGHTS ON A TRAIN

TOM HARRIS SAT BACK in the second-class carriage of the *pendolino*—the fast train from Venice to Naples—and looked out of the window as the buildings and fields flashed by. He was thinking about Alex Rider.

They had met two years ago at Brookland School. Tom—who was about half the size of anyone else in his year—had just been beaten up. This was something that seemed to happen to him rather often. In this case it was a bunch of sixteen-year-olds led by a boy named Michael Cook, who had suggested he should use his lunch money to buy them cigarettes. Tom had politely refused and a short while later Alex had come across him, sitting on the sidewalk, picking up his tattered books and wiping blood from his nose.

"You okay?"

"Yeah. I've got a broken nose. I've lost my lunch

money. And they've told me they're going to do it all again tomorrow. But otherwise I'm fine."

"Mike Cook?"

"Yeah."

"Maybe I should have a word with him."

"What makes you think he'll listen to you?"

"I've got a way with words."

Alex had met the bully and two of his friends behind the bike shed the following day. It was a short meeting, but Michael Cook never bothered anyone else again. It was also noticed that, for the following week, he limped and spoke in a strangely high-pitched voice.

It was the start of a close friendship. Tom and Alex lived near each other and often cycled home together. They were in lots of teams together—despite his size, Tom was extremely quick on his feet. When Tom's parents started talking about divorce, Alex was the only person he told.

In return, Tom probably knew more about Alex than anyone at Brookland. He had been to Alex's house a few times and had met Jack, the cheerful red-haired American girl who wasn't exactly his nanny or housekeeper but seemed to be looking after him somehow. Alex had no parents. Everyone knew that Alex had lived with his uncle—who must have been rich, judging from the house. But then he had died in a car accident. It had been announced at school assembly and Tom had gone over to the house a couple of times, hoping to find Alex, but he had never been in.

After that, Alex had changed. It had started with his first long absence from school in the Easter term and everyone assumed that he must have been knocked off balance by his uncle's death. But then he had disappeared twice in the summer term too. There was no explanation. Nobody seemed to have any idea where he was. When the two of them had finally met again, Tom had been surprised how much his friend had changed. He had been hurt. Tom had seen some of the scars when Alex was changing for games. And he seemed to have gotten a lot older. There was something in his eyes that hadn't been there before, as though he had seen things he would never be able to forget.

And now this business in Venice! Tom had barely slept a wink the night before, worrying about his friend. He had seen Alex disappear into the Widow's Palace and had known that their plan had worked. But after that . . . nothing! Alex hadn't returned to the youth hostel, and as dawn broke and the first light pushed the shadows back from the empty bed on the other side of the room, Tom had lain there, wondering if he should call the police or go back to the palace or—if necessary—leave Venice on his own.

In fact, Alex had turned up just as breakfast was about to start, limping into the hostel in old-fashioned jeans and a baggy jersey, both one size too big for him. He was dirty. His hair was matted and untidy. Tom glanced down and saw that he was barefoot. He looked worn-out.

"Alex . . . ?" Tom was almost too shocked to speak.

"Hi." Alex slumped onto his bed. "I'm back!"

"What happened to you? Where did you get those clothes? You're soaking wet!" Tom didn't know where to begin.

Alex helped him out. "I'm afraid I stole the clothes," he said. "I got them off a washing line. I couldn't get any shoes, though."

"Have you been swimming in the Grand Canal?"

"As a matter of fact, I have." Alex sighed. "I'll tell you on the train. What time does it leave?"

"Ten o'clock."

"Then I've got time for a shower."

He grabbed a towel and moved slowly toward the bathroom.

And now it was one o'clock and he was on the train with Tom, traveling through the Italian countryside. He had slept for the last two hours, his head cradled in his arms. Tom had spent the time listening to his Walkman, occasionally glancing at the silent figure of his friend on the other side of the table. A steward went past and he bought two sandwiches and sodas. At last Alex woke up.

"How are you doing?" Tom asked.

"I'm fine." Alex slowly uncurled himself. It was true. Already he was feeling better. The train hadn't just left Venice behind him but had carried him away from the experiences of the night before. He noticed the food waiting for him on the table.

"I thought you'd be hungry," Tom said.

"Thanks." Alex opened the can of soda. It was lukewarm, but he didn't mind. "Where are we?" he asked.

"We went through Rome about half an hour ago. I think we'll be there quite soon." Tom waited while Alex drank. He unplugged his Walkman and put it

away. "You look really terrible," he said. "Are you going to tell me what happened last night?"

"Sure." Alex knew that he was going to have to tell
Tom everything. He had promised as much the night
before. And anyway, he was tired of lying. "But I'm
not sure you're going to believe it," he added.

"Try me!"

Alex had only ever told one other person the truth
about himself and that had been his friend Sabina
Pleasure. She hadn't believed him . . . not until she'd
found herself knocked out and tied up in the basement of the country mansion owned by the mad multimillionaire Damian Cray. Now Alex told Tom everything he had told her, starting with the truth behind
the death of his uncle and continuing all his way up to
his escape from the flooded chamber the night before.
The strange thing was that he enjoyed telling his story.
He wasn't boasting about being a spy and working for
secret intelligence. Quite the opposite. For too long he
had been a prisoner of MI6, forced by them to keep
quiet about everything he had done. They had even
made him sign the Official Secrets Act. By telling the
truth, he was doing exactly what they didn't want him
to do and it came as a relief, a great weight off his

shoulders. It made him feel that he was the one in control.

". . . I was lucky to get out of the well alive. I swam across the canal and took some clothes off a washing line. I didn't like doing that, but I didn't have any choice. Then I made my way back to the hostel . . . and here I am!"

Alex finished and waited nervously for Tom's response. Tom had said nothing for the last twenty minutes. Would he, like Sabina, walk out on him?

Tom nodded slowly. "Well, that makes sense," he said.

Alex stared. "You believe me?"

"I can't think of any other reason to explain everything that's happened. Missing so much school. And all those injuries. I mean, I thought your housekeeper might be beating you up, but that didn't seem likely. So, yes. You must be a spy. But that's pretty heavy, Alex. I'm glad it's you, not me."

Alex couldn't help smiling. "Tom, you really are my best mate."

"I'm happy to help. But there's one thing you haven't told me. Why were you interested in Scorpia in the first place? And what are you doing now, coming to Naples?"

Alex hadn't mentioned his father. That was the one area that still troubled him. It had always been one area that was too private to share with anyone. But now he had no choice. He had promised to tell Tom the truth. "I've got to find Scorpia," he began. "I told you about Yassen Gregorovich. He was the man who killed my uncle. He was an assassin and I thought he was my enemy. But just before he died, he told me something. He knew my father. The two of them worked together. He even saved Yassen's life."

"But that means . . ."

"Yeah. I never knew my father. I never knew anything about him except that he was in the army once. Now it turns out that he wasn't a good guy. He was some sort of killer!"

"Maybe Yassen was lying."

"I don't think so. What would be the point? Anyway, he told me if I wanted proof, I had to go to Venice and find Scorpia. That's why I'm here."

"And that's why you dragged me with you."

"I'm sorry. I shouldn't have done that."

"No. It doesn't matter." Tom thought for a moment. "What happened to your father?" he asked.

Alex hesitated. This was worse than anything that had gone before. He glanced at Tom, who was watching him carefully. "I was always told that he died in a plane crash," he said. "But that wasn't true. Yassen told me the truth." He took a breath. "He was killed by MI6."

"MI6?" Tom gaped. "But I thought they were on your side."

"That's what I thought too." Alex felt the anger, deep and black, stirring inside him. "All the time they were lying to me, Tom. They killed him!"

Tom ran a hand through his hair. "Alex," he muttered. "This is all pretty serious."

"I know."

"So what are you going to do? Are you going to stay with me in Naples?"

Alex nodded. "I heard Mrs. Rothman talking about a company in Amalfi. That's not too far from Naples. I think it's called Consanto. I saw the same name in a sort of brochure in her desk and the person she was talking to . . . his photograph was inside. She said she'd be there in two days. That's tomorrow. I'd be interested to know why."

"But Alex . . ." Tom frowned. "You met this black guy, Nile . . ."

"Actually, he wasn't exactly black. He was more sort of . . . black and white."

"Well, the moment you mentioned Scorpia, he locked you in a cellar and tried to drown you. Why go back? I mean, it sounds to me that they're not that keen to meet you."

"I know." Alex knew Tom was right. He had learned very little about Julia Rothman. He couldn't even be certain that she was connected to Scorpia. The one thing he did know was that she—and the people who worked for her—were utterly ruthless. But he couldn't leave it. Not yet. Yassen Gregorovich had shown him a path. He had to follow it to the end. "I just want to take a look, that's all."

There was a brief silence. The train rushed through a station, a blur of neon and concrete, without stopping.

"It must mean a lot to you," Tom said. "Finding out about your dad."

"Yes. It does."

"My mum and dad have been shouting at each other for ages. All they ever do is fight. Now they're splitting up and they're fighting about that. I don't care about either of them anymore. I don't think I even like them." For a moment Tom looked sadder than Alex had ever seen him. "So I think I understand what you're saying and I hope you find out something good about your dad, because right now I can't think of anything good about mine."

Jerry Harris, Tom's older brother, met them at the station and took them by taxi to his apartment. He was twenty-two years old and had come to Naples, taking a year out of university to learn Italian. The only trouble was he had forgotten to go back. Alex liked him immediately. Jerry was totally laid-back, thin to the point of scrawny, with bleached hair and a lopsided smile. He was wearing baggy jeans and a sleeveless T-shirt that revealed a small broken-heart tattoo on his left shoulder.

He lived in the Spanish Quarter of the city. It was a typical Naples street; narrow, with buildings five and six stories high on both sides and washing lines strung out between them. Looking up, Alex saw a fantastic patchwork of crumbling plaster, wooden shutters, ornate railings, window boxes, and terraces with Italian women in their aprons leaning out to chat with their neighbors. Jerry was renting a top-floor apartment. There was no elevator. The three of them followed a twisting staircase with a different sound and smell on each floor: disinfectant and a baby crying on the first, tomato sauce and a violin playing on the second . . . and so on.

"This is it," Jerry said, unlocking a door. "Make yourselves at home."

Home was a single open space with hardly any furniture, white painted walls, a wooden floor, and views over the city. There was a kitchen in the corner, piled high with dirty plates, and a door leading to a small bedroom and bathroom. Somehow, someone had dragged a battered leather three-seater sofa all the way up. It sat in the middle of the floor surrounded by a tangle of sports equipment, only some of which Alex recognized. There were two skateboards, ropes and pitons, an oversized kite, a snowboard, and what looked like a parachute. Tom had already told Alex that his brother was into extreme sports. He was teaching English as a foreign language in Naples, but only to pay for his trips mountaineering, surfing, or whatever.

"You two hungry?" Jerry asked.

"Yeah." Tom slumped down on the sofa. "We've been on a train for, like, six hours. You got any food?"

"You've got to be kidding. No. We'll go out and get a pizza or something. How's things, Tom? How are Mum and Dad?"

"The same."

"As bad as that?" Jerry turned to Alex. "Our parents are complete crap. I'm sure my brother's told you. I mean, calling him Tom and me Jerry. How crap can you get?" He shrugged. "So what are you doing down here, Alex? You want to visit the coast?"

On the train, Alex had impressed on Tom the importance of not repeating anything he'd said. Now he winced as Tom announced, "Alex is a spy."

"Is he?"

"Yeah. He works for MI6."

"Wow. That's awesome."

"Thanks." Alex wasn't sure what to say.

"So what are you doing in Naples, Alex?"

Tom answered for him. "He wants to find out about a company. Constanza."

"Consanto," Alex said.

"Consanto Enterprises?" Jerry opened the fridge and took out a beer. Alex noticed that, apart from beer, there was nothing else in the fridge. "I know about them. I used to have one of their people learning English. He was a research chemist or something. I hope he was a better chemist than he was a linguist, because his English was awful."

"Who are Consanto?" Alex asked.

"I don't know. They're one of these big pharma-
ceutical companies. They make drugs and biological
stuff. They've got a plant just outside Amalfi."

"Can you get me in?" For a moment Alex was
hopeful.

"You've got to be kidding. I doubt the Pope could
get in. I drove past once and it's this really high-tech
sort of place. It looks like something out of a science-
fiction film. And it's got all these fences and security
cameras and stuff."

"They must have something to hide," Tom said.

"Of course they've got something to hide, you
dimwit," Jerry muttered. "All these drug companies
are coming up with new patents and they're worth a
fortune. I mean, like, if someone comes up with a cure
for AIDS or something, it would be worth billions.
That's why you can't get in. The guy I was teaching
never said anything about his work. He wasn't allowed to."

"Like Alex."

"What?"

"Being a spy. He's not allowed to say anything
about that either."

"Right." Jerry nodded.

Alex looked from one to the other. Despite the fact

that there were eight years between them, the two brothers were obviously close. He wished he could spend more time with them. He felt more relaxed now than he had in a long time. But that wasn't why he was here. "Can you take me to Amalfi?" he asked.

"Sure." Jerry shrugged and finished his beer. "I haven't got any lessons tomorrow. Would that be okay?"

"It would be great."

"It's only a couple of hours from Naples. I can borrow my girlfriend's car and drive you down. You can see Consanto for yourself. But I'm telling you now, Alex, there's definitely no way in."

7

CONSANTO

STANDING BESIDE THE CAR in the full heat of the midmorning sun, Alex had to admit that Jerry Harris was right. Consanto had certainly done everything it possibly could to protect whatever it was hiding.

There was a single main building, rectangular in shape and at least five hundred yards long. Alex had seen the picture in the brochure and he was struck by how much the actual building resembled it—as though the photograph had been blown up a thousand times, cut out, and somehow made to stand up. It wasn't quite real. Alex was looking at a wall of reflective glass, tapering to a point. Even the sunlight couldn't find a way in. It was a huge black and silver block with a single sign—CONSANTO—cut out of solid steel.

Jerry was standing next to him, dressed in knee-length shorts and a sleeveless T-shirt. He had brought along a pair of binoculars, and Alex examined the wide concrete steps that led up to the main entrance.

There were a few outlying buildings, warehouses, and ventilation plants, and a parking lot with about a hundred cars. He trained the binoculars back onto the roof of the main complex. He could see a pair of water tanks, a row of solar panels, and, next to them, a brick tower with a single open door. A fire escape? If he could reach it, he might just find a way in.

But it was obvious that he could get nowhere near. The entire plant was surrounded by a fence, more than sixty feet high and topped with razor wire. A single track led to a checkpoint with a second checkpoint right behind it. Every car that went in and out was searched. And just to be sure, cameras mounted on steel poles swiveled and rotated, the lenses sweeping over every inch of ground. Even a fly trying to get in would have been noticed. And swatted, Alex gloomily thought.

Consanto Enterprises had chosen its position carefully. Amalfi, the busy, densely populated Mediterranean port, was about two miles to the north. There were a few isolated villages to the south. The complex was in a sort of hole, a flat and rocky stretch of landscapes with few trees, few buildings, nowhere to hide. The Gulf of Salerno was to the east. Alex was standing with the sea behind him. There were sailing boats dotted about and a single ferry plowed through the water on its way to the island of Capri. But his main impression was that it would be impossible to approach Consanto from any direction without being noticed. He was probably being filmed even now.

"You see what I mean?" Jerry said.

Tom had his back to the buildings. He was looking at the sea. "Anyone fancy a swim?" he asked.

"Yeah." Jerry nodded slowly. "You bring any trunks?"

"No."

"It doesn't matter. We can swim in our underpants."

"I'm not wearing underpants."

Jerry glanced at his brother. "Charming!"

Alex watched as a supply van made its way past the first control post. It really did look impossible. Even if he managed to sneak into a car or a truck, he would be found when it was searched. There was no point waiting until nightfall. There were dozens of arc lamps arranged around the perimeter and they would flick on the moment it was dark. He could see uniformed guards moving through the grounds with German shepherd dogs on leashes. They would probably be there all night.

He was about to give up. He couldn't get in from the front or the sides. He couldn't climb the fence. He looked past the complex. It had been set against a sheer cliff. The rock face rose at least three hundred yards and he noticed a cluster of buildings, far away, at the very top.

He pointed. "What's that?" he asked.

Jerry followed the direction of his finger. "I don't know." He thought for a moment. "It's probably Ravello. It's a hilltop village."

"Can we go there?"

"Yeah. Sure. There's a road from Amalfi."

Alex put it all together in an instant. The flat rooftop with the fire escape, seemingly open. The village perched high up on the cliff. The equipment he had seen in Jerry's apartment in Naples. Suddenly it was very simple.

Consanto Enterprises might look impregnable. But he had found a way in.

The faded eighteenth-century villa stood some distance away from Ravello, reached by a path that twisted along the side of the mountain, high above the pine trees. It was a wonderful place to escape to, lost in its own world, far away from the crowds on the beaches and in the streets below. A cool evening breeze blew in from the sea and the light had turned from a blue to a mauve to a deep red as the sun slowly set. There was an ornamental garden with a long avenue running down the center and, at the far end, a terrace that appeared unexpectedly with white plaster heads mounted on the parapet. Beyond the terrace there was nothing. The garden simply came to an abrupt end with a sheer drop, straight down to the coastal road, the Consanto complex and the rocky flatlands 350 yards below.

The tourists had long ago left for the evening. The villa was about to close. Alex stood on his own, thinking about what he had to do. His mouth was dry and there was an unpleasant churning in his stomach. This was madness. There had to be another way . . .

No. He had examined all the possibilities. This was the only way.

He knew that BASE jumping was one of the most dangerous of all "extreme" sports, and that every BASE jumper would know someone who had been injured or killed. BASE stands for Buildings, Antennae, Spans, and Earth. It means, essentially, parachuting without the use of an aircraft. BASE jumpers will throw themselves off skyscrapers, dams, rock faces, and bridges. The jumps aren't actually against the law, but they're usually done without permission, often in the middle of the night. Trespassing, being outside the system, is all part of the fun.

Jerry Harris had driven all the way back to Naples to get the equipment, which he had agreed to lend to Alex. He had used the long journey to give Alex as much knowledge as he could about the techniques and the potential dangers. "A crash course," Tom had exclaimed cheerfully. Just what Alex didn't need.

"The first and most important rule is the one that beginners find hardest," he said. "When you jump, you've got to wait as long as possible before you release the canopy. The longer you wait, the farther you travel away from the side of the cliff. And you must keep your shoulders level. The last thing you need is a one-eighty onto a hard-core object."

"What's that in English?" Alex asked.

"It's what happens when you get an off-heading opening. Basically, it means you go the wrong way and hit the cliff."

"And what happens then?"

"Yeah. Well . . . You die."

Alex was wearing a helmet, knee pads, and shoulder pads. Jerry had also lent him a pair of sturdy hiking boots. But that was all. He would need to react instantly as he fell through the sky and too much protective gear would only slow him down. Besides, as Jerry had pointed out, nobody had ever made a BASE jump without basic training. If something went wrong, all the protective clothes in the world wouldn't do him one bit of good.

And the difference between life and death?

For Alex, it boiled down to 160 square feet of F111 nylon. Skydivers need one square foot of parachute for every pound of their body weight. But BASE jumpers need almost double that. Alex's chute had been designed for Jerry, who was quite a bit heavier than him. He would have plenty enough.

He was carrying a seven-cell Blackjack canopy, which Jerry had bought secondhand for a little under one thousand American dollars. An ordinary parachute normally contains nine cells—nine separate pockets. The larger BASE canopy is thought to be more docile, easier to fly and land accurately. Alex's own weight would drag it out of the deployment bag as he fell and it would inflate over his head, taking the shape of an aerofoil, the ram-air design of all modern parachutes.

Jerry stood next to him, pointing a black gadget

about the size and shape of a pair of binoculars at the ground. He was taking a reading. "Three hundred and fifty-seven meters," he said. He took out a laminated card—an Altitude Delay Planner—and quickly consulted it. "You can do an eight," he said. "It'll give you twenty-five seconds under canopy. A twelve, max. But that'll mean landing almost at once."

Alex understood what he was saying. He could free-fall for between eight and twelve seconds. The less time he spent dangling underneath the parachute, the less chance he would have of being spotted from below. On the other hand, the faster he arrived, the more chance he would have of breaking most of his bones.

"And when you get down there, remember . . ."

"Flaring."

"Yes. If you don't want to break both your legs, you have to slow yourself down about three or four seconds before impact."

"Not three or four seconds *after* impact," Tom added helpfully. "That'll be too late."

"Thanks!"

Alex looked around. There was nobody in sight. He half wished a policeman or somebody from the villa would come along and put a stop to this before he actually did it. But the gardens were empty. The white plaster heads stared past him, not remotely interested.

"You'll go from nought to sixty miles per hour in about three seconds," Jerry went on. "I've put on a mesh slider, but you're still going to feel the opening shock. At least that'll warn you you're about to land. That's when you get both feet and knees together. Put your chin on your chest. And try not to bite your tongue in half. I almost did on my first time."

"Yes." Single words were about all Alex could manage.

Jerry looked over the precipice. "The roof of Consanto is right underneath us and there's no wind. You won't have much time to steer, but you can try pulling on the toggles." He rested a hand on Alex's shoulder. "I could do this for you, if you like," he said. "I actually enjoy this kind of thing."

"No." Alex shook his head. "Thanks, Jerry. But it's down to me. It was my idea. . . ."

"Good luck."

"Break a leg!" Tom exclaimed with a grin. "Or rather . . . don't."

Alex moved to the edge between two of the statues and looked down. He was right over the complex, although from this height it looked tiny, like a silver Lego brick. Most of the workers would have left by now, but there would still be guards. He would just have to hope that nobody looked up in the twenty seconds it would take him to arrive. But that was what he had noticed earlier, outside the gate. Consanto faced the sea. The main road and the entrance were on the same side. That was where all attention would be focused, and if Alex was lucky, he would be able to drop in—quite literally—unnoticed.

His stomach heaved. There was no feeling in his legs. He felt as though he were floating. He tried to take a deep breath, but the air didn't seem to want to rise above his chest. Did it really matter to him so much, penetrating Scorpia, finding out how it might be involved with Consanto? What would Tom and his brother say if he changed his mind, even at this last minute?

To hell with it, he thought. Lots of teenagers do BASE jumps. Jerry himself had recently jumped the New River Gorge bridge in Virginia. It had been Bridge Day, the one day in the year when the jump was legal, and he had said there had been dozens of kids waiting in line. It was a sport. People did it for fun. If he hesitated even for one second more, he would never do it. It was time to get it over with.

With a single movement, he climbed onto the parapet, checked the line from the pilot chute, took one last look at the target, and jumped.

It was like nothing he had ever experienced.

It was like committing suicide.

Everything was a blur. There was the sky, the edge of the cliff, and (unless he imagined it) Tom's staring face. Then it all tilted. The blue rushed into the gray with the white of the roof punching up. The wind hammered into his face. His eyes were being sucked into the backs of their sockets with the sudden acceleration. How fast was he falling? Fifty feet a second? That was what it felt like. He had to deploy. No. Jerry had warned him about this. How long could he wait?

Now!

He threw out the pilot chute, hoping it would find the clean airflow that was meant to surround him. Had it worked? The chute had already disappeared, dragging with it the bridle line that would in turn suck the Blackjack canopy out of its pack. God! He'd left it too late. He was falling too fast. A long, silent scream with the wind in his ears, skin crawling, the fabric of the suit flapping and rattling. Where was the bloody chute? Where was up? Where was down? Falling . . .

And then there was a sudden, wrenching, braking sensation. He thought he was being pulled in half. He could see something—ropes and billowing material—just outside his vision. The canopy! But that didn't matter. Where was he going? He looked down and saw his own feet, dangling in space. A white rectangle was racing up to meet them. The roof of the complex—but it was too far away. He was going to miss. Quick. Pull the toggle. That's better. The roof tilted back toward him. What had he forgotten? Flaring! He pulled down on both toggles, dropping the tail of the canopy so that—like a plane landing—he came in at an upward angle. But had he left it too late?

All he could see was the surface of the roof. Then he hit it. He felt the shock travel through his ankles, his knees, and up into his thighs. He ran forward. The canopy was dragging him. Jerry had warned him about this. There might be a stronger breeze lower down, and if he wasn't careful, he would be pulled off the roof. He could see the edge racing toward him. He dug in his heels, reaching behind him for the risers. He caught hold of them and pulled them in. Stop running! With just inches to spare, he managed to get a grip with the balls of his feet. He leaned back, pulling the canopy toward him. He sat down hard.

He had arrived.

For a few seconds he did nothing. He was experiencing the massive high that all BASE jumpers know and that makes the sport so addictive. His body was releasing a flood of adrenaline and it was coursing through his entire system. His heart was pumping at double speed. He could feel every hair standing up on his skin. He looked back up at the cliff. There was no sign of Tom or his older brother. Even if they had been standing there, they would have been too small to see. Alex couldn't believe how far he'd traveled, or how quickly he'd arrived. And as far as he could tell, the guards had kept their heads down, their eyes on the ground, not the air. So much for Consanto's security!

Alex waited until his heart and pulse rate returned to normal, then pulled off the helmet and protective pads. He quickly folded the chute and packed it as best as he could inside the bag. He could taste blood in his mouth and realized that despite Jerry's warnings, he'd still managed to bite his tongue.

Keeping low, he carried the bag with the canopy over to the door that he had seen at ground level. He was going to have to leave Jerry's equipment up here on the roof until it was time to leave. He had more or less worked out how he was going to get out of Consanto. The easiest way would simply be to call the police and get himself arrested. At the very worst, he would be prosecuted for trespassing. But he was only fourteen. He doubted he would find himself in an Italian jail—more likely they would pack him off back to England.

The door was open. He had been right about that. A dozen cigarette butts on the roof told their own story. Despite all the security guards, the cameras, and the high-tech alarms, a single smoker in need of a nicotine fix had found his way up here and blown the whole place wide-open.

Well, that was fine. Alex slipped in through the door and found a flight of metal steps leading down. There was a set of more solid-looking doors—steel with small glass windows—and for a moment Alex thought his way was blocked. But there must have been some sort of sensor, because the doors slid open as he approached, then closed again after him. Perhaps the anonymous smoker had set it up that way. Alex turned around and waved a hand. The doors didn't move. A numerical keypad on the wall told him the bad news. Getting in this way was one thing. But to get out again, he would need some sort of code. He was trapped.

There was only one way to go. Forward.

He followed a blank white corridor down to another set of doors, which hissed open and shut as he passed through. He knew at once that he had entered the core of the complex. There was an immediate difference to the air quality. It was cold and smelled metallic. He looked up and saw a brightly polished silver duct running the full length of the passage. There were dials and monitors everywhere. Already, his head was beginning to ache. This place was just too clean.

He kept moving, wanting to see as much as possible before he was discovered. There didn't seem to be anyone around, but it could only be a matter of time before security looked in.

A door opened somewhere. Alex's heart leaped and he quickly searched for somewhere to hide. The corridor was bare, brightly lit by powerful neon lights behind glass panels. There wasn't so much as a shadow to give him cover. He saw a doorway and hurried over to it, but the door was locked. Someone turned the corner and Alex pressed himself against the door, hoping against hope that he wouldn't be seen.

A man turned the corner. At first it was hard to say that it was a man. The figure was wrapped in a pale blue protective suit that covered every inch of his body. He had a hood over his head and a glass mask in front of his face, obscuring most of his features— but then he turned sideways and Alex caught a glimpse of glasses and a beard. The man was pushing what looked like a huge tea urn, shining chrome, mounted on wheels. The urn was as tall as he was, with a series of valves and pipes on the lid. The man turned off down a second corridor and a moment later he was gone.

The door had provided Alex with minimal cover— but it had been enough. Now he looked through the door's thick glass window—like the front of a washing machine: There was a large room on the other side, still lit but empty. Alex supposed it must be a laboratory, but it looked more like a distillery with more urns, some of them suspended on chains. There was a metal staircase leading up to some sort of gantry and a whole wall lined with what looked like floor-to-ceiling fridge doors. All the metal looked brand-new, brilliantly polished. As he watched, a woman crossed the room. The complex obviously wasn't as deserted as he had thought! She was also dressed in a protective uniform with a mask across her face, and she was pushing a silver cart. Alex's breath frosted on the glass as he tried to see in. It didn't make any sense, but the woman seemed to be carrying eggs . . . hundreds of them, neatly lined up on trays. They were the size of ordinary chickens' eggs, every one of them pure white. Could the woman be part of the catering team? Alex doubted it. There was something almost sinister about the eggs. Perhaps it was their uniformity, the fact that they were all so obviously identical. The woman went behind some machinery and disappeared. Increasingly puzzled, Alex decided it was time to move on.

He went down a second corridor, following the direction of the man with the urn. Now he could hear machinery, a soft, rhythmic clattering. He came to a glass panel set in the wall and looked through it into a darkened room where a second woman sat in front of a bizarre, complicated machine that seemed to be sorting hundreds of test tubes, rotating them, counting them, labeling them, and finally delivering them into her hands.

What was being made at Consanto Enterprises? Chemical weapons, perhaps? And how in the world was he going to get out again? Alex glanced down and noticed his hands, still grubby from his BASE jump. He was dirty and sweaty and he was surprised he hadn't set off every single alarm in the building. Surrounded by these white paneled walls, with the air being sucked in and sterilized, he had become the equivalent of an enormous germ and the monitors should have screamed the moment he came near.

He came to another set of doors and was relieved when these slid open to allow him through. Perhaps he might be able to find his way to an exit after all. But the doors led only to another corridor, a little wider than the one he had just left but equally unpromising. It occurred to him that he was still on the top floor. There were no windows, but he had come in from the roof. So he needed to find an elevator or a staircase that would take him down. He took a step forward. Then a door about ten yards away opened and a man stepped out, staring at Alex in disbelief.

"Who the hell are you and what are you doing here?" he demanded.

Alex registered that the man was talking in English. At the same time, he recognized him: the bald head, the hooked nose, and the heavy black glasses. He was wearing a white laboratory coat hanging loose over a jacket and tie, but the last time Alex had seen him, he had been in costume. This was Dr. Liebermann, the man he had seen talking to Mrs. Rothman at the party in Venice.

"I . . ." Alex wasn't sure what to say. "I'm lost," he muttered helplessly.

"You can't come in here! This is a secure area! Who are you?"

"My name's Tom. My dad works here."

"What is his name? What's his department?" The man wasn't going to buy the little-boy-lost routine. "How did you get here?" he asked.

"My dad brought me. But if you'd like to show me the way out, that's fine by me."

"No! I'll call security. You can come with me!"

He took a step back toward the office or the laboratory from which he'd come. Alex wasn't sure what to do. Should he try to run? Once the alarm had gone off, it would only be a matter of minutes before he was caught. And what then? He had assumed that Consanto would simply hand him over to the police. But if they were hiding something here, if he had seen something secret, maybe he wouldn't be so fortunate.

Dr. Liebermann was reaching out for something and Alex saw an alarm button next to the door.

"It's all right, Harold. I'll deal with this."

The voice came from behind Alex.

Alex spun around and felt his heart sink. It was like a bad dream. Nile, the man who had knocked him out and left him to drown, was standing behind him, a smile on his face, totally relaxed. He too was wearing a white coat. In his case, it hung over jeans and a tight-fitting T-shirt. He had a gray attaché case in one hand, but as Alex watched, he set it down on the floor beside him.

"I wasn't expecting to see you." Harold Liebermann was puzzled.

"Mrs. Rothman sent me."

"Why?"

"Well, as you can see, Dr. Liebermann, there's been a very serious breakdown in security. She asked me to deal with it."

"Do you know this boy? Who is he?"

"His name is Alex Rider."

"He said his name was Tom."

"He's lying. He's a spy."

Alex was caught in the middle of this conversation with one man on either side of him. He was trapped between them. He felt dazed. And he knew there was nothing he could do. Nile was too fast and too strong for him. He had already proved that once.

"What are you going to do?" Liebermann demanded. He sounded peeved, as though neither Alex nor Nile had any right to be here.

"I just told you, Harold. We can't have security problems. I'm going to deal with it."

Nile reached under his coat and produced one of the most lethal-looking weapons Alex had ever seen. It was a samurai sword, very slightly curving, with a black ivory hilt and a flat, razor-sharp blade. But it was half-sized—somewhere between a sword and a dagger. Nile held it for a moment in his hand, obviously enjoying the fine balance, then raised it to the height of his shoulder. Now he could throw it or slash with it. Either way, Alex knew instantly, he was facing a master. He had perhaps seconds to live.

"You can't kill him here!" Liebermann exclaimed in an exasperated tone of voice. "You'll get blood everywhere!"

"Don't worry, Harold," Nile replied. "This is going through the neck and into the brain. There'll be very little blood."

Alex crouched down, preparing to duck, knowing that he wouldn't have a chance. Nile was still smiling, obviously enjoying himself.

He threw the sword.

There was a single movement. Alex hadn't even seen Nile take aim, but the blade was already a blur, flashing down the length of the passageway. It passed over Alex's shoulder. Had Nile missed? No. That was impossible. He suddenly realized that Nile hadn't been aiming at him.

Alex turned around and saw Dr. Liebermann already dead, still standing, a look of total surprise on his face. He had managed to bring one hand up so that it was lightly holding the blade of the sword that was now sticking out of the side of his neck. He pitched forward and lay still.

"Straight into the brain," Nile muttered. "Just like I said."

As Alex watched, utterly stunned, Nile ran forward and knelt down beside Dr. Liebermann. He pulled the sword out, used the dead man's tie to wipe it clean, and returned it to its sheath—which hung from his waist, underneath his coat. He looked up.

"Hello, Alex," he said cheerfully. "You're the last person I expected to see here. Mrs. Rothman will be pleased."

"You don't want to kill me?" Alex muttered. He still couldn't believe what had just happened.

"Not at all."

He went back to the attaché case and opened it. Alex was finding it very difficult to keep up with what was going on. Inside the case he saw a keyboard, a small computer screen, two square packets, and a series of wires. Nile knelt down and tapped on the keyboard. A series of codes appeared on the screen: black and white, like the fingers that were typing them. He continued talking as he worked.

"I hope you'll forgive me, Alex. I have to say, I'm terribly sorry for what happened at the Ca' Vedova. I didn't realize who you were . . . John Rider's son. I think it's brilliant how you managed to escape, by the way. I'd never have forgiven myself if I'd had to go in and fish you out with a boat hook." He finished typing, pressed enter, then closed the lid of the case. "But we can't really talk now. Mrs. Rothman is just down the coast . . . in Positano. She's dying to meet you. So let's go."

"Why did you kill Dr. Liebermann?" Alex asked.

"Because Mrs. Rothman told me to." Nile straightened up. "Look, I'm sure you've got a lot of questions, but I can't answer them right now. I've just set a bomb to blow this place to smithereens in"—he glanced at his watch—"ninety-two seconds' time. So I don't think we have time for a chat."

He slid the case so it lay near Dr. Liebermann's head, checked the dead man one last time, then walked away. Alex followed him. What else could he do? Nile came to a set of doors and tapped in a code. The doors opened and they went through. They were moving more quickly now. Nile had the athlete's ability to cover a lot of ground with no seeming effort at all. Here was the staircase that Alex had been looking for. They went down three floors and came to another door. Nile punched in another number and suddenly they were in the open air. There was a car—a two-seater Alfa Romeo Spider—waiting outside with the top down.

"Hop in!" Nile said. From the way he was talking, he and Alex could have just come from the cinema and been on their way home.

Alex got in next to Nile and they drove off. How much time had passed since Nile had set the bomb? It was dark outside. The sun had finally disappeared. They followed a tarmac drive to the main checkpoint. Nile smiled at the guard.

"Grazie. E'stato bello verdervi. . . ."

Thank you. It was good to see you. Alex already knew from their first meeting that Nile spoke Italian. The guard nodded and raised the barrier.

Nile gunned the accelerator and the car shot forward smoothly. Alex twisted around in his seat. They had driven only for a few seconds when there was an enormous explosion. It was as though a fist of orange flame had decided to punch its way out of the main complex. Windows shattered. Smoke and fire rushed out. Thousands of pieces of glass and steel, a deadly rainfall, showered down. Alarms—shrill and deafening—erupted. A huge bite had been taken out of the side and the roof of the building. Alex had seen the size of the bomb. It was hard to believe that it could have done so much damage.

Nile glanced in the mirror, examining his handiwork. He tutted.

"These industrial accidents," he muttered. "You can never tell when one is going to happen next."

He steered the Alfa Spider along the coastal road, already doing eighty miles per hour. Behind him, Consanto Enterprises burned, the flames leaping up and reflecting in the dark and silent sea.

8

DESIGNER LABELS

ALEX STOOD ON THE BALCONY with a sweeping view of the town of Positano and the black water of the Mediterranean beyond. Two hours had passed since sunset, but the warmth still hung in the air. He was dressed in a terry-cloth robe, his hair still wet from the power shower with its jets of steaming hot water blasting him from six directions. There was a glass of fresh lime juice and ice on the table next to him. From the moment he had met Nile for a second time, he had thought he was in a dream. Now that dream seemed to have taken him in a new and very strange direction.

The hotel, first. It was called The Sirenuse and, as Nile had been happy to tell him, it was one of the most luxurious in the whole of Southern Italy. Alex's room was huge and didn't look like a hotel room at all . . . more like a guest suite in an Italian palace. The bed was king-sized with pure white, Egyptian cotton sheets. He had his own desk, a thirty-six-inch TV with video and DVD, a sprawling leather sofa, and, on the other side of the floor-to-ceiling windows, his own private terrace. And the bathroom! As well as the power shower, there was a bath big enough for a football team, and a Jacuzzi. Everything in marble and handcrafted tiles. The millionaire suite. Alex shuddered to think how much it must cost a night.

Nile had driven him here from what was left of Consanto Enterprises. Neither of them had spoken on the short journey. There were a hundred things Alex wanted to ask Nile, but the rush of wind and the roar of the Alfa Spider's 126kW quad camshaft V6 engine made conversation impossible and anyway, Alex got the impression that Nile wasn't the one with the answers. It had only taken them twenty minutes, following the coast down from Amalfi, and suddenly they were there, parked in front of a hotel that was deceptively small and ordinary . . . from the outside.

While Alex signed in, Nile made a quick call on his cell phone.

"Mrs. Rothman is absolutely thrilled you're here," he said. "She's going to have dinner with you at nine o'clock. She's asked me to send up some clothes." He weighed Alex up. "I've got a good eye for size. Do you have any particular likes or dislikes when it comes to style?"

"Whatever you want," Alex said.

"Good. The bellboy will take you up to your room. I'm really so glad I ran into you, Alex. I know you and I are going to be friends. Enjoy your dinner. The food here is world-class."

He went back to the car and drove away.

"I know you and I are going to be friends." Alex shook his head in disbelief. Just a few days ago, the same man had knocked him out and left him in a subterranean cell to drown.

He was shaken out of these thoughts by the arrival of an elderly man in a uniform who gestured and then led Alex up to his room on the second floor, taking him along corridors filled with antiques and fine art. At last he was left on his own. He checked at once. The door was unlocked. The two telephones on the desk both had dial tones. He could presumably call anyone, anywhere in the world . . . and that included the police. He had, after all, just witnessed the destruction of a large part of Consanto Enterprises and the murder of Harold Liebermann. But Nile obviously trusted him to stay silent, at least until he had met with Mrs. Rothman. He could also walk out if he wanted

to. He could simply disappear. But again, they assumed he would want to stay. It was all very puzzling.

Alex sipped his drink and considered the view.

It was a beautiful night, the sky stretching to eternity with thousands of brilliant stars. He could hear
the waves rolling in, far below. The town of Positano
was built on a steep hillside with shops and restaurants, houses and apartments all piled up on top of
each other with a series of interlocking alleyways and
a single narrow street zigzagging all the way down to
the horseshoe bay below. There were lights everywhere. The holiday season was drawing to a close, but
the place was still crowded with people determined to
enjoy what the summer had to offer right to the end.

There was a knock at the door. Alex went back
into the room and walked across the shining marble
floor. A waiter in a white jacket and a black bow tie
had appeared. "Your clothes, sir," he said. He handed
Alex a case. "Mr. Nile suggested the suit for tonight,"
he added. He turned and left.

Alex opened the case. It was full of clothes, all of
them expensive, all of them brand-new. The suit was
on the top. He took it out and laid it on the bed. It was
charcoal gray, silk, with a Miu Miu label. There was a
white shirt to go with it: Armani. Underneath he

found a slim leather box. He opened it and gasped. They had even provided him with a new watch, a Baume & Mercier with a polished steel bracelet. He lifted it out and weighed it in his hand. It must have cost hundreds of dollars. First the room, now all this! He was certainly having money thrown at him—and like the water in the power shower, it was coming from all directions.

He thought for a moment. He wasn't sure what he was letting himself in for, but he might as well play along with it for the time being. It was almost nine o'clock and he was ravenous. He got dressed and examined himself in the mirror. The suit was in the classic mod style, with small lapels that barely came down to his chest and tightly fitted trousers. The tie was dark blue, narrow, and straight. Mrs. Rothman had also provided him with black suede shoes from D&G. It was quite an outfit. Alex barely recognized himself.

At exactly nine o'clock he entered the restaurant on the lower ground floor. The hotel, he now realized, was built on the side of the hill, so it was bigger than it seemed, with much of it on levels below the entrance and reception. He found himself in a long, arched room with tables spilling out onto another long terrace. It was lit by hundreds of tiny candles arranged in glass chandeliers. The place was crowded. Waiters were hurrying from table to table and the room was full of the clatter of knives against plates and the low murmur of conversation.

Julia Rothman had the best table, in the middle of the terrace, with views over Positano and out to sea. She was sitting on her own with a glass of champagne, waiting for him, wearing a low-cut black dress with a simple diamond necklace around her neck. She saw him, smiled, and waved. Alex walked over to her, feeling suddenly self-conscious in the suit. Most of the other diners seemed to be casually dressed. He wished now that he hadn't put on the tie.

"Alex, you look wonderful." She ran her dark eyes over him. "The suit fits you perfectly. It's Miu Miu, isn't it? I love the style. Please. Sit down."

Alex took his place at the table. He wondered what anyone watching might think. A mother and her son out for the evening? He felt like an extra in a film— and he was beginning to wish someone would show him the script.

"It's been a while since I ate dinner with my own boy toy. Will you have some champagne?"

"No, thank you."

"What, then?"

A waiter had appeared out of nowhere and was standing next to Alex, waiting to take the order.

"I'll have an orange juice, please. Freshly squeezed. With ice."

The waiter bowed and went to get it. Alex waited for Mrs. Rothman to speak. He was playing the game her way, but she was the one with the rules.

"The food here is absolutely wonderful," she said. "Some of the best cooking in Italy and, of course, Italian is the best food in the world. I hope you don't mind, I've already ordered for you. If there's anything you don't like, you can send it back."

"That's fine."

She lifted her glass of champagne. Alex could see the tiny bubbles rising to the surface in the honey-colored liquid. "I shall drink to your health," she said. "But first you have to say you've forgiven me. What happened to you at the Ca' Vedova was monstrous. I feel utterly embarrassed."

"You mean, trying to kill me," Alex said.

"My dear Alex! You came to my party without an invitation. You crept around the house and sneaked into my study. You mentioned a name that should have gotten you killed instantly and you're really very lucky that Nile decided to drown you rather than break your neck. So although what happened was very unfortunate, you can hardly say it was unprovoked. Of course, it would all have been different if we'd known who you were."

"I told Nile my name."

"It obviously didn't register with him and he didn't mention it to me until the morning afterward. I was shocked when I heard. I couldn't believe it. Alex Rider, the son of John Rider, in my house—and he'd been locked in that place and left to . . ." She closed her eyes for a moment. "We had to wait for the water to go down before we could open the door. I was sick with worry. I thought we were going to be too late. And then . . . ! We looked inside and there was nobody there. You'd done a Houdini and completely disappeared. I assume you swam down the well?"

"Yes."

"I'm amazed it was big enough. Anyway, I was furious with Nile. He wasn't thinking. The very fact that you were called Rider should have been enough. And for him to run into you a second time at Consanto! What were you doing there, by the way?"

"I was looking for you."

She thought for a moment. "You must have seen

the brochure in my desk. And did you overhear me talking to Harold Liebermann?" She didn't wait for an answer. "There's one thing I absolutely have to know. How did you get into the complex?"

"I jumped off the terrace at Ravello."

"With a parachute?"

"Of course."

Julia Rothman threw back her head and laughed out loud. At that moment, she looked more like a film star than anyone Alex had ever met. Not just beautiful, but supremely confident. "That's wonderful," she said. "That's really quite wonderful."

"It was a borrowed parachute," Alex said. "It belonged to a friend of mine. I've lost all his equipment. And he'll be wondering where I am."

"You'd better call him tonight and let him know you survived. And tomorrow I'll write him a check. It's the least I can do after everything that's happened."

The waiter arrived with Alex's orange juice and the first course: two plates of ravioli. The little white parcels were wonderfully fresh, filled with wild mushrooms, and served with a salad of mixed greens and parmesan cheese. Alex tasted one. He had to admit that the food was as delicious as Mrs. Rothman had promised.

"What's wrong with Nile?" he asked.

"He can be exceptionally stupid. Act first, ask questions later. He never stops to think."

"I meant his skin color."

"Oh, that! He suffers from vitiligo. I'm sure you've heard of it. It's an autoimmune disease. His antibodies are attacking his pigment cells or something like that. The singer Michael Jackson claims to have the same thing. Poor Nile! He was born black, but he'll die completely white. But let's not talk about him. There are so many other things we need to discuss."

"You knew my father," Alex said.

"I knew him very well, Alex. He was a good friend of mine. And I have to say, you're his spitting image. I can't tell you how strange it is to be sitting here with you. Here I am, fifteen years older. But you . . ." She looked deep into his eyes. Alex saw that she was examining him, but at the same time he felt as though she were sucking something out of him. "It's almost as though he's come back," she said.

"I want to know about him," Alex said.

"What can I tell you that you don't know already?"

"I don't know anything, except what Yassen told me." Alex paused. This was the moment he had been dreading. This was the reason he was here. "Was my father an assassin?" he asked.

But Mrs. Rothman didn't answer. Her eyes had momentarily slipped away. "You met Yassen Gregorovich," she said. "Was it he who led you to me?"

"I was there when he died."

"I was sorry about Yassen. I'd heard he'd been killed."

"I want to know about my father," Alex insisted. "He worked for an organization called Scorpia. He was a killer. Is that right?"

"Your father was my friend."

"You're not answering my question," Alex said, trying not to get angry. Mrs. Rothman seemed friendly enough, but he already knew that she was very rich and very ruthless. He suspected that he would regret it if he got on the wrong side of her.

Mrs. Rothman herself was perfectly calm. "I don't want to talk about him," she said. "Not yet. Not until I've had a chance to talk about you."

"What do you want to know about me?"

"I know a great deal about you already, Alex. You have an amazing reputation. That's the reason why we're sitting here tonight. I have an offer to make, something that may startle you. But I want you to understand, right from the start, that you're completely free. You can walk away from here anytime. I don't want to hurt you. Quite the opposite. All that I'm asking is that you consider what I have to say and then tell me what you think."

"And then you'll tell me about my dad?"

"Everything you want to know."

"All right."

Mrs. Rothman had finished her champagne. She gestured with one hand and immediately a waiter appeared to refill her glass. "I love champagne," she said. "Are you sure you won't change your mind?"

"I don't drink alcohol," Alex said.

"That's probably wise." Suddenly she was serious. "From what I understand, you've worked for the intelligence services in England four times," she began. "There was that business with the Stormbreaker computers. Then the school they sent you to in the South of France. Then you were in America. And fi-

nally you met up with Damian Cray. What I want to
know is, why did you do it? What did you get out of
it?"

"What do you mean?"

"Were you paid?"

Alex shook his head. "No."

Mrs. Rothman considered for a moment. "Then . . .
are you a patriot?"

Alex shrugged. "I like England," he said. "And I
suppose I'd fight for it if there was a war. But I
wouldn't call myself a patriot. No."

"Well, then, you need to answer my question.
What are you doing risking your life and getting hurt
for MI6? You're not going to tell me it's because
you're fond of Alan Blunt and Mrs. Jones. I've met
both of them and I can't say they did anything for me!
You've put your life on the line for them, Alex. You've
been hurt . . . nearly killed. Why?"

Alex was confused. "What are you getting at?"
he demanded. "Why are you asking me all this?"

"Because, as I said, I want to make you an offer."

"What offer?"

Mrs. Rothman ate some of her ravioli. She used
only a fork, cutting each pasta envelope in half, then
spearing it with the prongs. She ate very delicately.

Alex could see the pleasure in her eyes. It wasn't just food for her. It was a work of art.

"How would you like to work for me?" she asked.

"For Scorpia?"

"Yes."

"Like my father?"

"Yes."

"You're asking me to become a killer?"

"Perhaps." She smiled. "You have a great many skills, Alex. For a fourteen-year-old, you're quite re-markable and, of course, being so young, you could be very useful to us in all sorts of different ways. I imagine that's why Mr. Blunt has been so keen to hang on to you. You can do things and go places that an adult can't."

"What is Scorpia?" Alex demanded. "What were you doing at Consanto? What were they making in that complex? And why did you have to kill Dr. Liebermann?"

Mrs. Rothman finished eating her first course and laid down her fork. Alex found himself hypnotized by her necklace. It was reflecting the light of the can-dles, each diamond multiplying and magnifying the yellow flames.

"What a lot of questions!" she remarked. She

shrugged. "Consanto Enterprises is a perfectly ordinary biomedical company. If you want to know about
them, you can look them up in the telephone book.
They have offices all over Italy. As to what we were
doing there, I can't tell you. At the moment we're involved in an operation called Invisible Sword, but
there's no reason for you to know anything about it.
Not yet. I will, however, tell you why we had to kill Dr.
Liebermann. It's really very simple. It was because
he was unreliable. We paid him a great deal to help
us in a certain matter. He was worried about what he
was doing and at the same time he wanted more. A
man like that can be a danger to us all. It was safer to
be rid of him.

"But let's go back to your first question. You want
to know about Scorpia. That's why you were in
Venice and that's why you've followed me here. Very
well. I'll tell you."

She sipped her champagne, then set the glass
down. Alex realized that their table had been positioned so that they could talk without being overheard. Even so, Mrs. Rothman moved a little closer
before she spoke.

"Scorpia is a criminal organization," she began.
"Don't look so surprised, Alex. I'm sure you'd

guessed. The *S* stands for sabotage. The *CORP* comes from corruption. The *I* is intelligence . . . in other words, spying. And the *A* is for assassination. These are our main areas of expertise, although there are others. We are successful and that has made us powerful. We can be found all over the world. The secret services can't do anything about us. We're too big and they've left it too late. Anyway, occasionally some of them make use of us. They pay us to do their dirty work for them. We've learned to live side by side!"

"And you want me to join you?" Alex put down his knife and fork although he hadn't finished eating. "I'm not like you. I'm not like that at all."

"How strange. Your father was."

That hurt him. She was talking about a man he had never really met. But her words cut straight to the heart of who and what he was.

"Alex, you have to grow up a little bit and stop seeing things in black and white. You work for MI6. Do you think of them as the good guys, the ones in white hats? I suppose that makes me the bad guy. Maybe I should be sitting here in a wheelchair with a bald head and a scar down my face, stroking a cat." She laughed at the thought. "Unfortunately, it's not as simple as that anymore. Not in the twenty-first century. Think about Alan Blunt for a minute. Quite apart from the number of people he's had killed around the world, look at the way he's used *you*, for heaven's sake! Did he ask nicely before he pulled you out of school and turned you into a spy? I don't think so! You've been exploited, Alex. And you know it."

"I'm not a killer," Alex said. "I never could be."

"It's very strange that you should say that. I mean, I don't notice Damian Cray at the next table. I wonder what happened to him? Or how about that nice Dr. Grief? I understand he didn't quite survive his last meeting with you."

"They were accidents."

"You seem to have had an awful lot of accidents in the last few months."

She paused. When she spoke again, her voice was softer, like a teacher with a favorite child.

"I can see you're still upset about Dr. Liebermann," she said. "Well, let me assure you. He wasn't a nice man and I don't think anybody's going to miss him. In fact, I wouldn't be surprised if his wife sent us a thank-you card." She smiled as though at some private joke. "You could say his death was a shot in the arm for us all. And you have to remember, Alex. It was his choice. If he hadn't lied and cheated his company and come to work for us, he would still be alive. It wasn't all our fault."

"Of course it was your fault. You killed him!"

"Well, yes. I suppose that's true. But we're a very large, international business. And sometimes it does happen that people get in our way and they end up dead. I'm sorry, but it's just the way it is."

A waiter arrived and took away the plates. Alex finished his orange juice, hoping the ice would help clear his head.

"I still can't join Scorpia," he said.

"Why not?"

"I have to go back to school."

"I agree." Mrs. Rothman leaned forward. "We have a school. I want to send you there. It's just that our school will teach you things that you might find a little more useful than logarithms and English grammar."

"What sort of things?"

"How to kill. You say you could never do it, but how can you be sure? If you go to Malagosto, you'll find out. Nile was our star student there, a perfect killer . . . or he would be except that he has a single, rather irritating weakness."

"You mean . . . his disease?"

"No. It's rather more annoying than that." She paused. "You could be better than him, Alex, in time. And although I know you don't like me mentioning it, your father was actually an instructor there. A brilliant one. We were all devastated when he died."

And there it was again. Everything began and ended with John Rider. He couldn't avoid it any longer. He had to know.

"Tell me about my father," he said. "That's the reason I'm here. That's the only reason I came. How did he end up working for you? And how did he die?" Alex forced himself to go on. "I don't even know what his voice sounded like," he said. "I don't know anything about him at all."

"Are you sure you want to? It may hurt you."

Alex was silent.

The waiter arrived with the main course. Mrs. Rothman had chosen roast lamb for them both—the meat slightly pink and garlicky. A second waiter refilled her glass.

"All right," she said when they were gone. "Let's finish eating and talk about other things. You can tell me about Brookland. I want to know what music you listen to and what sports teams you support. Do you have a girlfriend? I'm sure a boy as handsome as you gets plenty of offers. Now I've made you blush. Have your dinner. I promise it's the best lamb you'll ever eat.

"And after we've finished, I'll take you upstairs and then I'll tell you everything you want to know."

9

ALBERT BRIDGE

SHE TOOK HIM TO A ROOM at the top of the hotel. There was no bed; just a trestle table with a DVD player, a few files, and two chairs.

"I had this flown down from Venice," Mrs. Rothman said. "As soon as I knew you were here. I thought it was something you'd want to see."

Alex nodded. After the bustle of the restaurant, he felt strange being here—like an actor onstage when the scenery has been removed. The room was wide with a high ceiling. Its emptiness made everything echo. He walked over to the table, suddenly nervous. In London, he had asked certain questions. Now he was going to be given the answers. Would he like what he heard?

Mrs. Rothman had walked with him, her high heels rapping on the marble floor. She seemed completely relaxed. "Sit down," she said.

Alex slipped off his jacket and hung it over the back of the chair. He loosened his tie, then sat. Mrs.

Rothman stood next to the table, studying him. It was a moment before she spoke.

"Alex," she began. "It's not too late to change your mind."

"I don't want to," Alex said.

"It's just that, if I'm going to talk to you about your father . . . I may say things that will upset you and I don't want to do that. Does the past really matter? Does it make any difference?"

"He was my father."

"Very well . . ."

She opened the file and took out a black-and-white photograph. It showed a very handsome man in military uniform, wearing a beret. He was looking straight at the camera with his shoulders forward and his hands behind his back. He was clean shaven, with watchful, intelligent eyes.

"This is your father, age twenty-six. The photograph was taken four years before you were born. Do you really know nothing about him?"

"My uncle spoke to me about him, a bit. I know he was in the army."

"Well, maybe I can fill in some gaps for you. I'm sure you know that he was born in London and went to a famous school . . . the Oratory. From there he went to Cambridge and got a degree in politics and economics. But his heart had always been set on joining the army. And that's what he did. He joined the Parachute Regiment at Aldershot. That in itself was quite an achievement. The Paras are the toughest regiment in the British army, second only to the SAS. And you don't just join them. You have to be invited.

"Your father spent three years with the Paras. He saw action in Northern Ireland, in Gambia, and he was part of the attack on Goose Green in the Falkland Islands in May 1982. He carried a wounded soldier to safety even though he was under fire, and as a result of this, he received a medal from the queen. He was also promoted to the rank of captain."

Alex had once seen the medal: the Military Cross. Ian Rider had always kept it in the top drawer of his desk.

"He returned to England and he got married," Mrs. Rothman went on. "He had met your mother at Cambridge. She was studying medicine and she eventually became a radiologist. But I can't tell you very much about her. We never met and he never spoke about her, not to me.

"Anyway, I'm afraid it was shortly after he got married that things started to go wrong . . . not, of

course, that I'm blaming your mother. But it was just
a few weeks after the wedding that your father found
himself in a pub in London and got involved in a fight.
There were some people making remarks about the
Falklands War. I don't know. They were probably
drunk. There was a skirmish and your father struck
a man and killed him. It was a single blow to the
throat . . . just like he had been trained. And that, I'm
afraid, was that."

Mrs. Rothman reached down and opened the file.
She took out a newspaper clipping and handed it to
Alex. The newspaper was at least ten years old. Alex
could tell from the old-fashioned newsprint and from
the way the paper had faded. He read the headline:

JAIL FOR "BRILLIANT SOLDIER"
WHO LOST HIS WAY

There was another photograph of John Rider, but
now he was in civilian dress, surrounded by photog-
raphers, getting out of a car. The picture was a little
blurred and it had been taken long ago, but looking at
it, Alex could almost feel the pain of the man, the
sense that the world had turned against him.

He read the article.

John Rider, described as a "brilliant soldier" by his commanding officer, was
sentenced to four years for manslaughter
following the death of Ed Savitt, a taxi
driver, nine months ago in a Soho bar.

The jury heard that Rider, 28, had been
drinking heavily when he became involved
in a fight with Savitt. Rider, who had been
decorated for valor in the Falklands War,
killed Savitt with a single blow to the head.
The jury heard that Rider was a highly
trained expert in several martial arts.

Summing up, Judge James Masterman
said: "Captain Rider has thrown away a
promising army career in a single moment
of madness. I have taken his distinguished
record into consideration. But he has
taken a life and society demands that he
pays the price. . . ."

"I'm sorry," Mrs. Rothman said. She had been
watching Alex closely. "You didn't know."

"My uncle showed me the medal once," Alex said.
He had to stop for a moment. His voice was hoarse.
"But he never showed me this."

"It wasn't your father's fault. He was provoked."

"What happened next?"

"He was sent to prison. There was quite an outcry about it. He had a lot of public sympathy. But the fact was that he had killed a man and he was guilty of manslaughter. The judge had no choice."

"And then?"

"They let him out after just a year. It was done very quietly. Your mother had stood by him. She never lost faith in him and he went back to live with her. Unfortunately, his army career was over. He had received a dishonorable discharge. He was very much on his own." She stopped to see how Alex would react.

"Go on." Alex's voice was cold.

"He found it difficult to get a job. But by this time, he had come to the attention of our personnel department." Mrs. Rothman paused. "Scorpia is always on the lookout for fresh talent," she explained. "It seemed quite obvious to us that your father had been unfairly treated. We thought he would be perfect for us."

"You approached him?"

"Yes. Your parents had very little money at this time. They were desperate. One of our people met your father and two weeks later, he came to us for evaluation." She smiled. "We test every new recruit,

Alex. If you decide to join us, and I still hope you will, we'll take you to the same place we took your father."

"Where is that?"

"I mentioned the name to you. Malagosto. It's near Venice." Mrs. Rothman wouldn't be any more precise than that. "We could see at once that your father was extremely tough and exceptionally talented," she went on. "He passed every test we threw at him with flying colors. We knew, by the way, that he had a brother—Ian Rider—working for MI6. I was always a little surprised that Ian didn't try to help him when he got into trouble, but I suppose there was nothing he could do. Anyway, it made no difference . . . the two of them being brothers. Your father was perfect for us. And after what had happened to him, I have to say that we were certainly perfect for him."

Alex was getting tired. It was almost eleven o'clock. But he knew there was no way he was leaving this room until the whole story had been told.

"So he joined Scorpia," Alex said.

"Yes. Your father worked for us as an assassin," Mrs. Rothman said. "He spent four months in the field."

"How many men did he kill?"

"Five or six. He was more interested in working as

an instructor in the training school where he had been evaluated. You might be interested to know, Alex, that Yassen Gregorovich was one of the assassins he helped train. Your father actually saved Yassen's life when they were on an assignment in the Amazon jungle."

Alex knew that Mrs. Rothman was telling the truth. Yassen had said as much himself in the last seconds before he had died.

"I got to know your father very well," Mrs. Rothman went on. "We had dinner together many times, once even in this hotel." She threw her head back, letting her black hair trail down her neck, and for a moment her eyes were far away. "I was very attracted to him. He was a very good-looking man. He was also intelligent and he made me laugh. It was just unfortunate that he was married to your mother."

"Did she know what he was doing? Did she know about you?"

"I very much hope not." Suddenly Mrs. Rothman was businesslike. "I have to tell you now how your father died. I wish you hadn't asked me to do this. Are you sure you want me to go on?"

"Yes."

"All right." She took a breath. "MI6 wanted him neutralized. He was one of our most effective operatives and he was training others who would become as effective as he was. And so they set about hunting him down. I won't go into the details, but they set a trap for him on the island of Malta. As it happened, Yassen Gregorovich was there too. He escaped—but your father was captured. We assumed that would be the last of him and that we would never see him again. You may think that the death penalty has been abolished in England, but—as they say—accidents happen. Then there was a development. . . .

"Scorpia had been involved in another operation. We had kidnapped the eighteen-year-old son of a senior British civil servant . . . a man with considerable influence in the government, or so we thought. Again, it's a complicated story and it's late, so I won't give you all the details. But the general idea was that if the father didn't do what we wanted, we would kill the son."

"That's what you do, is it?" Alex asked.

"Corruption and assassination, Alex. It's part of what we do. Anyway, as we quickly discovered, the civil servant was unable to do what we wanted. Unfortunately, this meant we would have to kill the son. You can't make a threat and then have second thoughts about it, because if you do, nobody will ever be afraid of you again. And so we were about to kill the boy in as dramatic a way as possible. But then, out of the blue, MI6 got in touch with us and offered us a deal.

"It was a straight swap. They'd give us back John Rider in return for the son. The executive board of Scorpia met and although it was only carried by a narrow vote, we decided to go ahead with the deal. Normally, we would never have allowed an operation to become entangled in this way, but your father had been extremely valuable to us and, as I said, I was personally very close to him. So it was agreed. We would make the exchange at six o'clock in the morning . . . this was March. And it would take place on Albert Bridge."

"March? What year was this?"

"It was fourteen years ago, Alex. March thirteenth. You were exactly two months old."

Mrs. Rothman stood up and leaned over the trestle table. She rested a hand on the television monitor.

"Scorpia has always made a practice of recording everything we do," she explained. "We film and we tape. There's a good reason for this. We're a criminal organization. It automatically follows that nobody trusts us . . . not even our clients. They'll assume we'll lie, cheat . . . whatever. We film what we do to prove that we are, in our own way, honest. We filmed the hand-over on Albert Bridge. If the civil servant's son had been hurt in some way, we would have been able to prove that it wasn't because of us."

She pressed a button and the screen flickered to life, showing images that had been taken in another world, when Alex was just eight weeks old. The first shot showed Albert Bridge, stretching over a chilly River Thames with Albert Park on one side and the lower reaches of Chelsea on the other. It was drizzling. Tiny specks of water hovered in the air.

"We had three cameras," Julia Rothman said. "We had to conceal them carefully or MI6 would have removed them. But as you'll see, they tell the whole tale."

The first image: Three men in suits and overcoats. With them, a young man with his hands tied in front of him. This must be the son. He looked even younger than eighteen years old. He was shivering.

"This is the southern end of the bridge," Mrs. Rothman explained. "It was how it had been agreed. Our agents would bring the son up from the park. MI6 and your father would be on the other bank. The two of them would walk across the bridge and the exchange would be made. As simple as that."

"There's no traffic?" Alex said.

"At six o'clock in the morning? There would have been little anyway. But I suspect MI6 had closed the roads."

The image changed. Alex felt something twist in his stomach. The camera was concealed somewhere on the edge of the bridge, high up. It was showing him his father, the first moving image of John Rider he had ever seen. He was wearing a thick padded jacket. He was looking around him, taking everything in. Alex wished the camera was closer. He wanted to see more of his father's face.

"This is the classic method of exchange," Mrs. Rothman said. "A bridge is a neutral area. The two participants—in this case, the boy and your father— are on their own. Nothing should go wrong."

She reached out with a single finger and pressed the pause button.

"Alex," she warned. "Your father died on Albert Bridge. I know you never knew him. You were just a baby when this happened. But I'm still not sure it's something you should see."

"Show me," Alex said. His voice sounded far away.

Mrs. Rothman nodded. She pressed PLAY.

The screen flickered back to life. The pictures were now being taken by a hidden camera, handheld, out of focus. Alex caught sight of the span of the bridge, hundreds of lightbulbs curving through the air. There was the river again and, caught briefly in the distance, the great chimneys of Albert Power Station. There was a cut. Now the picture was steady, a wide angle, perhaps taken from a boat.

The three men with the civil servant's son were at one end. His father was at the other. Alex could make out three figures behind him. Presumably they worked for MI6. The image quality was poor. Dawn was only just breaking and there was little light. The river water had no color, running gray. A signal must have been given because the teenager began to walk forward. At the same time, John Rider left the other group, also with his hands tied in front of him.

Alex wanted to reach out and touch the television screen. He was watching his father walk toward the three Scorpia men. But the figure in the picture was only an inch high. Alex knew it was his father. The face matched the photographs he had seen. But he was too far away. He couldn't see if John Rider was smiling or angry or nervous. Could he have had any idea of what was about to happen?

John Rider and the civil servant's son met in the middle of the bridge. They paused and seemed to speak to each other—but the only sound on the film was the soft patter of the rain and the occasional rush of an unseen speeding car. Then they began to walk again. The son was on the north side of the bridge, the side controlled by MI6. John Rider was moving south, a little faster now, heading for the waiting men.

"This is when it happened," Mrs. Rothman said softly.

Alex's father was almost running. He must have sensed that something was wrong. He moved awkwardly, his hands still clasped in front of him. On the north side of the bridge, one of the MI6 people took out a radio transmitter and spoke briefly. A second later, there was a single shot. John Rider seemed to stumble and Alex realized he had been hit in the back. He took two more steps, twisted, and collapsed.

"Do you want me to turn it off, Alex?"

"No."

"There's a closer shot. . . ."

The camera angle was lower. Alex could see his father lying on his side. The three Scorpia men had produced guns. They were running forward, aiming at the son of the civil servant. Alex wondered why. The teenager hadn't had anything to do with what had just happened.

But then he understood. MI6 had shot John Rider. They hadn't kept their side of the bargain. So the son had to die too.

Yet the son had reacted incredibly quickly. He was already running, zigzagging across the bridge, his head down. He seemed to know exactly what was happening. One of the Scorpia men fired and missed. Then there was a sudden explosion, a machine gun opening fire. Alex saw bullets ricocheting off the iron girders of the bridge. Lightbulbs smashed. The tarmac surface seemed to leap up. The men hesitated and fell back. Meanwhile, the son had reached the far end of the bridge. A car surged forward. It had come from nowhere. Alex saw the door open and he was pulled inside.

Mrs. Rothman froze the image.

"It seems that MI6 wanted the son back, but they weren't prepared to pay with your father's freedom," she said. "They double-crossed us and shot him in front of our eyes. You saw for yourself."

Alex said nothing. The room seemed to have grown darker, shadows chasing in from the corners. He felt cold from head to foot.

"There is one last part of the film," Mrs. Rothman went on. "I hate seeing you like this, Alex. I hate having to show you. But you've seen this much. You might as well see the rest."

The last section of the film replayed the final moments of John Rider's life. Once again he was on his feet, beginning to run, while the civil servant's son hurried the other way.

"Look at the MI6 agent who gave the order to fire," Mrs. Rothman said.

Alex gazed at the tiny figures on the bridge.

Mrs. Rothman pointed. "We had the image computer enhanced."

Sure enough, the camera leaped in closer and now Alex could see that the MI6 agent with the transmitter was in fact a woman wearing a black raincoat.

"We can get in closer."

The camera jumped forward again.

"And closer."

The same action, repeated a third or fourth time. The woman taking out her radio transmitter. But now her face filled the screen. Alex could see her fingers, holding the device in front of her mouth. There was no sound, but he saw her lips move, giving the order, and he understood perfectly what she said.

"Shoot him."

"There was a sniper in an office on the north bank of the Thames," Mrs. Rothman explained. "It was really just a matter of timing. The woman you're looking at masterminded the operation. It was one of her early successes in the field, one of the reasons why she was promoted. You know who she is, of course."

Alex had known at once. She was fourteen years younger on the television screen, but she hadn't changed all that much. And there could be no mistaking the black hair—cut short—the pale, businesslike face, eyes that could have belonged to an eagle or a crow.

Mrs. Jones, the head of operations at MI6.

Mrs. Jones, who had been there when Alex was first recruited and who had always pretended she was his friend. When he had returned to London, hurt and exhausted after his fight with Damian Cray, she had come looking for him and tried to help him. She had said she was worried about him. And all the time she had been lying. She had sat opposite him and smiled at him, knowing that she had taken his father from him just weeks after he was born.

Julia Rothman turned the television off.

There was a long silence.

"They told me he died in a plane crash," Alex said in a voice that wasn't his own.

"Of course. They didn't want you to know."

"So what happened to my mother?" He felt a sudden spurt of hope. If they had been lying about him, then maybe she wasn't dead. Could it be at all possible? Was his mother somewhere in England, still alive?

"I'm so sorry, Alex. There *was* a plane crash. It happened a few months later. It was a private plane, and she was on her own, going to France." Mrs. Rothman rested a hand on his arm. "Nothing can make up for what's been done to you, for all the lies you've been told. If you want to go back to England, back to school, I'll understand that. I'm sure you just want to forget the whole lot of us. But if it's any consolation, I adored your father. I still miss him. This was the last thing he sent me, just before he was taken prisoner in Malta."

She had opened the file and taken out a postcard. It showed a strip of coastline, a setting sun. There were just a few lines, handwritten.

My dearest Julia—

A dreary time without you. Can't wait to be at the Ca' Vedova with you again.

John R.

Alex recognized the handwriting although he had never seen it before, and in that instant any last, lingering doubt was swept away.

The writing was his father's. It had to be.

It was identical to his own.

"It's very late," Mrs. Rothman said. "You really ought to get to bed. We can talk again tomorrow."

Alex looked at the television screen as though expecting to see Mrs. Jones, mocking him across fourteen years, destroying his life before it had even really begun. For a long minute he didn't speak. Then he stood up.

"I want to join Scorpia," he said.

"Are you sure?"

"Yes."

Go to Venice and find your destiny, Yassen had told him. And that was what had happened. He had made up his mind. There could be no going back.

10

HOW TO KILL

THE ISLAND WAS ONLY a few miles from Venice, but it had been forgotten for a hundred years. Its name was Malagosto and it was shaped roughly like a crescent moon, just half a mile long. There were six buildings on the island, surrounded by wild grass and poplar trees, and they all looked condemned. The largest of them was a monastery, built around a court-yard, with a redbrick bell tower, slanting very slightly, next to it. There was a crumbling hospital and then a row of what looked like apartment blocks with shat-tered windows and gaping holes in the roofs. A few boats went past Malagosto but never landed there. It was forbidden. And the place had a bad reputation.

There had once been a small, thriving community there. But that had been long ago . . . in the Middle Ages. It had been ransacked in 1380 during the war with Genova, and after that it had been used for plague victims. Sneeze in Venice, it was said, and you

would end up in Malagosto. When the plague dried
out, it became a quarantine center and then, in the
eighteenth century, a sanctuary for the insane. Finally,
it had been abandoned and left to rot. But there were
fishermen who claimed that, on a cold winter's night,
you could still hear the screams and the demented
laughter of the lunatics who had been the island's last
residents.

Malagosto was the perfect base for Scorpia's
Training and Assessment Center. They bought the island on a lease from the Italian government in 1987
and they had been there ever since. If anyone asked
what was happening there, they would be told that it
was now a business center where lawyers, bankers,
and office managers could come for motivation and
bonding sessions. This was, of course, a lie. Scorpia
sent new recruits to the school that they ran on
Malagosto. It was here that they learned how to kill.

Alex Rider sat at the front of the motorboat,
watching as the island drew nearer. It was the same
motorboat that had led him to the Ca' Vedova, and the
silver scorpion on the bow glistened in the sun. Nile
was sitting opposite him, totally relaxed, dressed in
white trousers and a blazer.

"I spent three months being trained here," he

shouted over the noise of the engine. "You're going to love it!"

Alex nodded but said nothing. He could see the bell tower looming up, rising crookedly over the level of the trees. The wind chased through his hair and the spray danced in his eyes.

Julia Rothman had left Positano earlier that morning, returning to Venice, where she was involved in something that needed her presence. They had met briefly after breakfast and this time she had been more serious and businesslike. Alex would spend the next few days on Malagosto, she said—not for full training but for an initial assessment that would include a medical examination, psychological testing, and a general overview of his fitness and aptitude. It would also give Alex time to reflect on his decision.

Alex's mind was dead. He had made his decision, and as far as he was concerned, nothing else mattered. Only one good thing had come out of the night before. He hadn't forgotten Tom Harris and his brother. They had heard nothing from him since he had broken into Consanto—and there was still the question of all Jerry's equipment, left behind on the roof.

Mrs. Rothman had been sympathetic. "Of course you must call them," she had said. "Apart from anything else, we don't want them worrying about you and raising the alarm. As for the parachute and all the rest of it, I already told you. I'll send your friend a check to cover the amount. Five thousand dollars? That should do it." She smiled. "You see, Alex? That's what I mean. We want to look after you."

After she had gone, Alex called Tom from his bedroom. Tom was delighted to hear from him.

"We saw you land, so we knew you hadn't gotten splatted," he said. "Then nothing happened for a bit. And then the whole place blew up. Was that you?"

"Not exactly," Alex said.

"Where are you?"

"I'm in Positano. I'm okay. But Tom, listen to me—"

"I know." Tom's voice was heavy. "You're not coming back to school."

"Not for a bit."

"Is this MI6 again?"

"Sort of. I'll tell you one day." That was a lie. Alex knew he would never see his friend again. "Just tell Jerry that he's going to get a check soon to pay for all his stuff. And tell him thanks from me."

"Alex . . . you sound strange. Are you sure you're all right?"

"I'm fine, Tom. Good-bye. . . ."

He hung up and felt a wave of sadness. It was as though Tom was the last link to the world he had known—and he had just ended the connection.

The boat pulled in. There was a jetty carefully concealed in a natural fault line in the rock so that nobody could be watched coming or leaving the island. Nile sprang ashore. He had the ease and the grace of a ballet dancer. Alex had noticed the same thing once about Yassen Gregorovich.

"This way, Alex."

Alex followed. The two of them walked up a twisting path between the trees. For a moment the buildings were hidden.

"Can I tell you something?" Nile said. He flashed Alex his friendliest smile. "I was just delighted you decided to join us. It's great to have you on the winning side."

"Thank you."

"But I hope you never change your mind, Alex. I hope you never disappoint us. After what happened at the Ca' Vedova—I'd hate to have to murder you again."

"Yes. It wasn't much fun the last time," Alex agreed.

"It would really upset me. Mrs. Rothman is expecting great things from you. I hope you don't let her down."

They had passed through the copse and there was the monastery with its great walls peeling from age and neglect. There was a heavy wooden door with a smaller door set in it and, next to it, the one sign that the building might, after all, have adapted itself to modern times: a keypad with a built-in video camera. Nile tapped in a code. There was an electronic buzz and the smaller door opened.

"Welcome back to school!" Nile said.

Alex hesitated. The new term at Brookland would start in two days' time. And here he was about to enter a school of a very different kind. But it was too late for second thoughts. He was following the path his father had set out for him.

Nile was waiting. Alex went in.

He found himself in a courtyard with cloisters on three sides and the bell tower rising up above the fourth. The ground was a neat rectangle of grass with two cypress trees side by side at one end, the whole thing enclosed by a tile roof that slanted in, like an old-fashioned tennis court. Four men, all dressed in white robes, were standing around an instructor, an older man dressed in black. As Alex and Nile entered, they stepped forward as one, lashed out with their fists, and shouted the *"Kiai"* that Alex knew from karate.

"Sometimes, with the silent kill, it is not possible to shout out," the instructor said. He spoke with a Russian or an Eastern European accent. "But remember the power of the silent kiai. Use it to drive your *chi* into the strike zone. Do not underestimate its power at the moment of the kill."

"That's Professor Yermalov," Nile said. "He taught me when I was here. You don't want to get on the wrong side of him, Alex. I've seen him finish a fight with a single finger. Fast as a snake and about as friendly . . ."

They crossed the courtyard, walking through an archway into a vast room with a multicolored mosaic floor, ornate windows, pillars, and intricate wooden angels carved into the walls. This might once have been a place of worship. Now it was used as a refectory and meeting place with long tables, modern sofas, and a hatch leading into a kitchen beyond. The ceiling was domed and carried the faint remnants of a fresco. There had been angels here once too, but they had long ago faded.

There was a door on the far side. Nile went over to it and knocked.

"Entrez!" The voice was friendly. The language, Alex recognized even from one word, was French.

They went into a tall, octagonal room with books lining five of the eight walls. It rose up at least twenty yards to a ceiling painted blue with silver stars. There was a ladder on wheels, leading up to the top shelves. Two windows looked out onto more woodland, but much of the light was blocked out by leaves, and an iron chandelier with about a dozen electric bulbs hung down on a heavy chain. The center of the room was taken up by a solid-looking table with two antique chairs in front of it and one behind. This third chair was occupied by a small, plump man in a suit and waistcoat. He was working at a laptop computer, his short fingers moving at great speed. He was peering at the screen through gold-rimmed glasses perched on a hooked nose. He had a neat black beard coming to a point underneath his chin. The rest of his hair was gray.

"Alex Rider! Please . . . come in." The man looked up from his computer with obvious pleasure. "I would have recognized you at once. I knew your father very well and you're the spitting image." Apart from a slight French accent, his English was perfect. "My name is Oliver D'Arc. I am, you might say, the prin-

cipal of this establishment . . . the head teacher, perhaps. I was just looking at your personal details on the
Internet."

Alex sat down on one of the antique chairs. "I
wouldn't have thought they'd be posted on the Internet," he said.

"It depends which search engine you use." D'Arc
gave Alex a sly smile. "I know that Mrs. Rothman told
you that your father was an instructor here. I worked
with him and he was a good friend to me, but I never
dreamed that I would one day meet his son. And it is
Nile who brings you here. Nile graduated from here a
few years ago. He was a brilliant student . . . number
two in his class."

Alex glanced at Nile and for the first time saw a
note of annoyance in the man's face. He remembered
what Mrs. Rothman had said—something about Nile
having a weakness—and he wondered what it was
that had prevented him from becoming number one.

"Are you thirsty after your journey?" D'Arc asked.
"Can I get you anything? A *sirop of grenadine*, perhaps?"

Alex started. The red fruit juice was his favorite
drink when he was abroad. Had D'Arc gotten that off
the Internet too?

"It was what your father always drank," D'Arc explained, reading his thoughts.

"I'm all right, thank you."

"Then let me tell you the program. Nile will introduce you to the other students who are here at Malagosto. There are never more than fifteen at one time and at the moment there are only ten. Eight men and two women. You will join in with them and over the next few days we will examine your progress. Eventually, if I consider you have the ability to become part of Scorpia, I will write a report and your real training will begin. But I have no doubts, Alex. You are very young . . . only fourteen. But you are John Rider's son and he was the very best."

"There's something I have to tell you," Alex said.

"Please. Go ahead." D'Arc sat back, beaming.

"I want to join Scorpia. I want to be part of what you do. But you might as well know now that I don't think I could kill anybody. I told Mrs. Rothman and she didn't believe me. She said I'd only be doing what my dad had done, but I know how I am inside and I know I'm different from him."

Alex hadn't been sure how D'Arc would react. But he seemed completely unconcerned. "There are a great many things that Scorpia does that do not involve killing," he said. "You could be very useful to us, for example, for blackmail. Or as a courier. Who would suspect that a fourteen-year-old on a school trip was carrying drugs or plastic explosive? But these are early days, Alex. You have to trust us. We will discover what you can and can't do and we will find the work that suits you best."

"I was eighteen when I killed my first man," Nile said. "That's only four years older than you are now."

"But Nile, you were always exceptional," D'Arc purred.

There was a knock at the door and a moment later it opened and a woman came in. She was a Thai—slender and delicate and several inches shorter than Alex. She had long, very black hair, dark, intelligent eyes, and lips that could have been drawn with an artist's pencil. She stopped and made the traditional greeting of the Thai people, bringing her hands together as though in prayer and bowing her head.

"*Sawasdee*, Alex," she said. "It is very nice to meet you." She had a very gentle voice and, like the principal, her English was excellent.

"This is Miss Binnag," D'Arc said.

"My name is Eijit. But you can call me Jet. I have come to take you to your room."

"You can rest this afternoon and I will see you again at dinner." D'Arc stood up. He was very short. His pointed beard only just rose above the level of the table. "I'm so glad you're here, Alex. Welcome to Malagosto."

The woman called Jet led Alex out of the room, back across the main hall, and down a corridor with a high, vaulted ceiling and bare plaster walls.

"What do you do here?" Alex asked.

"I teach botany."

"Botany?" Alex couldn't keep the surprise out of his voice.

"It is a very important part of the syllabus," Jet retorted. "There are many plants that can be useful to our work. The oleander bush, for example. You can extract a poison similar to digitalis from the leaves and this will paralyze the nervous system and cause immediate death. The berries of the mistletoe can also be fatal. You must learn how to grow the rosary pea. Just one pea can kill an adult in minutes. Tomorrow you can come to my greenhouse, Alex. Every flower there is another funeral."

She spoke in a way that was completely matter-of-fact. Once again, Alex felt a sense of unease. But he said nothing.

They passed a classroom that might once have been a chapel, with no windows and more faded frescoes on the walls. Another teacher, with ginger hair and a ruddy, weather-beaten face, was standing in front of a blackboard, talking to half a dozen students, two of them women. There was a complicated diagram on the blackboard and each student had what looked like a cigar box on the desk in front of them.

". . . and you can lead the main circuit through the lid and back into the plastic explosive," he was saying. "And it's right here, in front of the lock, that I always put the trembler switch . . ."

Jet had paused briefly at the door. "This is Mr. Ross," she whispered. "Technical specialist. He's from your country, from Glasgow. You'll meet him tonight."

They moved on. Behind him, Alex heard Mr. Ross speaking again.

"Do try and concentrate, please, Miss Craig. We don't want you blowing us all up . . ."

They came out of the main building and walked over to the nearest apartment block that Alex had seen from the boat. Once again, the building looked dilapidated from the outside but was elegant and modern once they were in. Jet showed Alex to an

air-conditioned room on the second floor. It was on
two levels with a king-size bed overlooking a large living space with sofas and a desk. There was a window
with a balcony and a sea view.

"I'll come back for you at four o'clock," Jet told
him. "You have an appointment with the doctor. Mrs.
Rothman wants you to have a complete examination.
We meet for drinks before dinner at six and dinner is
early . . . at seven. There's a night exercise tonight.
The students are diving. But don't worry. You won't
be taking part."

She bowed a second time and backed out of the
room. Alex was left alone. He sat down on one of the
sofas, noticing that the room had a fridge, a television,
and even a PlayStation 2—which he presumed was
there for his benefit.

What had he gotten himself into? Had he done the
right thing? Dark uncertainties rose up in his mind
and he deliberately forced them back again. He remembered the video he had been shown, the terrible
images he had seen. Mrs. Jones mouthing the two
words into the radio transmitter. He closed his eyes.

Outside, the waves broke against the island shore
and the students in their white robes went once again
through the motions of the silent kill.

* * *

Six hundred miles away, the woman who had been so much in Alex's thoughts was examining a photograph. There was a single sheet of paper attached to it and both were stamped with the words top secret in red. The woman knew what the photograph meant. Only one course of action was open to her. But for once—and for her it really was a first time—she was reluctant. She couldn't allow emotion to get in the way. That was when mistakes were made and in her line of work that might be disastrous. But even so . . .

Mrs. Jones took off her reading glasses and rubbed her eyes. She had received the photograph and the report a few minutes ago. Since then, she had made two telephone calls, hoping against hope that there might have been a mistake. But there could be no doubt. The evidence was right there in front of her. She reached out and pressed a button on her telephone, then spoke.

"William—is Mr. Blunt in his office?"

In an outer office, her personal assistant, William Dearly, glanced at his computer screen. He was twenty-three, an Oxford graduate. He was in a wheelchair. "He hasn't left the building yet, Mrs. Jones."

"Any meetings?"

"Nothing scheduled."

"Right. I'm going down there now."

It had to be done. Mrs. Jones took the photograph and the typed sheet and walked down the corridor on the twelfth floor of the building that pretended to be an international bank but which was in fact the headquarters of MI6—Special Operations. Alan Blunt was her immediate superior, the chief executive. She wondered how he would react to the news that Alex Rider had joined Scorpia.

Blunt's office was at the very end of the corridor with views overlooking Liverpool Street. Mrs. Jones went in without knocking. There was no need. William would have rung to say she was coming. And sure enough, Blunt registered no surprise as the door opened and she came in. Not that his round, strangely featureless face ever showed any emotion anyway. He too had been reading a report, several inches thick. She could see he had made neat notes using a fountain pen and green ink for instant recognition.

"Yes?" he asked as she sat down.

"This just came in from SatInt. I thought you should see it." SatInt was satellite intelligence. She passed it across.

Mrs. Jones watched Alan Blunt carefully as he read the single page. She had been his deputy for seven years and had worked with him for another ten before that. She had never been to his home. She had never met his wife. But she probably knew him better than anyone in the building. And she was worried about him. Quite recently, he had made a huge mistake, refusing to believe Alex when it came to that business with Damian Cray. As a result, Cray had come within minutes of destroying half the world. Blunt had been given a severe dressing-down by the home secretary, but it wasn't just that that he was finding hard to live with. It was the fact that he, the head of Special Operations, had been bettered by a fourteen-year-old boy. Mrs. Jones wondered how much longer he would stay.

Now he examined the photograph, his eyes unblinking behind his steel-frame spectacles. The pictures showed two figures, a man and a boy, getting out of a boat. It had been taken above Malagosto and blown up many times. Both the faces were blurred.

"Alex Rider?" Blunt asked. There was a dead tone to his voice.

"The picture was taken by a spy satellite," Mrs. Jones said. "But Smithers ran it through one of his computers and it's definitely him."

"Who is the man with him?"

"We think it could be a Scorpia agent called Nile. It's hard to tell. The photograph is black-and-white, but so is he. I've downloaded his details for you."

"Are we to infer that Rider has decided to switch sides?"

"I've spoken to his housekeeper, the American girl . . . Jack Starbright. It seems that a week ago Alex decided to go on vacation with a friend. To Venice."

"The choice could have been a coincidence."

"I don't think so."

"Is it possible that the boy has somehow become involved with Scorpia and that they've taken him by force?"

"I'd like to believe it." Mrs. Jones sighed. It couldn't be avoided any longer. "But there was always a possibility that Yassen Gregorovich managed to speak to Alex before he died," she went on. "When I met him after the Cray business, I knew something was wrong. I think Yassen must have told him about John Rider."

"Albert Bridge."

"Yes."

"That's very unfortunate."

There was a long silence. Mrs. Jones knew that Blunt would be turning over a dozen possibilities, considering and eliminating each one in a matter of seconds. She had never met anyone with such an analytical mind.

"Scorpia haven't been very active recently," he said.

"It's true. They've been very quiet. We think they may have been involved in a piece of sabotage at Consanto, near Amalfi."

"The biomedical people?"

"Yes. We've only just received the reports and we're looking into them. There may be a link."

"If Scorpia have turned Alex, they'll use him against us."

"I know."

Blunt took a last look at the photograph. "This is Malagosto," he said. "And that means that he isn't their prisoner. They're training him. I think we should step up your security rating with immediate effect."

"And yours?"

"I wasn't on Albert Bridge." He laid the photo-graph down. "I want all local agents in Venice placed on immediate alert and we'd better talk to airports and all points of entry into the UK. I want Alex Rider found and I want him brought in."

"Unharmed." The single word was spoken as a challenge.

Blunt looked at her with empty eyes. "Whatever it takes."

11

THE BELL TOWER

"So tell me, Alex. What do you see?"

Alex was sitting in a leather chair in a plain, white-washed room at the back of the monastery. He was on one side of a desk, facing a smiling, middle-aged man who sat on the other. The man's name was Dr. Karl Steiner, and although he spoke with a slight German accent, he had come to the island from South Africa. He was a psychiatrist and looked it—with silver glasses, thinning hair, and eyes that were always more inquisitive than friendly. Dr. Steiner was holding a white card with a black shape on it. The shape looked like nothing at all. It was just a series of blobs. But Alex was supposed to be able to interpret it.

He thought for a moment. He knew that this was called a Rorschach test. He had seen it being done once in a film. He supposed it must be important. But he wasn't sure that he saw anything in particular on the card. Eventually he spoke.

"I suppose it's a man flying through the sky," he said. "He's wearing a backpack."

"That's excellent. Very good!" Dr. Steiner put down the card and picked up another. "How about this one?"

The second shape was easier. "It's a soccer ball being pumped up," Alex said.

"Good, thank you."

Dr. Steiner laid the second card down and for a moment there was silence in the office. Outside, Alex could hear guns being fired. The other students were doing target practice. But there was no view of the firing range from the doctor's window. Perhaps the room had been designed like that.

"So, how are you settling in?" Dr. Steiner asked.

Alex shrugged. "Okay."

"You have no anxieties? Nothing you wish to discuss?"

"No. I'm fine, thank you, Dr. Steiner."

"Good. That's good." The psychologist seemed determined to be friendly. Alex wondered if the interview was over, but then the man opened a file. "I have your medical report here," he said.

For a moment, Alex was nervous. He had been physically examined on his first day on the island. Stripped down to his underwear, he had been put through a whole series of tests by a nurse or a matron who spoke little English and who seemed to have been brought across from Venice. Blood and urine samples had been taken, his blood pressure and pulse measured, his sight, hearing, and reflexes checked. He wondered now if they had found something wrong.

But Dr. Steiner was still smiling. "You're in very good shape, Alex," he said. "I'm glad you've been looking after yourself. Not too much fast food. No cigarettes. Very sensible."

He opened a drawer in his desk and took out a hypodermic syringe and a little bottle. As Alex watched, he inserted the needle into the bottle and filled it.

"What's that?" Alex asked.

"According to your medical report, you're a little run-down. I suppose it's to be expected after all you've been through. And I'm sure it's very demanding, being here on this island. The doctor has suggested a vitamin booster. That's all this is." He held the needle up to the light and squirted a little of the amber-colored liquid out of the tip. "Would you mind rolling up your sleeve?"

Alex hesitated. "I thought you were a psychiatrist," he said.

"I'm perfectly qualified to give you an injection,"

Dr. Steiner said. He raised an accusing finger. "You're not going to tell me you're afraid of a little prick?"

"I wouldn't call you that," Alex muttered. He rolled up his right sleeve.

Two minutes later, he was back outside.

He had been missing gun practice because of his medical appointment and he joined the other students on the firing range. This was on the western side of the island—the side that faced away from Venice. Although Scorpia were legally permitted to be on Malagosto, they hadn't wanted to draw attention to themselves with the sound of gunfire, and the woodland provided a natural screen. There was a strip of the island that was long and flat with nothing growing apart from wild grass, and the school had built a cut-out town, offices and shops that were nothing more than fronts, like a movie set. Alex had already been through it twice, using a handgun to shoot at paper targets—black rings with a red bull's-eye—that popped up in the windows and doors.

Gordon Ross, the ginger-haired technical specialist who seemed to have picked up most of his skills in Scotland's tougher jails, was in charge of the shooting range. He nodded as he saw Alex approach.

"Good afternoon, Mr. Rider. How was your visit

to the shrink? Did he tell you that you were mad? If not, I wonder what the hell you're doing here!"

A number of other students stood around him, unloading and adjusting their weapons. Alex knew all of them by now. There was Klaus, a German mercenary who had trained with the Taliban in Afghanistan. Walker, who had spent five years with the CIA in Washington before he had decided he could earn more working for the other side. One of the two women he had seen on his first day had become quite close to him. He wondered if she had been specially chosen to look after him. Her name was Amanda and she had been a soldier with the Israeli army, in the occupied Gaza Strip. Seeing him, she raised a hand in greeting. She seemed genuinely pleased to see him.

But then they all did. That was the strange thing. He had been accepted into the day-to-day life of Malagosto without any problem. That in itself was remarkable. Alex remembered the time when MI6 had sent him for training with the SAS in Wales. He had been an outsider from the day he arrived, unwanted and unwelcome, a child in an adult world. He was by far the youngest person here too, but that didn't seem to matter. Quite the opposite. He was accepted and liked by the other students.

"You're just in time to show us what you can do before lunch," Gordon Ross said. His Scottish accent made almost everything sound like a challenge. "You got a high score the day before yesterday. In fact, you were second in the class. Let's see if you can do even better today. But this time, I may have built in a little surprise!"

He handed Alex a gun, a Belgian-made FN semi-automatic pistol. Alex weighed it in his hand, trying to find the balance between himself and his weapon. Ross had explained that this was essential to the technique that he called "instinctive firing."

"Remember—you have to shoot instantly. You can't stop to take aim. If you do, you're dead. In a real combat situation, you don't have time to mess around. You and the gun are one. And if you believe that you can hit the target, you will hit the target. That's what instinctive firing is all about."

Now Alex stepped forward, the gun at his side, watching the mocked-up doors and windows in front of him. He knew there would be no warning. At any time, a target would appear. He would be expected to turn and fire.

He waited. He was aware of the other students watching him. Out of the corner of his eye he could just make out the shape of Gordon Ross. Was the teacher smiling?

A sudden movement.

A target had appeared in an upper window and in the blink of an eye Alex saw that the bull's-eye targets with their innocent rings had been replaced. A photograph had appeared instead. It was a life-size color picture of a young man. Alex didn't know who he was—but that didn't matter. He was a target.

There was no time to hesitate.

Alex raised the gun and fired.

Later that day, Oliver D'Arc, the principal of Scorpia's Training and Assessment Center, sat in his office, talking to Julia Rothman. Her image filled the screen of the laptop computer on his desk in the office in Malagosto. There was a webcam perched on a shelf and his own image would be appearing simultaneously somewhere in the Ca' Vedova, just across the water in Venice. Mrs. Rothman never came to the island. She knew it was under surveillance by both the American and the English intelligence services and one day one of them might be tempted to target the island with a non-nuclear ballistic missile. It was too dangerous.

It was only the second time they had spoken since Alex had arrived. The time was exactly seven o'clock in the evening. Outside, the sun had begun to set.

"So how is he progressing?" Mrs. Rothman asked. Her own webcam didn't flatter her. Her face on the screen looked cold and colorless.

D'Arc considered. He ran a thumb and a single finger down the sides of his chin, stroking his beard. "The boy is certainly exceptional," he murmured. "Of course, his uncle, Ian Rider, trained him all his life . . . almost from the moment he was born. But I have to say, he did a good job."

"And . . . ?"

"He is very intelligent. Quick-witted. Everyone here at Malagosto genuinely likes him. Unfortunately, though, I have my doubts about his usefulness to us."

"I am very sorry to hear that, Professor D'Arc. Please explain."

"I will give you two examples, Mrs. Rothman. This afternoon, Alex returned to the shooting range. We've put him through a course of instinctive firing. It's something he had never done before and, I have to say, it takes many of our students several weeks to master the art. After just a few hours on the range, Alex was already achieving impressive results. At the

end of his second day, he scored seventy-two percent."

"I don't see anything wrong with that."

D'Arc shifted in his seat. He was already small and,
in his formal suit and tie, shrunk down to fit Rothman's
computer screen, he looked rather like a ventriloquist's
dummy. "Today we switched the targets," he explained.
"Instead of black-and-white rings, Alex was asked to
fire at photographs of men and women. He was told to
aim at the vital points: the heart . . . between the eyes."

"How did he do?"

"That's the point. His score dropped to forty-six
percent. He missed several targets altogether." D'Arc
took off his glasses and wiped them with a cloth. "I
also have the results of his Rorschach psychological
test," he went on. "He was asked to identify certain
shapes—"

"I do know what a Rorschach test is, Professor."

"Of course. Forgive me. Well, there was one shape
that every student who has ever come here has iden-
tified as a man lying in a pool of blood. But not Alex.
He said he thought it was a man flying in the air with
a backpack. Another shape, which is invariably seen as
a gun pointing at someone's head, he believed to be
someone pumping up a soccer ball. On the very first

day he came here, Alex told me that he couldn't kill for us and I have to say that, psychologically speaking, he seems to lack what might be called the killer instinct."

There was a long pause. The image on the computer screen flickered.

"It's very disappointing," D'Arc went on. "Having met Alex, I must say that a teenage assassin would be extremely useful to us. The possibilities are almost limitless. I think we should make it a high priority to find one of our own."

"I doubt that there are many teenagers quite as experienced as Alex."

"That's what I began by saying. But even so . . ."

There was another pause. Mrs. Rothman came to a decision. "Did Alex see the doctor?" she asked.

"Yes. Everything was done exactly as you instructed."

"Good." She nodded. "You say that Alex won't kill for us, but you could still be proved wrong. It's just a question of giving him the right target . . . and this time I'm not talking about paper."

"You want to send him on an assignment?"

"As you know, Invisible Sword is about to enter its second critical phase. Introducing Alex Rider into the mix right now might provide an interesting distraction

at the very least. And if he did succeed, which I believe
he might, he could be very useful indeed. All in all, the
timing couldn't be better."

Julia Rothman leaned forward so that her eyes almost filled the screen.

"This is what I want you to do . . ."

There were 247 steps to the top of the bell tower. Alex
knew because he had counted every one of them. The
bottom of the tower was empty; a single chamber with
bare brick walls and a damp smell. It had clearly been
abandoned years ago. The bells themselves had either
been stolen or had fallen down and been lost. The
stairs were made of stone and twisted upward, following the edges of the tower with small windows al-
lowing just enough light to see. There was a door at
the top. Alex wondered if it would be locked. The
tower was used occasionally when there were camou-
flage exercises with the students moving from one side
of the island to the other. It was a useful lookout post.
But he hadn't been up here yet himself.

The door was open. It led to a square platform,
about thirty feet wide, out in the open air. Once there
might have been a metal balustrade enclosing the platform and making it safe. But at some time it had been

removed and now the stone floor simply ended. If Alex took three paces forward, he would simply step into nothing. He would fall to his death.

Cautiously, Alex moved to the edge and glanced down. He was right above the monastery courtyard. He could see the *makiwara*, which had been set up there earlier in the afternoon. This was a heavy pole with a thick leather pad wrapped around it at head height. It was used to practice kickboxing and karate strikes. But there was nobody in sight. Lessons for the day had ended and the other students were resting before dinner.

He looked across, over the woodland that surrounded the building, already dark and impenetrable. The sun was sinking into the sea, spilling the last of its light onto the black water. In the distance he could see the twinkling lights that he knew belonged to the city of Venice. What would be happening there right now? Tourists would be leaving their hotels, searching out the restaurants and bars. There might be concerts in some of the churches. The gondoliers would be tying up their boats. Winter was still a long way off, but already it was too cold for most people to set out on an evening cruise. Alex still found it hard to believe that this island with all its secrets could exist so close to one of the world's most popular vacation destinations. Two worlds. Side by side. But one of them was blind, utterly unaware of the existence of the other.

He stood there, unmoving, feeling the breeze rippling through his hair. He was wearing only a long-sleeved shirt and jeans and he was aware of the evening chill. But somehow it was distant. It was as though he had become part of the tower—a statue or a gargoyle. He was there because he had nowhere else to go. He no longer had any choice.

He thought back over the last few days. How long had he been on the island now? He no longer had any idea. In many ways it was just like being at school. There were teachers and classrooms and separate lessons and one day more or less blurred into the next. Only the subjects here were nothing like the ones he had studied at Brookland.

First there was history—also taught by Gordon Ross. But his version of history had nothing to do with kings and queens, battles and treaties. Ross specialized in the history of weapons.

"Now, this is the double-edged commando knife, developed in the Second World War by Fairbairn and Sykes. One was a silent killing specialist and the other a crack shot with the rifle. Isn't it a beauty? You'll see it has an eight-inch blade with a cross piece and a ribbed center on both sides. It's designed to fit exactly into the palm of your hand. You may find it a little heavy, Alex, as your hand isn't fully developed. But this is still the greatest murder weapon ever invented. Guns are noisy. Guns can jam. But the commando knife is a true friend. It will do its job instantly and it will never let you down."

Then there was fieldwork with Professor Yermalov. As Nile had said, he was the least friendly member of the staff at Malagosto, a scowling, silent man in his fifties who had little time for Alex. But Alex soon found out why. Yermalov was from the province of Chechnya and had lost his entire family in the war with Russia.

"Today I am going to show you how to make yourself invisible," he said.

Alex couldn't resist a half smile.

Yermalov saw it. "You think I am making a joke with you, Mr. Rider? You think I am talking about children's books, a cloak of invisibility, perhaps? You are wrong. I am teaching you the skills of the ninjas, the greatest spies who ever lived. The ninja assassins of feudal Japan were reputed to have the ability to vanish into thin air. In fact, they used the five elements of

escape—the *gotonpo*—not magic, but science. They
might hide underwater, breathing through a tube.
They might bury themselves a few inches below the
surface of the earth. Wearing protective clothing, they
might hide inside a fire. To vanish into the air, they
carried a rope or even a hidden ladder. And there were
other possibilities. They developed the art of sight re-
movers or eye blinders. Blind your enemy with smoke
or with chemicals and you will become invisible. That
is what I will show you now, and this afternoon Miss
Binnag will be demonstrating how to make a blinding powder from hot peppers. . . ."

There had been other exercises too. How to as-
semble and dismantle an automatic pistol, blind-
folded. (Alex had dropped all the pieces, much to the
amusement of the other students.) How to use fear.
How to use surprise. How to target aggression. There
were textbooks—a manual on the most vulnerable
parts of the human body, written by a Dr. Three—as
well as blackboards and even written exams. They sat
in classrooms with ordinary desks. There was just one
difference. This was a school for assassination.

And then there had been the demonstration. It was
something Alex would never forget.

One afternoon, the students had assembled in the

main courtyard, where Oliver D'Arc was standing with Nile, who was dressed in white judo robes with a black belt around his waist. It was odd how often the two colors seemed to surround him as though perpetually mocking his disease.

"Nile was one of our most successful students," D'Arc explained. "Since his time here, he has risen up the ranks of Scorpia with successful assignments in Washington, London, Bangkok, Sydney . . . in fact, all over the world. He has kindly agreed to show you a few of his techniques. I'm sure you'll all learn something from him." He bowed. "Thank you, Nile."

In the next thirty minutes, Alex saw a display of strength and fitness he would never forget. Nile smashed bricks and planks with his elbows, his fists, and his bare feet. Three students with long wooden staffs closed in on him. Unarmed, he beat them all, weaving in and out, moving so fast that at times his hands were no more than a blur. Then he moved on to demonstrate a variety of ninja weapons: knives, swords, spears, and chains. Alex watched him throw a dozen *shuriken* at a wooden target. These were the deadly, star-shaped projectiles that spun through the air, each steel point razor-sharp. One after another, they thudded into the wood, hitting the inner circle. Nile never missed. And this was a man with some sort of secret weakness? Alex couldn't see it—and he understood now how he had been beaten so easily at the Ca' Vedova. Against a man like Nile, he wouldn't stand a chance.

But they were on the same side.

Alex reminded himself of that now as he stood at the top of the bell tower, watching the night draw in and darkness take hold. He had made his choice. He was part of Scorpia now.

Like his father.

He couldn't get the images out of his mind. The three Scorpia agents waiting at one end of the bridge. Mrs. Jones talking into the radio transmitter. The betrayal. John Rider pitching forward and lying still.

Alex felt hatred welling up inside him. It was stronger than anything he had ever felt in his life. He wondered if it would ever be possible to live an ordinary life again. There seemed to be nowhere for him to go. Maybe it would be better for everyone if he just took one step forward. He was already on the very edge of the tower. Why couldn't he just let the night take him?

"Alex?"

He hadn't heard anyone approach. He looked around and saw Nile standing in the doorway, one hand resting against the frame.

"I've been looking for you, Alex. What are you doing?"

"I was just thinking."

"Professor Yermalov said he thought he saw you come up here. You shouldn't really be here." Alex expected Nile to come forward, but he stayed where he was, the hand still holding on to the wood.

"I just wanted to be alone," Alex said.

"I think you should come down. You could fall."

Alex hesitated. Then he nodded. "All right."

He followed Nile back down the twisting staircase and at last they emerged at ground level. "Monsieur D'Arc wants to see you," Nile said.

"To fail me?"

"Whatever gave you that idea? You've done very well. Everyone is very pleased with you. You've only been here a week, but you've made great progress."

They walked back together. A couple of students passed them and raised a hand in greeting. Only the day before, Alex had seen them fight a ferocious duel with fencing swords. They were deadly killers. And they were his friends. He shook his head and followed Nile back into the monastery and through to D'Arc's study.

As usual, the principal was sitting behind his desk.

He was looking as neat as ever, the beard perfectly trimmed.

"Do please sit down, Alex," he said. He tapped a few keys on his computer and glanced at the screen through his gold-rimmed spectacles. "I have some of your results here," he went on. "You'll be pleased to know that all the teachers speak very highly of you." He frowned. "We do have one small problem, however. Your psychological profile . . ."

Alex said nothing.

"This business of killing," D'Arc said. "I heard what you said when you first came to my office and, as I told you, there are many other things you could do for Scorpia. But here's the problem, my dear boy. You're afraid of killing, so you're afraid of us. You are not quite one of us—and I fear you never will be. That is not satisfactory."

"Are you asking me to leave?" Alex said.

"Not at all. I'm asking you only to trust us a little more. I'm searching for a way to make you feel more that you belong with us. And I think I have the answer."

D'Arc turned off the computer and walked around from behind the table. He was dressed in another suit—he wore a different suit every day. This one was brown with a herringbone pattern.

"You must learn to kill," he said suddenly. "You'll have to do it without any hesitation. Because as soon as you've done it once, you'll see that actually it wasn't such a big deal. It's the same as jumping into a swimming pool. As easy as that. But you have to cross the psychological barrier, Alex, if you are to become one of us." He raised a hand. "I know you are very young. I know this isn't easy. But I want to help you. I want to make it less painful for you. And I think I can.

"I am going to send you to England tomorrow. This is your first mission for Scorpia, and if you succeed, there will be no going back. You will know that you are truly one of us and we will know that we can trust you. But here is the good news." D'Arc smiled, showing teeth that didn't look quite real. "We have chosen the one person in the world who—we think you will agree—most deserves to die. It is someone you have every reason to despise and we hope that your hatred and your anger will steer you forward, removing any last doubts you may have.

"The deputy head of MI6: Special Operations. Mrs. Jones. She is the one we want you to kill."

12

"DEAR PRIME MINISTER . . ."

JUST AFTER HALF PAST SEVEN in the morning, a man got out of a taxi in Whitehall, paid with a brand-new ten-pound note, and began to walk the short distance to Downing Street, home to the British prime minister. The man had started his journey at Paddington, but that wasn't where he lived. Nor had he come into London on a train. He was about thirty years old with short, fair hair. He was wearing a suit and tie.

It is not possible to walk into Downing Street, nor has it been since Margaret Thatcher erected huge anti-terrorist gates. Britain is the only democracy whose leaders feel a need to hide behind bars. As always, a policeman was there, just coming to the end of the eight-hour shift that had taken him through the night.

The man walked up to him, at the same time producing a plain white envelope, made from the very finest paper. Later, when the envelope was analyzed, it would be found to have come from a supplier in Naples.

There would be no fingerprints, even though the man who had delivered it was not wearing gloves. He had no fingerprints. They had been surgically removed.

"Good morning," he said. He had no accent of any kind. His voice was pleasant and polite.

"Good morning, sir."

"I have a letter for the prime minister."

The policeman had heard it a hundred times. There were cranks and pressure groups, people with grievances, people needing help. Often they came here with letters and petitions, hoping they would reach the prime minister's desk. The policeman was friendly. As he was trained to be.

"Thank you, sir. If you'd like to leave it with me, I'll see it goes through."

The policeman took the letter—and his would be the only fingerprints that would show up later. Written on the front of the envelope in neat, flowing handwriting were the words: *For the attention of the Prime Minister of Great Britain, First Lord of the Admiralty, 10 Downing Street.* He carried it into the long, narrow office that is little more than a Portacabin and that all members of the public must pass through before they can enter the famous street. This was as close as the letter would normally get to number ten. It would be rerouted to an office where a secretary—one of a dozen—would open and read it. If necessary, it might be passed on to the appropriate department. More likely, after a few weeks, the sender would receive a standard, word-processed reply.

This letter was different.

As the duty officer received it, he turned it over, and that was when he saw the silver scorpion embossed on the other side. There are many symbols and code words used by criminal and terrorist organizations. They are designed to make themselves instantly identifiable so that the authorities will treat them seriously. The duty officer knew at once that he was holding a communication from Scorpia and pressed the panic button, alerting half a dozen policemen outside.

"Who delivered this?" he demanded.

"It was just someone . . ." The policeman was old and getting toward the end of his career. After today, that end would be considerably nearer. "He was young. Fair-haired. He was wearing a suit."

"Get out there and see if you can find him."

But it was already too late. Seconds after the man in the suit had delivered the letter, a second taxi had drawn up and he had gotten in. This taxi was not in fact licensed and its license plate was fake. After less

than half a mile, the man had gotten out again, disappearing into the crowds coming out of Charing
Cross Station. His hair was now dark brown. He had
discarded his jacket and was wearing sunglasses. He
would never be seen again.

By ten o'clock that morning, the letter had been
photographed, the paper analyzed, the envelope
checked for any trace of biochemical agents. The
prime minister was not in the country. He had gone
to Mexico City to be photographed with other world
leaders at a summit meeting about the environment.
It was the middle of the night in Central America, but
he had been woken up and told about the letter. Already he was on his way home.

Meanwhile, two men were sitting in his private office. One was the permanent secretary to the cabinet
office. The other was the director of communications.
They each had a copy of the letter—three typewritten
sheets, unsigned—in front of them.

This is what they had read.

Dear Prime Minister,

*It is with regret that we must inform you that we
are about to bring terror to your land.*

We are acting on the instructions of an overseas

client who wishes to make certain adjustments to the balance of world power. He makes four demands:

1. The Americans must withdraw all their troops and secret service personnel from every country around the world. Never again will the Americans act as "international policemen."

2. The Americans must announce that they intend to destroy their entire nuclear weapons program as well as their long-range conventional weapons systems. We will allow six months for this process to be put into effect and completed. By the end of that time, America must have disarmed.

3. The sum of one billion dollars must be paid to the World Bank, this money to be used to rebuild poor countries, and countries damaged by recent wars.

4. The president of the United States must resign at once.

Prime Minister, you may wonder why this letter is addressed to you when our demands are directed entirely at the American government.

The reason for this is simple. You are America's "best friend." You have always supported their foreign policy. Now it is time to see if they will be as loyal to you as you have been to them.

Should they fail, it is you who will pay the price.

We will wait three days. To be more precise, we are prepared to give you exactly seventy hours, starting from the moment this letter was delivered. In that time, we expect to hear the president of the United States agree to our terms. If he fails to do so, we will inflict a terrible punishment on the people of the United Kingdom.

We must inform you, Prime Minister, that we have developed a new weapon that we call "Invisible Sword." This weapon is now primed and operational. If the president of the United States chooses not to respond to all four of our demands in the allotted time, then—at exactly four o'clock next Thursday afternoon— many thousands and perhaps as many as a hundred thousand schoolchildren in London will die. Let me assure you, most sincerely, that this cannot be avoided. The technology is in place. The targets have been selected. This is not a hollow threat.

Even so, we understand that you may doubt the power of Invisible Sword.

We have therefore arranged a demonstration. This afternoon, the English reserve soccer team will be returning to Britain from Nigeria, where they have been playing a number of exhibition games. As you read this

*letter, they will already be in the air. They are due to
arrive at Heathrow Airport at five minutes past two.*

*At exactly 2:15, all eighteen members of this team,
including the coaches and the reserves, will be killed.
You cannot save them. You cannot protect them. You
can only watch. We hope that by this action, you will
understand that we are to be taken seriously and that
you will therefore act quickly to persuade the Americans to act. By doing so, you will avoid the terrible and
pointless massacre of many thousands of your young
people.*

*We have taken the liberty of forwarding a copy of
this letter to the American ambassador in London. We
will be watching the news channels on television,
where we will be expecting an announcement to be
made. You will receive no further communication from
us. We repeat: These demands cannot be negotiated.
The countdown has already begun.*

*Yours faithfully,
SCORPIA*

There was a long silence, broken only by the ticking of an antique clock, as both men studied the let-

ter for a fourth and a fifth time. Each was aware of the other, wondering how he would react. The two men could not have been more different. Nor could they have disliked each other more.

Sir Graham Adair, the permanent secretary to the cabinet office, had been a civil servant for as long as anyone could remember . . . not part of any government, but always serving it, advising it, and (some people said) controlling it. He was now in his sixties with long, silvery gray hair and a face well used to disguising its emotions. He was dressed, as always, in a dark, old-fashioned suit. He was the sort of man who moved very little and never said anything until he had thoroughly considered it first. He had worked with five different prime ministers in his lifetime and had different opinions about them all. But he had never told anyone, not even his wife, his innermost thoughts. He was the perfect public servant. One of the most powerful people in the country, he was delighted that very few people even knew his name.

The director of communications hadn't even been born when Sir Graham had first entered Downing Street. Mark Kellner was one of the many "special advisers" with whom the prime minister liked to surround himself . . . and he was also the most influential. He had been at university—studying politics and economics—with the prime minister's wife. For a time he had worked in television until he had been invited to try his luck in the corridors of power. He was a small, thin man with too much curly hair and glasses. He was also wearing a suit. There was dandruff on both of his shoulders.

It was Kellner who broke the silence with a single four-letter word. Sir Graham glanced at him. He never used that sort of language himself.

"You don't believe any of this rubbish, do you?" Kellner demanded.

"This letter came from Scorpia," Sir Graham replied. "I have had direct dealings with them in the past and I have to tell you that they're not known to make idle threats."

"You accept that they've invented some sort of secret weapon? An invisible sword?" Kellner couldn't keep the contempt out of his voice. "So what's going to happen? They're going to wave some sort of magic wand and everyone is going to fall down dead?"

"As I've already said, Mr. Kellner, in my opinion Scorpia would not have sent this letter if they didn't have the means to back it up. They are probably the most dangerous criminal organization in the world. Bigger than the mafia, more ruthless than the triads."

"But you tell me, what sort of weapon could target children? A thousand . . . maybe a hundred thousand school kids. That's what they say. So what are they going to do? Set off some sort of dirty bomb in the playground? Or maybe they're going to go around schools with hand grenades!"

"They say the weapon is primed and operational."

"The weapon doesn't exist!" Kellner slammed his hand down on his copy of the letter. "And even if it did, these demands are ridiculous. The Americans are never going to withdraw their troops from anywhere. And as for the suggestion that they dismantle their weapons systems . . . does Scorpia really think for a single minute that they're going to even consider it? The Americans love weapons! We show this letter to the president, he'll laugh at us."

"MI6 isn't prepared to rule out the possibility that the weapon exists."

"You've spoken to them?"

"I had a telephone conversation with Alan Blunt this morning. I have also sent him a copy of the letter.

He believes, like me, that we should treat this matter with the utmost seriousness."

"The prime minister has cut short his visit to Mexico," Kellner muttered. "He's flying home even as we speak. You don't get much more serious than that!"

"I'm sure we're all grateful to the prime minister for interrupting his conference," Sir Graham retorted dryly. "But I would have said that it is the aircraft carrying these soccer players we should be considering. I've also spoken to British Airways. Flight 0074 was delayed at Lagos airport yesterday and only left this morning . . . at nine o'clock our time. It will be touching down at Heathrow Airport at five past two, just like the letter says. And the English reserve soccer team is on board."

"So what are you suggesting we do?" Kellner demanded.

"It's very simple. The threat to the plane is at Heathrow. Scorpia has helped us at least by giving us the place and the time. We must therefore reroute the plane at once. It can land at Birmingham or Manchester. Our first priority is to make sure the players are safe."

"I'm afraid I don't agree."

Sir Graham Adair glanced at the communications officer, his eyes filled with an icy contempt. He had spoken at length with Alan Blunt that morning. The two men knew each other well. Both of them had been expecting this.

"Let me tell you my way of thinking," Kellner said. He held his two index fingers in the air, as though to frame what he had to say. "I know you're scared of Scorpia. You've made that much clear. Well, I've read their demands and personally I think they're a bunch of idiots. But either way, they've given us a chance to call their bluff. Redirecting the team is the last thing we want to do! We can use the arrival of the plane to test this so-called Invisible Sword. And by half past two we'll know it doesn't exist and we can put Scorpia's letter where it deserves to be . . . in the trash!"

"You're willing to risk the lives of the players?"

"There is no risk. We'll throw a security blanket around Heathrow Airport, making it impossible for anyone to get near them. The letter says the players are going to be hit at exactly two-fifteen. We can find out exactly who's on the plane. Then we can make sure that there are a hundred armed soldiers surrounding it when it lands. Scorpia can bring out their weapon and we'll see exactly what it is and how it works. Anyone tries to set foot in the airport, we'll arrest them and throw them in jail. End of story. End of threat."

"And how are you going to put a hundred extra armed guards into Heathrow Airport?" Sir Graham asked. "You'll start a national panic."

Kellner grinned. "You think I can't make up some sort of spin to take care of that? I'll say it's a training exercise. Nobody will even blink."

Sir Graham sighed. There were times when he wondered if he wasn't getting too old for this sort of work—and this was definitely one of them. There was only one more thing to ask. But he already knew the answer.

"Have you put this to the prime minister?" he asked.

"Yes. While you were speaking to MI6, I was talking to him. And he agrees with me. So I'm afraid on this matter you're overruled, Sir Graham."

"He's aware of the risks?"

"I don't believe there are any risks, actually. But it's really very simple. If we don't act now, we'll lose the chance to see this weapon in action. If we do this my way, we force Scorpia to show its hand."

Sir Graham Adair stood up. "There doesn't seem to be anything more to discuss," he said.

"You'd better get onto MI6. They'll be in charge of security at the airport."

"Of course." Sir Graham moved to the door. He stopped and turned around. "And what happens if you're wrong?" he inquired. "What happens if these soccer players do somehow get killed?"

Kellner shrugged. "At least we'll know what we're dealing with," he said. "And they lost every single one of their games while they were in Nigeria. I'm sure we can put together another team."

The plane landing at Heathrow Airport was a Boeing 747—flight number BA 0074 from Lagos. It had been in the air for six hours and thirty-five minutes. It had left late. There had been a seemingly endless delay at Lagos Airport: some sort of technical fault. Scorpia had arranged that, of course. It was important that the plane followed the schedule that they had imposed. It had to land at two o'clock. In fact, it hit the runway at five minutes to.

There were eighteen members of the English reserve soccer team sitting in business class. They were blank-faced and bleary-eyed . . . not just from the long flight, but from the series of defeats they had left behind them. The Nigerian tour had been a disaster from start to finish. These were only exhibition games. The results weren't meant to matter, but the tour had been something of a humiliation.

As they gazed out of the windows, looking at the gray light and the gray tarmac of a Heathrow afternoon, the captain's voice came over the intercom.

"Well, good morning, ladies and gentlemen, and welcome to Heathrow. Once again, I'm sorry for the late running of this aircraft. I'm afraid I've just had the control tower onto me and for some reason we're being rerouted away from the main terminal, so we're going to be out here a little longer. Can you please remain in your seats with your seat belts fastened and we'll have you out of here as soon as we possibly can."

And here was something strange. As the plane taxied forward, two army jeeps appeared from nowhere, one on each side, escorting them along the runway. There were soldiers with machine guns in the back. Following instructions from the control tower, the plane turned off and began to move away from the main buildings. The two jeeps went with it.

Alan Blunt stood behind an observation window, watching the 747 through a pair of miniature binoculars. He didn't move as the plane trundled toward a square, concrete holding area. When he lowered the binoculars, his eyes still remained fixed in the distance. He hadn't spoken for several minutes. He'd barely even breathed. There is nothing more dangerous than a government that does not trust its own security services. Unfortunately, as Blunt was only too well aware, the prime minister had made his dislike of both MI5 and MI6 clear almost from the day he had come to office. This was the result.

"So what now?" Sir Graham Adair was standing next to him. The permanent secretary to the cabinet office knew Alan Blunt very well. They met once a month, formally, to discuss security matters. But they were also members of the same club and occasionally played bridge. Now he stood, watching the sky and the runway as though expecting to see a missile shooting toward the slowly moving plane.

"We are about to watch eighteen people die."

Sir Graham didn't want to believe him. "Kellner is a fool," he muttered. "But even so, I can't see how they're going to do it. The airport has been cut off since midday. We've trebled the security. Everyone is on the highest possible alert. You looked at the passenger list?"

Blunt knew just about everything about every man, woman, and child who had boarded the plane at Lagos. Hundreds of agents had spent the morning checking and cross-checking their details, looking for anything remotely suspicious. If there were assassins or terrorists on the plane, they were deep undercover. At the same time, the pilots and cabin staff had been alerted to look out for anything amiss. If anyone so much as stood up before the players had disembarked, they would raise the alarm.

"Of course we did," Blunt said irritably.

"And?"

"Tourists. Businessmen. Families. Two weather forecasters and a celebrity chef. Nobody seems to have any understanding of what we're up against."

"Tell me."

"Scorpia will do what they said they would do. It's as simple as that. They never fail."

"They may not find it so easy this time." Sir Graham looked at his watch. It was nine minutes past two. "It's still possible they made a mistake warning us."

"They only warned you because they knew there was nothing you could do."

The plane came to a halt with the two jeeps on either side. At the same time, more armed soldiers appeared. They were everywhere. Some were in clusters on the ground, watching the plane through the telescopic sights of their automatic weapons. There were single snipers on the roofs, all of them linked by radio. Armed policemen with sniffer dogs waited at the entrance to the main terminal. Every door was guarded. Nobody was being allowed in or out.

Sixty more seconds had passed. There were just five minutes to the deadline: a quarter past two.

On the plane, the captain turned off the engines. Normally, the passengers would already be standing up, reaching for their bags, anxious to get off. But by now they all knew something was wrong. The plane seemed to have stopped in the middle of nowhere. There was no tunnel connecting the door with the terminal. A vehicle drove slowly forward, bringing with it a flight of steps. Armed soldiers in khaki uniforms with helmets and visors crept along beside it. Whatever window the passengers looked out of, they could see security forces totally surrounding the plane.

The captain spoke again, his voice deliberately matter-of-fact and calm.

"Well, ladies and gentlemen, it seems we have a situation here at Heathrow but the control tower assures me that it's all routine . . . there's nothing to worry about. We're going to be opening the main door in a moment, but I must ask you to remain in your seats until you're given the instruction to leave. We're going to be disembarking our passengers in business class first, starting with passengers in rows seven to nine. A bus will be arriving to take the rest of you very shortly. Please, can I ask for your patience for just a few minutes more."

Numbers seven to nine. The pilot had already been told. These were the seats taken by the team. None of them had been informed what was happening.

There were four minutes left.

The engines had been switched off. The players and coaches stood up and began to collect their carry-on luggage, a variety of sports bags and souvenirs: brightly colored clothes and wooden carvings. They were glad they had been chosen to leave first. Some of them were thinking that it was all quite fun.

The steps connected with the side of the plane. Blunt watched as a man in orange overalls ran up to stand next to the door. The man looked like an airport technician, but in fact he worked for MI6. A dozen soldiers, hooded and with gas masks, ran forward and formed a circle around the steps, their guns pointing outward so that they resembled a human porcupine. Every angle was covered. The nearest building was more than fifty yards away.

At the same time, a bus appeared. The bus was one of two that were kept at Heathrow for exceptional circumstances such as this. It looked ordinary, but its body was made of reinforced steel and its windows were bulletproof. Blunt had been in charge of all these preparations, working with the police and airport authorities. As soon as all eighteen men were on board, it would leave the airport, not bothering with customs or passport control. Black Mercedes limousines were waiting on the other side of the perimeter fence. They would whisk the team members, two or three at a time, to a secret location in London. By then, they would be safe.

Or so everyone hoped. Blunt alone was less sure.

"There's nothing," Sir Graham muttered. "There's nobody even close."

It was true. The area surrounding the plane was empty. There were maybe fifty soldiers and policemen in view. But nobody else.

"Scorpia will have been expecting this."

"Maybe one of the soldiers . . ." Sir Graham hadn't thought of this until now—when it was almost too late.

"They've all been checked," Blunt said. "I went through the list personally."

"Then for heaven's sake—"

The door of the plane opened.

A stewardess appeared at the top of the stairs, blinking nervously in the afternoon light. Only now could she see how serious the situation must be. It was as though the plane had landed in a battlefield. It was totally surrounded. There were men with guns everywhere.

The MI6 agent in the orange overalls spoke briefly with her and she went back inside the plane. Then the first of the players appeared.

"That's Hill-Smith," Sir Graham said. "He's the team captain."

Blunt looked at his watch. It was fourteen minutes past two.

Edmund Hill-Smith was slim, dark-haired, a well-built man with a sports bag over his shoulder. He was looking around him, obviously puzzled. He was followed out of the plane by the other team members. A black player in sunglasses, Jackson Burke, the goalie. Then one of the coaches. A man with gray hair, holding a straw hat, something he must have bought in a Nigerian market. One by one, they appeared in the door and began to move down the stairs to the waiting bus.

Blunt said nothing. A tiny pulse was beating in the side of his head. All eighteen men were out in the open now. Sir Graham looked left and right. Where was the attack going to come from? There was nothing anybody could do. Hill-Smith and Burke had already reached the bus. They were safely inside.

Blunt turned his wrist.

The second hand on his watch passed the twelve.

One of the players, just coming out of the plane, seemed to stumble. Sir Graham saw one of the soldiers turn, alarmed. On the bus, Burke suddenly jerked backward, his shoulders slamming into the glass. Another player, halfway down the stairs, dropped his bag and clutched his chest, his face distorted in pain. He pitched forward, knocking into the two men in front of him. But they too seemed to have been gripped by some invisible force. . . .

One after another the players crumpled. The soldiers were shouting, gesticulating. What was happening was impossible. There was no enemy. Nobody had done anything. But eighteen healthy men, athletes, were collapsing in front of their eyes. Sir Graham saw one of the soldiers speaking frantically into a radio transmitter and a second later a fleet of ambulances appeared, lights blazing, speeding toward the plane. So somebody had been prepared for the worst. Sir Graham glanced at Blunt and knew it had been him.

The ambulances were already too late. By the time they arrived, Burke was on his back, gasping his last few breaths. Hill-Smith, the captain of the team, had joined him, dropping to the floor of the bus, his lips mauve, his eyes empty. The steps were strewn with bodies, one or two of them feebly kicking, the others deadly still. The man with the gray hair was lost in a tangle of bodies. The straw hat had rolled away, blown across the runway by the breeze.

"What . . . ?" Sir Graham rasped. "How?" He couldn't find the words.

"Invisible Sword," Blunt said.

At exactly that moment, a quarter of a mile away in Terminal Two, the passengers were just arriving on a flight from Rome. At passport control, the officer noticed a mother and a father returning with their son. The boy was about fourteen years old. He was overweight, with black, curly hair, thick glasses, and terrible skin. There was a slight mustache on his upper lip. The boy was Italian. His passport gave his name as Federico Casali.

The passport officer might have looked more closely at the boy. There was some sort of alert on for a fourteen-year-old named Alex Rider. But he knew what was happening out on the runway. Everyone knew. The whole airport was in a state of panic and right now he was distracted. He didn't even bother comparing the face in front of him with the picture that had been circulated. What was happening outside was much more important.

Scorpia had timed it perfectly.

The boy took his passport back and slouched forward, through customs and out of the airport.

Alex Rider had come home.

13

PIZZA DELIVERY

SPIES HAVE TO BE careful where they live.

An ordinary person will choose a house or an apartment because it has nice views, because they like the shape of the rooms, because it feels like home. For spies, the first consideration is security. There's a comfortable sitting room—but will the window offer a target for a possible sniper's bullet? A backyard is fine—so long as the fence is high enough and there aren't too many shrubs providing cover for an intruder. The neighbors, of course, will be checked. So will the postman, the milkman, the window cleaner, and anyone else who comes to the front door. The front door itself may have as many as five separate locks and there will be alarm systems, night cameras, and panic buttons too. Someone once said that an Englishman's home is his castle. For a spy, it can be his prison too.

Mrs. Jones lived in the penthouse apartment on

the ninth floor of a building in Clerkenwell, not far from the old meat market at Smithfields. There were forty apartments altogether and the security check run by MI6 had shown that the majority of the residents were bankers or lawyers, working in the city. Melbourne House was not a cheap place to live. Mrs. Jones had ten thousand square feet and two private balconies on the top floor . . . a great deal of living space, particularly as she lived alone. On the open market, it would have cost her in excess of a million dollars when she bought it seven years ago. But as it happened, MI6 had a file on the developer. The developer had seen it and had been glad to make a deal.

The apartment was secure. And from the moment Alan Blunt had decided his second-in-command might need protection, it had become more so.

The front doors opened onto a long, rather stark reception area with a desk, two fig trees, and a single elevator at the far end. There were closed-circuit television cameras above the desk and outside on the street, recording everyone who came in. Melbourne House had porters working twenty-four hours, seven days a week—but until the crisis was over, Blunt had replaced them with agents from his own office. He had also installed a metal detector next to the reception desk, identical to the sort you would find in an airport. All visitors had to pass through it.

It was impossible to get into the building without passing the two agents on the front desk. There was a service entrance at the back, but it was locked and alarmed. The building couldn't be climbed. The walls had no footholds of any sort and anyway, there were four more agents on constant patrol. Finally, there was an agent on duty outside Mrs. Jones's front door. Hers was the only apartment on the ninth floor and he had a clear view of the corridor in both directions. There was nowhere to hide. The agent—in radio contact with the people downstairs—was armed with a high-tech, fingerprint-sensitive automatic weapon. Only he could fire it, so if—impossibly—he were overpowered, his gun would be useless.

Mrs. Jones had protested about all these arrangements. It was one of the very few times she had ever argued with her superior.

"For heaven's sake, Alan. We're talking about Alex Rider!"

"No, Mrs. Jones. We're talking about Scorpia."

There had been no more discussion after that.

At eight o'clock in the evening, the day after the deaths at Heathrow Airport, two agents were sitting behind the reception desk, discussing the news. Both of them were in their twenties, dressed in the uniform of security guards. One was plump, with short-cut, fair hair and a childish face that looked as though it would never need a shave. His name was Lloyd. He had been thrilled to get into the secret service straight from university, but he was fast getting disappointed. This sort of work, for example. It wasn't what he had expected. The other man was dark and looked foreign . . . he could have been mistaken for a Brazilian soccer player. He was smoking a cigarette even though it wasn't allowed in the building and annoyed Lloyd. His name was Ramirez. The two men had just begun the night shift. They would be there until seven o'clock the next morning, when Mrs. Jones left.

They were bored. As far as they were concerned, there was no chance of anyone getting anywhere near their boss on the ninth floor. And as though to add insult to injury, they had been told to look out for a fourteen-year-old boy. They had been given a photograph of Alex Rider and they both agreed . . . it was crazy. Why would a schoolboy be gunning for the deputy head of Special Operations?

"Maybe she's his aunt," Lloyd said. "Maybe she's forgotten his birthday and he's out for revenge."

Ramirez blew smoke. "You really think that?"

"I don't know. What do you think?"

"I don't care. It's just a waste of time."

They had been talking about the news. Even though they were part of MI6, they were too junior to know what had really happened to the soccer team. According to the papers, the players had picked up a rare disease in Nigeria. Quite how they had all managed to die at the same moment hadn't been explained.

"It was probably malaria," Lloyd said. "They've got these new mosquitoes out there."

"Mosquitoes?"

"Super-mosquitoes. Genetically modified."

"Yeah. Sure!"

Just then, the front door opened and a young man came into the reception area, dressed in motorbike leathers, with a helmet in one hand and a canvas sack over his shoulder. There was a logo on his chest, repeated on the bag:

Perelli's Pizzas
Grab yourself a pizza the action

The agents ran an eye over him. About seventeen or eighteen years old. Short, frizzy hair and a wispy beard. A gold tooth. A twisting scar on one cheek. And lots of attitude. He was smiling crookedly, as though he wasn't just delivering fast food to a fancy apartment. As though he lived here.

Lloyd stopped him. "Who are you delivering to?" he demanded.

The delivery man looked surprised. He dug into his top pocket and pulled out a grubby sheet of paper. "Foster," he said. "A pizza wanted on the sixth floor." He had a strong Scottish accent.

Ramirez was also taking an interest. It had been a long evening. Nobody had come in or out. "We're going to have to take a look in that bag," he said.

The delivery man rolled his eyes. "Are you joking? It's just a pizza—that's all. What is this place? Like . . . Fort Knox or something?"

"We need to take a look inside," Lloyd repeated.

"Okay! Okay! Whatever you say!"

The delivery man opened the bag and took out a liter bottle of Coca-Cola, which he set upright on the desk.

"I thought you said you only had a pizza," Lloyd said.

"One pizza. One bottle of Coke. You want to call my boss?"

The two agents exchanged a glance. "What else have you got in there?" Lloyd asked.

"You want to see everything?"

"Yes. As a matter of fact, we do."

The delivery man put down his helmet next to the bottle. He produced a handful of drinking straws, still in their paper wrappers. Next out was a rectangular card, about six inches long. Lloyd took it. "What's this?"

"What does it look like?" The delivery man sighed. "I'm meant to leave it behind. It's like . . . a promotion. Can't you read?"

"You want to come into this place, you mind your manners."

"It's a promotion! We leave them all over town."

Lloyd examined the card. There were pictures of pizzas on both sides and a series of special offers. Family-sized pizza, Coke, and garlic bread for just $12.50. Order before seven o'clock and get $1.00 off.

"You want to order a pizza?" the delivery man asked.

He was rubbing the two agents the wrong way. "No," Lloyd said. "But we want to see the pizza you're delivering."

"You can't do that! That's not hygienic!"

"We don't see it, you don't deliver it."

The delivery man shook his head. "You know, I've been delivering all over London and I've never had this before."

With a scowl, he took out a cardboard box, warm to the touch, and laid it on the reception desk. Lloyd pried open the lid and there was the pizza—a Four Seasons, with ham, cheese, tomato, and black olives. The smell of melted mozzarella wafted upward.

"You want to taste it too?" the delivery man asked sarcastically.

"No. What else have you got in the bag?"

"There is nothing else. The bag is empty." The delivery man pulled open the canvas bag to show them. "You know, if you're so worried about security, why don't you deliver it yourself?"

Lloyd closed the box. In a way, he knew he should have done just that. But he was a secret agent, not a pizza boy! And anyway, the pizza was only going as far as the sixth floor. He could see the elevator from where he was standing. There was a steel panel next to the door marked with the letter G and then the numbers from one to nine. Each number lit up as the elevator traveled, and if the pizza delivery man tried to go any farther, he would see. As for the stairs between the floors, they had been equipped with pressure pads and security cameras. Even the air-conditioning ducts running through the building had been alarmed.

It was safe.

"Okay," he said. "You can go up. You go straight to floor number six. You do not go anywhere else. Do you understand that?"

"Why should I want to go anywhere else? I've got a pizza for someone named Foster and she's on the sixth floor."

The delivery man loaded up the sack and walked forward.

"You go through the metal detector," Ramirez said.

"You got a metal detector? I thought this was a block of apartments. Not Edinburgh Airport."

The delivery man handed his helmet to Ramirez and, with the canvas bag over his shoulder, walked through the metal frame. The machine was silent.

"There you are!" he said. "I'm clean. Now, can I deliver the pizza or are you going to strip-search me first?"

"Wait a minute!" The fair-haired agent—Lloyd—sounded threatening. "You forgot the Coke—and your promotions card," he said. He picked the two items up from the reception desk and handed them over.

"Yeah. Thanks." The delivery man began to walk toward the elevator.

He had known he would be stopped.

Behind the wig and the makeup, Alex Rider heaved a sigh of relief. The disguise had worked. Nile had told him it would and he'd had no reason to doubt it. He had been careful to make his voice sound older, with a fair imitation of a Scottish accent. The motorbike leathers had thickened out his body and he was wearing special shoes that had added an inch to his height. He hadn't been worried about his bag being searched. The moment he had set eyes on them, he had known that Lloyd and Ramirez were new to the game, with little field experience.

If they had taken him up on his offer and demanded to call the pizza company, Alex would have given them a business card with the telephone number. But it would have been Scorpia who would have answered. If they had been smart, the two agents might have telephoned up to the sixth floor. But Sarah Foster—the owner of the apartment—was out of London. Her telephone line had been switched from outside. The call would have been redirected . . . again to Scorpia.

Everything had gone exactly as planned.

After Alex had left Venice, he had been taken through Heathrow Airport with two Scorpia people he had never met before. They had been with him at passport control, checking to see there was no problem. How could there have been? Alex was in disguise. He had a false passport. And there seemed to be some sort of security alert at the airport. Everyone was running around in circles. Doubtless it had been engineered by Scorpia.

From Heathrow, he had been taken to a house in the middle of London, only glimpsing the front door and the quiet, leafy road as he was whisked in. Nile had been waiting for him there, sitting on an antique chair with his legs crossed.

"Federico!" He greeted Alex with the name from the fake passport.

Alex said little. Nile briefed him. He would be given another disguise—the pizza delivery costume—as well as everything he would need to break into Mrs. Jones's apartment and kill her. How he got out again would be his own problem.

"It'll be easy," Nile said. "You'll just walk out the

way you came in. And if there is any trouble, I'm sure you'll cope, Alex. I have every faith in you."

Scorpia had already reconnoitered the apartment. Nile showed him the plans. They knew where the cameras were, how many pressure pads had been installed, how many agents had been commandeered. And everything had been worked out . . . right down to the Coke bottle that Alex had purposefully left on the reception desk and that had been handed back to him *without passing through the metal detector frame.* It was simple psychology. A plastic bottle filled with liquid. How could it possibly contain anything metallic?

Alex reached the elevator and stopped. This was the vital moment.

He had his back to the two secret service agents. He was standing between them and the elevator, blocking their line of vision. As he walked, he had already slipped the special offers card out of the canvas bag, and he was holding it in both hands. In fact, one side of the card peeled off to reveal a thin silver plate with the letter *G* and the numbers one to nine. It was identical to the plate beside the elevator. The other side was magnetic. Casually, Alex leaned forward and placed the fake panel over the real one. It held in place immediately. Sticking it there had also activated it. Now it was just a matter of timing.

The elevator doors opened and he got in. As he turned around, he saw the two agents watching him. He reached out and pressed the button for the ninth floor. The elevator doors slid shut, cutting them out. A second later, the elevator jerked and moved up.

The two agents saw the numbers changing beside the elevator door. Ground . . . one . . . two . . . What they didn't realize was, they weren't following the real progress of the elevator. A tiny chip and a watch battery inside the silver plate were illuminating the fake numbers. The real numbers were blocked out behind.

Alex arrived at the ninth floor.

The silver panel showed he had stopped at floor six.

It had taken thirty seconds to travel up from the ground floor. In that time, Alex had removed the motorbike leathers, revealing clothes that were loose, light-wearing, and black. The uniform of the ninja assassin. He dragged off his wig and grabbed hold of the latex covering his face. It came off almost in one piece, taking the fake scar with it. Finally, he removed the gold tooth. The doors slid open. Once again he was himself.

He had already been shown a floor map of the entire building. Mrs. Jones's apartment was to the right . . . and there were two unforgivable lapses of security. Although there were closed-circuit television cameras in the fire escapes, there were none in the corridor. And the agent standing in front of the door could see all the way from one end to the other, but he couldn't see into the elevator. Two blind spots. Alex was about to take advantage of them both.

The agent on the ninth floor had heard the elevator arrive. Like Lloyd and Ramirez downstairs, he was new to the job. He wondered why they had sent the elevator up. Perhaps he should radio down and find out. At that moment, a boy with light brown hair and death in his eyes stepped out. Alex was holding one of the drinking straws that the two agents had seen but not examined. He had unwrapped it. It was already between his lips. He blew.

The *fukidake*—or blowgun—was another lethal weapon used by the ninjas. A needle-sharp dart fired into a major artery could kill instantly. But there were also darts that had been hollowed out and filled with poison. A ninja could hit a man without making any sound at all—over a distance of twenty yards or more. Alex was much closer than that. Fortunately for the agent, the dart that he fired out of the straw contained only a tranquilizer. It hit the side of his cheek. The agent opened his mouth as though to cry out, stared stupidly at Alex, then collapsed.

Alex knew he had to move quickly. The two agents downstairs would allow him a couple of minutes, but then they would expect the elevator to return. He grabbed the Coke bottle and opened it—not turning the lid but the bottle itself. The bottle came apart in two halves. Dark brown liquid poured out, soaking into the carpet in the elevator. Inside the bottle was a package wrapped in brown plastic, the same color as the Coke. With the label covering most of it, the package had been completely invisible. Alex tore it open. There was a gun inside.

It was a Kahr P9 double-action semi-automatic, manufactured in America. It was six inches long and—with its stainless steel and polymer construction—it weighed just twenty-five ounces, making it one of the smallest, lightest pistols in the world. The in-line magazine could have held seven bullets. To keep the weight down, Scorpia had provided just one. It was all Alex would need.

Taking the canvas bag with the pizza, he went past the sleeping agent and over to Mrs. Jones's door. It had three locks, as he had been told. He opened the pizza and removed three of the black olives from the top, squeezing each one against a lock. The canvas bag had a false bottom. He opened it and trailed out three wires, which he connected to the olives. A plastic box and a button were built into the bottom of the bag. Crouching down, Alex pressed it. The olives—which weren't olives at all—exploded silently, each one a brilliant flare, burning into the locks. The sharp smell of molten metal rose in the air.

Alex pushed and the door swung open.

Holding the gun ahead of him, he stepped into a single large room with gray curtains along the far wall, a dining table, and a suite of leather sofas. It was lit by a soft, yellow glow coming from a single lamp. The room was modern and sparsely furnished. There was little in it that told him any more about Mrs. Jones than he already knew. Even the pictures on the walls were abstracts, blobs of color that gave nothing away. But there were clues. He saw a photograph on a shelf, a younger Mrs. Jones, actually smiling, with two children, a boy and a girl aged about six and four. A nephew and a niece? They looked a lot like her.

Mrs. Jones read books. She had an expensive television and a DVD player. And there was a chess-board. She was halfway through a game. But who with? Alex wondered. Nile had told him she lived alone. There was a soft purring and he noticed a Siamese cat stretched out on one of the sofas. That was a surprise. He hadn't expected the deputy head of MI6 Special Operations to need companionship of any sort.

The purring grew louder. It was as though the cat were trying to warn its owner that he was there, and sure enough, a door opened on the other side of the room.

"What is it, Q?"

Mrs. Jones came into the room. She had heard the cat and walked toward it. Then she saw Alex and stopped.

"Alex! . . ."

"Mrs. Jones."

She was wearing a gray silk dressing gown. Alex suddenly saw a picture of her life and the emptiness at the heart of it. She came home from work, had a shower, ate dinner on her own. Then there was the chess game . . . maybe she was playing over the Internet. News at ten on the television. And the cat.

She stopped in the middle of the room. She didn't seem alarmed. There was nothing she could do—certainly no panic button or alarm she could reach. Her hair was still wet from the shower. Alex noticed her bare feet. He lifted his hand and she saw the gun.

"Did Scorpia send you?" she asked.

"Yes."

"To kill me."

"Yes."

She nodded as though she understood why this should be so. "They told you about your father," she said.

"Yes."

"I'm sorry, Alex."

"Sorry you killed him?"

"Sorry I didn't tell you myself."

She didn't try to move. She simply stood there, facing him. Alex knew that he didn't have much time. Any moment now the elevator would return to the ground floor. As soon as the agents saw he wasn't in it, they would raise the alarm. They might already be on their way up.

"What happened to Winters?" she asked. Alex didn't know who she meant. "He was outside the door," she explained.

Winters was the third agent.

"I knocked him out," Alex said.

"So you got past the two downstairs. You got up here. And you broke in." Mrs. Jones shrugged. "Scorpia has trained you well."

"It wasn't Scorpia who trained me, Mrs. Jones. It was you."

"But now you've joined Scorpia?"

Alex nodded.

"I can't quite see you as an assassin, Alex. I know you don't like me—or Alan Blunt. I can understand that. But I know you. I don't think you have any idea what you've gotten yourself into. I bet Scorpia was all smiles. I'm sure they were delighted to see you. But they've been lying to you—"

"Stop it!" Alex's finger tightened on the trigger. He knew that she was trying to make it difficult for him. He had been warned that this was what she would do. By talking to him, by using his first name, she was reminding him that she wasn't just a paper cutout, a target. She was sowing doubts in his mind. And, of course, she was playing for time.

Nile had told him to do it quickly, the moment they met. Alex realized that this had already gone wrong, that she had already gained the upper hand . . .

even though he was the one with the gun. He reminded himself of what Julia Rothman had shown
him on the television screen. Albert Bridge. The death
of his father. He was facing the woman who had given
the order to shoot.

"Why did you do it?" he demanded. His voice had
become a whisper. He was trying to channel the hatred through him, to give him the strength to do what
he had been sent here for.

"Why did I do what, Alex?"

"You killed my father."

Mrs. Jones looked at him for a long moment and
it was impossible to tell what was going on in those
black eyes. But he could see that she was making
some sort of calculation. Of course, her entire life was
a series of calculations—and once she'd worked out
the figures, someone would usually die. The only difference here was that the death was her own.

She seemed to come to a decision.

"Do you want me to apologize to you, Alex?" she
asked, suddenly hard. "We're talking about John
Rider, a man you never knew. You never spoke to
him. You have no memory of him. You know nothing
about him."

"He was still my dad!"

"He was a killer. He worked for Scorpia. Do you want to know how many people he murdered?"

Five or six. That was what Mrs. Rothman had told him.

"There was the millionaire working in Singapore. He was a married man with a son of your age. There was the aid worker in Brazil. He was trying to help the street children, but unfortunately he'd made too many enemies, so he had to be taken out. There were two agents. One English, one American. There was a woman . . . she was about to blow the whistle on a big corporation in Sydney. She was only twenty-six, Alex, and he shot her as she was getting out of her car—"

"That's enough!" Now Alex was holding the gun in both hands. "I don't want to hear any of this."

"Yes, you do, Alex. You asked me. You wanted to know why he had to be stopped. And that's what you're going to become, isn't it? Following in your father's footsteps? I'm sure they'll send you all over the world, killing people you know nothing about. And I'm sure you'll be very good at it. Your father was one of the best."

"You cheated him. He was your prisoner and you said you were going to let him go. You were going to swap him for someone else. But you shot him in the back. I saw—"

"I always wondered if they kept a video," Mrs. Jones muttered. She gestured with her hands and Alex stiffened, wondering if she was trying to keep him talking while help arrived. But they were still alone. The cat had gone to sleep. Nobody was approaching the room. "I'll give you some advice," she said. "You'll need it if you're going to work with Scorpia. Once you join the other side, there are no rules. They don't believe in fair play. Nor do we.

"They had kidnapped an eighteen-year-old," she continued. Alex remembered the figure on the bridge. "He was the son of a civil servant working with the British government. They were going to kill him. But they were going to torture him first. We had to get him back—so, yes, I arranged the exchange. But there was no way I was ever going to release your father. He was too dangerous. Too many more people would have died. And so I arranged a double-cross. Two men on a bridge. A sniper. It worked perfectly and I'm glad. You can shoot me if it really makes you feel any better, Alex. But I'm telling you. You didn't know your father. And if I had to do it all again, I'd do it exactly the same."

"If you're saying my father was so evil . . . what do you think that makes me?" Alex was trying to will himself to shoot. He had thought anger would give him strength. But he was more tired than angry. So now he searched for another way to persuade himself to pull the trigger. He was his father's son. It was in his blood.

Mrs. Jones took a step toward him.

"Stay where you are!" The gun was less than a yard away from her, aiming straight at her head.

"I don't think you're a killer, Alex. You never knew your father. Why do you have to be like him? Do you think every child is *made* the moment they're born? I think you have a choice—"

"I never chose to work for you."

"Didn't you? After Stormbreaker, you could have walked away. We never needed to meet again. But if you remember, you *chose* to get tangled up with drug dealers and we had to bail you out. And then there was Wimbledon. We didn't make you go undercover. You agreed to go . . . and if you hadn't locked a Chinese gangster in a deep freeze, we wouldn't have had to send you to America."

"You're twisting everything!"

"And finally, Damian Cray. You went after him on

your own and we're very grateful to you, Alex. But you ask me—what do I think you are? I think you're too smart to pull that trigger. You're not going to shoot me. Now or ever."

"You're wrong," Alex said. He lifted the gun one last time. She was lying to him, he knew that. She had always lied to him. He could do this. He had to do it.

He aimed the gun straight at her.

He let the hatred take him.

And fired.

The air in front of him seemed to explode into fragments.

Mrs. Jones had tricked him. She had been tricking him all along. Although he hadn't seen it, the room was divided into two parts. A huge pane of transparent, bulletproof glass ran from one corner to the other, stretching from the floor to the ceiling. She had been on one side. He had been on the other. In the half-light it had been invisible, but now the glass frosted, a thousand cracks spiraling outward from the dent made by the bullet. Mrs. Jones had almost disappeared from sight, her face broken up as though she had become a smashed picture of herself. At the same time, an alarm rang, the door flew open, and Alex was grabbed and thrown sideways, onto the sofa. The gun went flying. Somebody shouted something in his ear, but he couldn't understand the words. The cat snarled and leaped past his head. His arms were wrenched behind him, a knee pressed into his back, and he felt cold steel against his wrists. There was a click. He could no longer move his hands.

Now there seemed to be several voices in the room.

"Are you all right, Mrs. Jones?"

"We're sorry, ma'am . . ."

"We've got the car waiting outside . . ."

"Don't hurt him!"

Alex was jerked off the sofa with his hands chained behind him. He felt wretched and sick. He had failed Scorpia. He had failed his father. He had failed himself.

He didn't cry out. He didn't resist. Limp and unmoving, he allowed himself to be dragged out of the room, back down the corridor, and into the night.

14

COBRA

THE ROOM WAS A BARE white box, designed to intimidate. Alex had measured out the space: ten paces one way, four paces across. There was a narrow bunk with no sheets or blankets and, behind a partition, a toilet. But that was all. The door had no handle and fitted so flush to the wall that it was almost invisible. There was no window. Light came from behind a square panel in the ceiling and was controlled from outside.

Alex had no idea how long he had been here. Someone, at some time, must have taken his watch.

After he had been taken down from Mrs. Jones's penthouse apartment, he had been bundled into a car and driven at speed across London, the black cloth bag still over his head. He had no idea where he was going. They drove for about half an hour, then slowed down. Alex felt his stomach sink and knew they were driving down some sort of ramp. Had they taken him to the basement of the Liverpool Street HQ? He had been there once before, but this time he was being given no chance to gather his bearings. The car stopped. The door opened and he felt himself being grabbed and dragged out. Nobody spoke to him. He was taken along another corridor— pinned between two men—and down a flight of stairs. Then his hands were unlocked. The bag was pulled off. He just had time to glimpse Lloyd and Ramirez—the two agents from the reception desk— as they walked out. Then the door closed and he was on his own.

He lay on his back, remembering the final moments in the apartment. He was amazed that he hadn't seen the glass barrier until it was too late. Had Mrs. Jones's voice been amplified in some way? It didn't matter. He had tried to kill her. He had finally found the strength to pull the trigger, proving that Scorpia had been right about him all along.

"He was a killer. Do you know how many people he murdered?"

Alex remembered what she had said about his father. She was the one who had given the order for John Rider's own death. She had arranged it. She deserved to die.

Or so he tried to persuade himself. But the worst of it was, he half understood how she felt. Suppose his father hadn't been killed on Albert Bridge. Suppose Alex had grown up and somehow found out what his father did for a living. How would Alex have felt about it? Would he have been able to forgive the man himself?

Sitting on his own in this cruel, white room, Alex thought back to the moment when he had fired the gun. At the very last second, almost unconsciously, he had changed his aim. He knew that now. He remembered the slight shudder in his hand as his conscience forbade him to do what his heart most wanted. He hadn't been aiming at Mrs. Jones. The bullet would have gone past her, over her head.

Not that it would have made any difference. Mrs. Jones had been safe all along. Once again he saw the invisible glass screen crack but not break. Good old Smithers! It was almost certainly the MI6 gadget master who had fixed it up.

He wondered what would happen to him now. Would MI6 prosecute him? More likely, they would interrogate him. They would want to know about Malagosto, about Mrs. Rothman and Nile. But maybe after that, at last, they would leave him alone. After what had happened, they would never trust him again.

He fell asleep . . . not just exhausted but drained. It was a black and empty sleep, without dreams, without any feeling of comfort or warmth.

The sound of the door opening woke him up. He opened his eyes and blinked. It was disconcerting having no idea of the time. He could have slept for a few hours or it could have been all night. He wasn't feeling rested. There was a crick in his neck. But without a window, it was impossible to tell night from day.

"You need the toilet?"

"No."

"Then come with me."

The man at the door wasn't Lloyd or Ramirez or anyone Alex had ever met at MI6. He had a blank, uninteresting face and Alex knew that if they met the next day, he would already have forgotten him. He got off the bunk and walked toward the door, suddenly nervous. Nobody knew he was here. Not Tom, not Jack Starbright . . . none of his friends. MI6 could make him disappear. Permanently. Nobody would ever find out what had happened to him. Maybe that was what they had in mind.

But there was nothing he could do. He followed the agent along a curving corridor with a steel mesh floor and fat pipes following the line of the ceiling. He could have been in the engine room of a ship.

"I'm hungry," he said. He was. But he also wanted to show this agent that he wasn't afraid.

"I'm taking you to breakfast."

Breakfast! So he had slept through the night.

"Don't worry," Alex said. "You can drop me off at a McDonald's."

"I'm afraid that's not possible. In here . . ."

They had arrived at a second door and Alex went through and into a strange, curving room—obviously still underground. There were thick glass panels built into the ceiling and he could see the shapes of people—commuters—walking overhead. The room was underneath a sidewalk. Feet of different sizes and shapes touched, briefly, against the glass. Above them, the commuters were like ghosts, twisting, rippling, moving soundlessly by as they made their way to work.

There was a table with fruit salad, cereal, milk, croissants, and coffee. Alex welcomed the sight of breakfast but lost some of his appetite when he saw who he was supposed to share it with. Alan Blunt was waiting for him, sitting in a chair on the other side of the table, dressed in yet another of his neat gray suits. He really did look like the bank manager that he had once pretended to be, a man in his fifties, more comfortable with figures and statistics than with human beings.

"Good morning, Alex," he said.

Alex didn't reply.

"You can leave us, Burns. Thank you."

The agent nodded and backed out. The door swung shut. Alex walked forward and sat down.

"Are you hungry, Alex? Please. Help yourself."

"No, thanks." Alex was hungry. But he wouldn't feel comfortable eating in front of this man.

"Don't be stupid. You need your breakfast. You have a very busy day ahead of you." Blunt waited for Alex to respond. Alex said nothing. "Do you know how much trouble you're in?" Blunt demanded.

"Perhaps I will have some cornflakes after all," Alex said.

He helped himself. Blunt watched him coldly.

"We have very little time," Blunt said as Alex ate. "I have some questions for you. You will answer them fully and honestly."

"And if I don't?"

"What do you think? Do you think I'll give you a truth serum or something? You'll answer my questions because it's in your interest to do so. Right now, you don't know anything. You have no idea what's at stake. But believe me when I tell you that this meeting is vital. We have to know what you know. More lives than you can imagine may depend on it."

Alex lowered his spoon and nodded. "Go on."

"You were recruited by Julia Rothman?"

"You know who she is?"

"Of course we do."

"Yes. I was."

"You were taken to Malagosto?"

"Yes."

"And you were sent to kill Mrs. Jones."

Alex felt a need to defend himself. "She killed my dad."

"That's not the issue."

"Not for you."

"Just answer the question."

"Yes. I was sent to kill Mrs. Jones."

"Good." Blunt nodded. "I need to know who brought you to London. What you were told. And what you were to do when you completed your mission."

Alex hesitated. Telling Blunt all this, he knew he would be betraying Scorpia. But suddenly he didn't care. He had been drawn into a world where everyone betrayed everyone. He just wanted to get out.

"They had a layout of her apartment," he said. "They knew everything . . . except for the glass screen. All I had to do was wait for her to come in. Two of their agents took me through Heathrow Airport. They never told me their real names, but we came in as an Italian family. I had a fake passport . . ."

"Where did they take you?"

"I don't know. It was a house somewhere. I didn't have time to see the address." Alex paused. "Where is Mrs. Jones?"

"She didn't want to see you."

Alex nodded. "I can understand that."

"After killing her . . . what were you supposed to do?"

"They gave me a telephone number. I was meant to call it the moment I'd done what they wanted. But they'll know you've got me now. I expect they were watching the apartment."

There was a long silence. Blunt was examining Alex minutely, like a scientist with an interesting laboratory specimen. Alex twisted uncomfortably in his chair.

"Do you want to work for Scorpia?" Blunt demanded.

"I don't know," Alex said. "I'm not sure it's any different than working for you."

"You don't believe that. You can't believe that."

"Why not? You're all killers in the end. Are you really going to tell me you're any better than they are?" Blunt said nothing, but his eyes were fixed on Alex. "I don't want to work for either of you!" Alex finished. "I just want to go back to school. I don't want to see any of you ever again."

"I wish that were possible, Alex." For once, Blunt actually sounded sincere. "Let me tell you something that may surprise you. It's been six . . . seven months since we first met. In that time, you've proved yourself to be remarkably useful. You've been more successful than I could possibly have calculated. And yet, in truth, I wish we had never met."

"Why?"

"Because there has to be something wrong—seriously wrong—when the security of the entire world rests on the shoulders of a fourteen-year-old boy. Believe me, right now I would be very glad to let you walk out of here. You don't belong in my world any more than I belong in yours. But I can't let you go back to school because in a little over twenty-four hours every child in that school could be dead. Thousands of children in London could have joined them. This is what your friends in Scorpia have promised and I have no doubt at all that they mean what they say."

"Thousands . . . ?" Alex had gone pale. He hadn't expected anything like this. What had he walked into?

"Maybe more. Maybe tens of thousands."

"How?"

"We don't know. You may. All I can tell you now is that Scorpia has made a series of demands. We cannot give them what they want. And they're going to make us pay a heavy price."

"What do you want from me?" Alex asked. All the strength seemed to have drained out of him.

"Scorpia has made one mistake. They've sent you to us. I want to know everything you've seen . . . everything Julia Rothman told you. We still have no idea what we're up against, Alex. You may at least be able to give us a clue."

Thousands of children in London.

"Sometimes, unfortunately, killing people is what we have to do."

That was what she had said.

This was what she meant.

"I don't know anything," Alex said.

"You may know more than you think. Right now, you're all that stands between Scorpia and an unimaginable bloodbath. I know what you think about me. I know how you feel about MI6. But are you willing to help?"

Alex slowly raised his eyes. He examined the man sitting opposite him and at that moment he saw something he would never have believed.

Alan Blunt was afraid.

"Yes," he said. "I'll help you."

"Good. Then finish your breakfast, have a shower, and get changed. The prime minister has called a meeting of COBRA. I want you to attend."

COBRA.

The word stands for Cabinet Office Briefing Room, which is where, at 10 Downing Street, the meetings take place. COBRA is an emergency council, the government's ultimate response to any major crisis.

The prime minister is, of course, present when COBRA sits. So are most of his senior ministers, his director of communications, his chief of staff, and representatives from the police, the army, and the intelligence services. Finally, there are the civil servants, men in dark suits with long and meaningless job titles. Everything that happens, everything that's said, is recorded, minuted, and then filed away for thirty years under the Official Secrets Act. Politics may be a game, but COBRA is deadly serious. Decisions made here can bring down a government. The wrong decision could destroy the entire country.

Alex Rider had been shown into another room and left to shower and change into fresh clothes. He recognized the Pepe jeans and the Reebok World Cup rugby shirt. They were his own. Somebody must have been around to his home to get them, and seeing them laid out on a chair, he felt a pang of guilt. He hadn't spoken to Jack Starbright for weeks, not since he had left for Venice. He wondered if anyone from MI6 had told his friend and housekeeper what was happening. He doubted it. MI6 never told anyone anything unless they had to.

But as he pulled on the shirt, he felt something rustle in the breast pocket. He dipped his hand in and took out a folded sheet of paper. He opened it and recognized Jack's handwriting.

Alex—

What have you gotten yourself mixed up in this time? Two secret agents [spies] waiting downstairs. Suits and sunglasses. Think they're smart, but I bet they don't look in the top pocket.

Thinking of you. Take care of yourself. Try and come home in one piece.

Love you.

Jack

That made him smile. It seemed it had been a long time since anything had happened to cheer him up.

As he had thought, the cell and interrogation room were beneath Liverpool Street. He was led out to a garage where a navy blue Jaguar XJ6 was waiting and the two of them were driven up the ramp and into Liverpool Street itself. Alex settled into the leather seat. He found it strange to be sitting so close to the head of MI6 Special Operations. It was the first time they had ever been alone together—and without a table or a desk between them.

Blunt was in no mood to talk.

"You'll be brought up-to-date at COBRA," he muttered briefly. "But while we're driving there, I want you to think of everything that happened to you

while you were with Scorpia. Everything you overheard. If I had more time, I'd debrief you myself. But
COBRA won't wait."

After that, he buried himself in a report that he
took from his briefcase and Alex might as well have
been alone. He looked out of the window as the
chauffeur drove them west, across London. It was a
quarter past nine. People were still hurrying to work.
Shops were opening. On one side of the glass, life was
going on as normal. But once again Alex was on the
wrong side, sitting in this car with this man, heading
into God knows what.

He watched as they arrived at Charing Cross and
stopped at the lights at Trafalgar Square. Blunt was
still reading. Suddenly there was something Alex
wanted to know.

"Is Mrs. Jones married?" he asked.

Blunt looked up. "She was."

"In her apartment, I saw a photograph of her with
two children."

"They were hers. They'd be your age now. But she
lost them."

"They died?"

"They were taken."

Alex digested this. Blunt's replies were leaving him hardly any the wiser. "Are you married?" he asked.

Blunt turned away. "I don't discuss my personal life."

Alex shrugged. Frankly, he was surprised that Blunt had one.

They drove down Whitehall and then turned right, through the gates that were already open to receive them. The car stopped and Alex got out, his head spinning. He was standing in front of probably the most famous front door in the world. And the door was open. A policeman was ushering him in. Blunt had already disappeared ahead. Alex followed.

The first surprise was how large 10 Downing Street was inside. It was two or three times bigger than he had expected, opening out in all directions with high ceilings and a corridor stretching improbably into the distance. Chandeliers hung from the ceiling. Works of art, borrowed from museums, lined the walls.

Blunt had been stopped by a tall, gray-haired man in a suit and striped tie. The man had the sort of face that should have looked out of a gold frame: a Victorian portrait. It belonged to another world and like an old painting it seemed to have faded. Only the eyes, small and dark, showed any life. The eyes flickered over Alex and seemed to know him at once.

"So this is Alex Rider," the man said. He held out a hand. "My name is Graham Adair."

He was looking at Alex as though he knew him—but Alex was sure the two of them had never met before.

"Sir Graham is permanent secretary to the cabinet office," Blunt explained.

"I've heard a great deal about you, Alex. I have to say, I'm pleased to meet you. I owe you a great deal. More, I think, than you can imagine."

"Thanks." Alex was puzzled. He didn't know what Sir Graham meant and wondered if the man had been involved in some way in one of his other assignments.

"I understand you're joining us at COBRA. I'm very glad—although I should warn you that there may be one or two people there who know less about you and may resent your presence."

"I'm used to it," Alex said.

"I'm sure. Well, come this way. I hope you can help us. We're up against something very different and none of is quite sure what to do."

Alex followed the cabinet secretary along the cor-

ridor, through an archway, and into a large, wood-
paneled room with at least forty people gathered
around a huge conference table. Alex's first impression was that they were all middle-aged and, with only
a few exceptions, male and white. Then he realized
how many faces he recognized. The prime minister
was sitting at the head of the table. The deputy prime
minister—fat and jowly—was next to him. The foreign secretary was fiddling nervously with his tie. Another man who might have been the defense secretary
was opposite him. Most of the men were in suits, but
there were also uniforms—army and police. Everyone
in the room had a thick file in front of them. Two
elderly women, dressed in black suits with white
shirts, sat in the corners, their fingers poised over
what looked like miniature typewriters.

Blunt gestured Alex to an empty chair at the table
and sat down next to him. Alex noticed a few heads
turn in his direction, but nobody said anything.

The prime minister stood up and Alex felt the
same buzz he'd had when he first met Damian
Cray—the realization that he was seeing, in the flesh,
a face known all over the world. The prime minister
looked older and shabbier than he did on television.

Here there was no makeup, no subtle lighting. He looked defeated.

"Good morning," he said, and everyone in the room fell silent.

The meeting of COBRA had begun.

15

REMOTE CONTROL

THEY HAD BEEN talking for three hours.

The prime minister had read out the contents of
Scorpia's letter and copies had been passed around.
Even Alex had a copy in front of him and he had read
it with a feeling of sick disbelief. Eighteen innocent
people had already died and nobody in the room had
any idea how it had happened. Would Scorpia go
ahead with its threat to target children in London?
Alex had no doubt of it, but nobody had asked for his
opinion and the first hour had been taken up discussing the question over and over again. At least half
the people in the room thought it was a bluff. The
other half wanted to put pressure on the Americans—
to make them agree to Scorpia's demands.

But there was no chance of that happening. The
foreign secretary had already met with the American
ambassador. The prime minister had spent several
hours on the telephone with the president of the

United States. This was the American position: Scorpia was asking the impossible. The Americans considered their demands to be laughable . . . quite possibly insane. The president had offered the help of the CIA to track Scorpia down. Two hundred American agents were already on their way to London. But there was nothing more he could do. England was on its own.

The response caused a great deal of debate at COBRA. The deputy prime minister crashed his fist against the table.

"It's incredible! It's a bloody scandal! We help the Americans. We're their closest allies. And now they turn around and tell us to jump in the lake!"

"That's not quite what they've said." The foreign secretary was more cautious. "And I don't know what else they could do. The president has a point. These demands are impossible."

"They could try to negotiate!"

"But the letter says there will be no negotiation—"

"That's what it says. But they could still try!"

Alex listened as the two men argued, neither of them really listening to what the other had to say. So this was how government worked! It was incredible. Nobody seemed to have any idea what to do.

Next up was a science officer with a report on how the soccer players had died.

"They were all poisoned," he said. He was a short man, bald, with a round, pink face. He had put on a crumpled suit for the meeting, but somehow Alex could tell he spent most of his life in a white coat. "We found traces of cyanide that seem to have been delivered straight to the heart. The amounts were very small—but they were enough."

"How were they delivered?" someone—the police chief—asked.

"We don't yet know. They hadn't been shot, that's for sure. There were no unexplained perforations on their skin and there's only one thing we've come up with that's rather odd. We found tiny traces of gold in their blood."

"Gold?" The director of communications had spoken for the first time and Alex noticed him, sitting next to the prime minister. He was the smallest—and in many ways seemed to be the least imposing —man in the room. And yet, at his single word, every head had turned.

"Yes, Mr. Kellner. We don't believe the gold particles contributed to their death. But every single one of the players was the same—"

"Well, it all seems pretty obvious to me," Kellner said, and there was a sneer in his voice. He stood up and looked around the crowded table with cold, superior eyes. Alex disliked him at once. He had seen kids like him at Brookland. Small and spiteful, always winding people up. But running in tears to the teachers the moment they got whacked. "All these people died at exactly the same time," he continued. "So it's pretty obvious they were all poisoned at the same time. When could that have been? Well, obviously, when they were on the plane! I've already checked. The flight lasted six hours, thirty-five minutes and they were given a meal just after they left Lagos. There must have been cyanide in the food and it kicked in just after they arrived at Heathrow."

"Are you saying there is no secret weapon?" the deputy prime minister asked. He blinked heavily. "What does Scorpia mean by 'Invisible Sword,' then?"

"It's a trick. They're trying to make us think they can kill people by some sort of remote control . . ."

Remote control. That meant something to Alex. He remembered something he had seen when he had first broken into the Ca' Vedova. What was it?

"There is no 'Invisible Sword,' " Kellner continued. "They're just trying to frighten us."

"I'm not sure I agree with you, Mr. Kellner." The medical officer seemed nervous of the director of communications. "They could all have taken the poison at the same time, I suppose. But each one of those men had his own metabolism. The poison would have reacted more quickly in some than in others."

"They were all athletes. Their metabolisms would have been more or less the same."

"No, Mr. Kellner. There were also two coaches and a manager—"

"To hell with them. There is no 'Invisible Sword.' These people are playing games with us. They make demands they know the Americans can't possibly meet and they threaten us with something that simply isn't going to happen."

"That isn't normally Scorpia's way." Alex was surprised to see that it was Blunt who had spoken. The head of MI6 Special Operations was sitting on his left. His voice was quiet and very even. "We've had dealings with them before and they've never yet made a hollow threat."

"You were at Heathrow, Mr. Blunt. What do you think happened?"

"I don't know."

"Well, that's very helpful, isn't it. Secret intelli-

gence comes to the table and they don't have any intelligence to offer. And since you're here . . ." Mark
Kellner seemed to have noticed Alex for the first time.
"I'd be fascinated to know why you've brought along
a schoolboy. Is it Take Your Son to Work Day?"

"This is Alex Rider." This time it was Sir Graham
Adair who had spoken. His dark eyes settled on the
head of communications. "As you know, Alex has
helped us on several occasions. He also happens to be
the last person to have had contact with Scorpia."

"Really? And how was that?"

"I sent him to Venice, undercover," Blunt said,
and Alex was surprised at how fluently he lied. "Scorpia has a training school on the island of Malagosto
and we needed to know certain details. Alex trained
there for a week."

One of the politicians coughed. "Is that really necessary, Mr. Blunt?" he asked. "I mean, if it was
known that the government was using school-age
children for this sort of work, it might not look very
good for us."

"I hardly think that's relevant right now," Blunt
replied.

The police chief looked puzzled. He was an elderly
man in a blue uniform with brightly polished silver

buttons. "If you know about Scorpia, if you even know where to find them, why can't you take them out?" he asked. "Why can't we just send in the SAS and kill the whole lot of them?"

"The Italian government might not be too amused to have their territory invaded," Blunt replied. "And anyway, it's not as simple as that. Scorpia is a world-wide organization. We know some of the leaders, but not all of them. If we take out one branch, another one will simply take over the operation. And then they'll come for revenge. Scorpia never forgives or forgets. You have to remember, they may be the ones who are threatening us. But they'll be working for a client and it is the client who is our real enemy."

"And what did Alex Rider find out when he was on Malagosto?" Kellner asked. He wasn't going to allow himself to be knocked off his pedestal. Not by Alan Blunt. And certainly not by a fourteen-year-old boy.

Alex felt all eyes on him. He shifted uncomfort-ably. "Mrs. Rothman took me out for dinner and she mentioned Invisible Sword," he said. "But she wouldn't tell me what it was."

"Who exactly is Mrs. Rothman?" Kellner de-manded.

"Julia Rothman sits on the executive board of

Scorpia," Blunt said. "She is one of nine senior officers. Alex met her when he was in Italy."

"Well, that's very helpful," Kellner said. "But if that's all Alex has to offer, we really don't need him here anymore."

"There was something about a cold chain." Alex remembered the conversation he had overheard at the Ca' Vedova. "I didn't know what it meant, but it may have had something to do with it."

In the corner of the room, a young, smartly dressed woman with long black hair sat up in her chair and looked at Alex with sudden interest.

But Kellner had already moved on. "We're being asked to believe that Scorpia can somehow poison thousands of children and arrange for them all to keel over at exactly four o'clock on Thursday—"

"They'll all be coming out of school," one of the army men said.

"It can't be done! The soccer team was a stunt. They want to panic us into going public with this, and if we do that, the entire credibility of the government will be undermined. *That's* what they want!"

"Then what are you suggesting we do?" Sir Graham Adair asked. The permanent secretary was trying hard to keep the contempt out of his voice. But he remembered what he had seen at Heathrow Airport. He didn't want to see it again all over London.

"Ignore them. Tell them to get lost."

"We can't!" Like everyone else, the foreign secretary was afraid of Kellner. But he was determined to have his say. "We can't take that risk!"

"There is no risk. Think about it for a minute. The soccer team was poisoned with cyanide. They were all on the same plane at the same time. It wasn't difficult. But if you wanted to poison a hundred thousand kids, how could you possibly do it?"

"Injections," Alex said.

Everyone stopped and looked at him again.

He had worked it out in a split second. It had suddenly come to him, as though spoken by someone else. He had been thinking about a trip he had once made to South America . . . a long time ago. And then he had remembered what he had seen at Consanto. The little test tubes. All the machinery . . . everything utterly sterile. What was it for? Now he understood the link with Dr. Liebermann. And there was something else. When he was in the restaurant with Julia Rothman, she had made a joke about the scientist.

"You could say his death was a shot in the arm for all of us."

A shot in the arm. An injection.

"Every schoolkid in London gets injected," Alex said. He was aware that he was now the center of attention. The prime minister, half the cabinet, the police and army chiefs, the civil servants . . . all the most powerful people in the country were there in the room. He was surrounded by them. And they were all listening to him. "When I was at Consanto, I saw test tubes with liquid in them," he went on. "And there were trays with what looked like eggs."

"Some vaccines are grown on eggs," the medical officer said. "And Consanto does supply vaccines all over the world." He nodded as he was struck by another thought. "That would also explain what you heard. Of course! The cold chain! It refers to the transportation of vaccines. They have to be kept at a certain temperature all the time. If you break the chain, the vaccine is no use."

"Go on, Alex," Sir Graham Adair said.

"I saw them kill a man called Dr. Liebermann," Alex explained. "He worked at Consanto and Julia Rothman told me she'd paid him a lot of money to help them. Maybe he put something in a whole load of vaccines. Some sort of poison. It would be injected in schoolkids. There are always injections at the start of term. . . ."

Adair glanced at the medical officer, who nodded. "It's true. There were BCG injections in London about a week ago."

"A week ago!" the director of communications cut in. Mark Kellner's tone of voice hadn't changed. He wasn't accepting any of it. "If they were injected with cyanide one week ago, how come they haven't all dropped dead already? How is this 'Julia Rothman' going to arrange for the poison to work on Thursday afternoon?" A few heads around the table nodded in agreement, and he went on. "And I don't suppose the English soccer team had BCG injections while they were away. Or are you going to tell me I'm wrong?"

"Of course they'd have had injections," the permanent secretary snapped, and Alex saw that he was no longer able to hide his anger. He wasn't even trying. "They were in Nigeria. They wouldn't have been allowed into the country without being inoculated."

"Yes!" The medical officer couldn't keep the excitement out of his voice. "They'd have been inoculated against yellow fever."

"A month ago!" Kellner insisted.

"Then the question isn't how did they administer the poison," Sir Graham said. "The question is—how do they prevent it from working until a time of their choosing? That's the secret of Invisible Sword."

"What else can you tell us, Alex?" Blunt asked. Even the head of MI6 seemed to be on his side.

"You were talking about a remote control," Alex said. "Well, Mrs. Rothman kept a wild animal in her office. It was a white tiger. It attacked me and I thought I was going to be killed—"

"Are you seriously asking us to believe this?" Kellner asked.

Alex ignored him. "But then someone came in and pressed a button on what looked like a remote control device. You know . . . for a TV. The tiger just sat down and went to sleep."

"Nanoshells."

The young woman who had been sitting against the wall—and who had been examining Alex earlier—had spoken the single word. She obviously hadn't been considered important enough to be given a place at the table, but now she stood up and walked forward. She was about thirty years old; after Alex the youngest person in the room, slim and pale, wearing a suit with a white shirt and a silver chain around her neck.

"What the hell are nanoshells?" the deputy prime minister demanded. "And for that matter—who are you?"

"This is Dr. Rachel Stephenson," the medical officer said. "She works in my department. She's a writer and a researcher . . . a specialist in the field of nanotechnology."

"Oh—so now we're moving into science fiction," Kellner complained.

"There's no fiction about it," Dr. Stephenson replied, refusing to be intimidated. "Nanotechnology is about manipulating matter at the atomic level, and it's already out there in more ways than you would believe. Universities, food companies, drug agencies, and—of course—the military are all spending billions of dollars a year on development programs and they all agree. In less time than you think, the life of every human being on this planet is going to change forever."

Kellner took this as a personal insult. "I don't see—" he began.

"Tell us about nanoshells," the prime minister

said, and it occurred to Alex that this was the first time he had spoken in a while.

"Yes, sir." Dr. Stephenson collected her thoughts.

"I was already thinking about nanoshells when I heard about the gold particles, but Alex has made it all clear. It's quite complicated and I know we don't have a lot of time, but I'll try to make it as simple as I can.

"Injections must be the answer. What these people have done is to inject first the soccer players and then goodness knows how many children with gold-coated nanoshells." She paused. "What we're talking about here are tiny bullets—and by tiny I mean about a hundred nanometers across. Just so you know, one nanometer is a billionth of a meter. Or to put it another way, a single hair on your head is about one hundred thousand nanometers wide. So each one of these bullets is a thousand times smaller than the tip of a human hair."

She leaned forward, resting her hands on the table. Nobody moved. Alex couldn't hear anyone so much as breathe.

"What would these bullets consist of?" Dr. Stephenson continued. "Well, it's anyone's guess. But if you imagine an M&M, it would be a bit like that.

The inside would be what we call a polymer bead and might be made of something not very different from a supermarket shopping bag. Don't forget, though, I'm only talking about a few molecules. The polymer would hold everything together and it would be quite easy to mix in the cyanide. When the polymer and the cyanide are released, the person dies.

"And what prevents it from being released? Well, that's the colored shell on the outside of the M&M— except what we're talking about here is gold. A solid gold shell, but so tiny, you could never see it. All of this would have been done by Dr. Liebermann, the man who was killed, using highly advanced collodial chemistry." She stopped again. "I'm sorry. I'm probably making it sound more complicated than it really is. Basically, what you've got is a bullet with the poison inside, and after that, you fix a protein onto the outside, onto the shell."

"What does the protein do?" someone asked.

"It guides the whole thing, a bit like a heat-seeking missile. It would take too long to explain how it works, but proteins can find their way around the human body. They know exactly where to go. And once the nanoshell was injected, the right protein would direct it straight to the heart."

"How many of these nanoshells would you need to inject?" Blunt asked.

"That's impossible to answer," Dr. Stephenson replied. "They'd be sitting right inside the heart. Once the poison was released, it would act almost immediately and you wouldn't need very much of it. As a matter of fact, we've studied the effect of nanoshells on the human body, developing them as a cure for cancer. Of course, this is rather different because Scorpia is only interested in killing, but let me see . . ." She thought for a moment. "There's not very much liquid in a BCG injection. Only about a fiftieth of a teaspoon. At a guess, I'd say you'd only need to add one part cyanide for every one hundred parts of the actual vaccine." She had worked it out and nodded. "That adds up to about one billion nanoshells," she said. "Just enough to cover the head of a pin."

"But you said that the poison is safe. It's protected by the gold."

"Yes. That's where these people have been so clever. The polymer-and-poison mix is contained in the gold. It's sitting inside the heart and it's not doing anyone any harm. If you leave it alone, it'll just pass out of the system in a little while and nobody will be any the wiser.

"But the gold is easy to break up. That's why Scorpia has chosen it. They can do it, just like Alex said, by remote control. Have you ever put an egg in a microwave? After a few moments, it explodes. It's exactly the same here. It could be microwave technology that they're planning to use." Stephenson shook her head, her long hair swaying. "No. Microwaves would be too low frequency. I'm sorry. I'm not really an expert on plasmon resonance." She thought for a moment. "A terahertz beam might be the answer."

"I'm sorry, Dr. Stephenson," the foreign secretary said. "You're losing me. What are terahertz beams?"

"They're not used much yet. They sit between the infrared and the microwave bands of the electromagnetic spectrum and they're being developed for medical imaging and satellite communications."

"So you're saying that Scorpia could send out a signal using a satellite and it would break up the gold, releasing the poison."

"Yes, sir. Except they wouldn't actually need to use a satellite. In fact, they couldn't. The beams wouldn't be strong enough. If you ask me, when those poor men got off the plane at Heathrow, there must have been some sort of radar dish erected. It was probably put there a long time ago, on one of the buildings or perhaps up a mast, and they'll have taken it down by now. But all they had to do was throw a switch, the terahertz beams would have broken down the gold, and . . . well . . . you know the result."

"Is there any chance that the nanoshells could be broken up accidentally?" Sir Graham Adair asked.

"No. That's what's so brilliant about the whole thing. You'd need to know the exact thickness of the gold. That tells you what frequency to use. It's just like when you shatter a glass by singing the right note. If you ask me, Alex saw the same technology at work with the tiger in Venice. The animal must have had some sort of sedative in its bloodstream. They just had to press a button and it fell asleep."

"So if they're not using a satellite, what are we looking for?"

"A saucer. It would look much the same as the sort of thing you'd have for satellite TV, only quite a bit bigger. They've said they're targeting London kids, so it will have to be somewhere high up in London. Probably mounted on the side of an office building. They may call it Invisible Sword, but I'd say it's more like invisible arrows being fired out of satellite dishes. They shoot out in a straight line. And they need to be able to see their targets."

"And how long will it take for the gold to break up once the switch is thrown?"

"A few minutes. Maybe less. Once the gold breaks, the children will die."

Dr. Stephenson backed away from the table and sat down again. She had nothing more to say. Immediately, everyone began to talk at once. Alex noticed some of the civil servants talking into cell phones. The two women in black and white were typing furiously, trying to keep up with the babble of conversation. Meanwhile, the permanent secretary had leaned across Alex, talking quickly and quietly to Alan Blunt. Alex saw the spy chief nod. Then the prime minister held up a hand for silence.

It took a few moments for the clamor to die down.

The prime minister glanced at his head of communications, who was looking down, biting his nails. Everyone was waiting for him to speak.

"All right," he said. "We know what we're up against. We know about Invisible Sword. The question is—what are we going to do?"

16

DEADLINE

ALEX SAID NOTHING AS HE and Blunt drove back to Liverpool Street. Blunt hadn't spoken either, apart from once, just as they were pulling out of Downing Street.

"You did very well in there, Alex," he said.

"Thank you."

It was the first time the head of MI6 had ever complimented him.

Finally they arrived back at the room on the sixteenth floor, the office he knew all too well. Mrs. Jones was waiting for them. Alex hadn't seen her since he had broken into her apartment. She looked exactly the same as he had always remembered her. It was as though nothing had happened between them. She was dressed in black, her legs crossed. She was even sucking one of her peppermint candies.

There was a brief silence as Alex came in.

"Hello, Alex," she said.

"Mrs. Jones." Alex felt uncomfortable, unsure what to say. "I'm sorry about what happened," he muttered.

"I think we should forget about it." Mrs. Jones looked him directly in the eye. "I know you didn't really try to kill me. We've worked out the angles and the bullet wouldn't have come close. I can understand how much you must hate me—and I suppose you've every right to—but you still weren't able to shoot me in cold blood."

"I don't hate you," Alex said. It was true. He felt nothing.

"Well, you don't need to hate yourself either. Whatever Scorpia may have told you, you're not one of them."

"Shall we get down to business?" Blunt took his place behind his desk. Quickly, he outlined the COBRA meeting. He told Mrs. Jones what the scientist, Dr. Stephenson, had said. Finally, he described the last fifteen minutes before he and Alex had left.

"Sir Graham wanted to evacuate London," he began. "And of course, that would have been the right thing to do. But the police weren't sure they could handle an evacuation on that scale. Not in less than twenty-four hours."

"But they can't leave any children out on the street!"

"The prime minister felt he couldn't go public. He might start a national panic. And if he went on television and tried to warn everyone, Scorpia might release Invisible Sword there and then. That was also Mark Kellner's view."

"It would be!" Mrs. Jones couldn't keep the contempt out of her voice. "And did Mr. Kellner have any bright ideas?"

"I'm afraid so."

It had been Kellner, of course, who had persuaded the prime minister to do things his way. According to Dr. Stephenson, the nanoshells would be activated by satellite dishes mounted on skyscrapers. To work, they would have to be at least a thousand feet above street level.

But every satellite dish in London has been authorized. That was what Kellner had realized. So it was easy. All the police had to do was find any unauthorized satellite dish that had been mounted on an office or any other tall building in the last couple of months and then tear it down. And while they were working, the government would find out exactly who had received inoculations developed by Consanto.

Every single name and address. That might tell them in which part of London the satellite dishes had been located.

"They've got twenty thousand men working around the clock," Blunt concluded. "Police officers. Soldiers. Our friends in MI5. They're playing a gigantic game of hide-and-seek and every child in London could die if they lose."

"They'll never do it!" Mrs. Jones looked shocked. Alex had never seen her like this before. "There must be three or four hundred office buildings and apartments in London. And even if they do manage to search them all, they may not find the satellite dishes. Scorpia is cleverer than that."

"I'm well aware of that, Mrs. Jones." Blunt frowned. "That's why I left Downing Street and came here. With Alex . . ."

There was a sudden silence. Both adults were looking at Alex.

"You want me to go back," he said.

"Yes."

Alex had already guessed that this is what they would want. It was the only way. Find Mrs. Rothman and they might be able to find the satellite dishes. But right now, he was their only link with her. He had a

telephone number. Mrs. Rothman was expecting his
call.

"She'll know I failed," he said. "At least, she'll
know I was taken prisoner by you."

"You could escape," Mrs. Jones suggested. "Mrs.
Rothman doesn't know if I'm alive or dead. You could
tell her you killed me and that you managed to escape
from us later."

"She might not believe it."

"You'll have to make her." Mrs. Jones hesitated. "I
know it's a lot to ask, Alex," she went on. "After everything that's happened, I'm sure you never want to see
any of us again. But you know the stakes now. If there
was any other way . . ."

"There isn't," Alex said. He had already made up
his mind, before he had even gotten into the car. "I
can call them. I don't know if it'll work. I don't know
if they'll even answer. But I can try."

"We'll just have to hope that they take you to Mrs.
Rothman. Right now, it's our only chance of finding
her." Blunt reached out and pressed a button on his
telephone. "Please, could you send Smithers up," he
muttered into the machine.

Smithers. Alex almost smiled. It struck him that
Alan Blunt and Mrs. Jones had already planned this.

They had known they would be sending him back and they had already told Smithers to come up with whatever gadgets he would need. That was typical of MI6. They were always one step ahead. Not just planning the future but controlling it.

"This is what I want you to do," Blunt explained. "We'll arrange an escape for you. If we make it spectacular enough, we can even get it on the news. You'll make the telephone call to Scorpia. You can tell them that you shot Mrs. Jones. You'll sound nervous, on the edge of panic. You'll ask them to bring you in."

"You think they'll come?"

"Let's hope so. If you can somehow make contact with Julia Rothman, you may be able to find out where the satellite dishes are located. And the moment you know, you get in contact with us. We'll do the rest."

"You'll have to be very careful," Mrs. Jones said. "Scorpia isn't stupid. They sent you to us and when you go back, they'll be very careful indeed. You'll be searched, Alex. Everything you do and say will be examined. You'll have to lie to them. Do you think you can get away with it?"

"How will I get in touch with you?" Alex asked. "I doubt if they'll let me use a telephone."

As though in answer to the question, the door opened and Smithers came in. In a strange way, Alex was pleased to see him. Smithers was so fat and jolly that it was hard to believe that he was part of MI6 at all. He was wearing a tweed suit that was at least fifty years out of date. With his bald head, his several chins, and his open, smiling face, he could have been anybody's uncle, the sort who liked to do magic tricks at parties.

And yet, for once, even he was serious. "Alex, my dear boy," he exclaimed. "This is all a bit of a mess, isn't it! How are you keeping? Are you in good shape?"

"Hello, Mr. Smithers," Alex said.

"I'm sorry to hear you've been tangling with Scorpia. They're a very, very nasty piece of work. Worse than the Russians ever were. Some of the things they get up to . . . well, quite frankly it's criminal." He was out of breath and sat down heavily in an empty seat. "Sabotage and corruption. Intelligence and assassination. Whatever next?" he demanded.

"What have you got for us, Smithers?" Blunt asked.

"Well, you're always asking the impossible, Mr.

Blunt, and this time it's even worse. There are all sorts of gadgets I'd like to give young Alex. I'm always working on new ideas. I've just finished work on a pair of roller blades. The blades are actually hidden in the wheels and they'll cut through anything. I've got a very nice iPod hand grenade. But as I understand it, these people aren't going to let him keep anything when he turns up again. If there's anything remotely suspicious, they're going to examine it and then they'll know he's working with us."

"He needs to have a homing device," Mrs. Jones said. "We have to be able to track him wherever he goes. And he has to be able to signal us when it's time for us to move in."

"I know," Smithers said. He reached into his pocket. "And I think I may have come up with the answer. It's the last thing they'd expect . . . but at the same time, it's exactly what you would expect a teenage boy to have."

He had taken out a clear plastic bag, and inside the bag Alex saw a small metal and plastic object. He couldn't help smiling. The last time he had seen one of these had been at the dentist.

It was a retainer. For his teeth.

"We may have to make a few adjustments, but it

should fit snugly into your mouth," Smithers said. He tapped the bag. "The wire going over your teeth is white, so it will hardly be noticed. It's actually a looped radio antenna. The retainer will begin transmitting the moment you put it in." He turned the bag over in his pudgy fingers and pointed to the bottom. "There's a little switch here," he continued. "You activate it with your tongue. As soon as you do that, you send out a distress signal and we can come rushing in."

Mrs. Jones nodded. "Well done, Smithers. That's first-rate."

Smithers sighed. "I feel really terrible sending Alex in without any weapons. And I've got a marvelous new device for him too! I've been working on a Palm organizer that's actually a flamethrower. I call it the Napalm Organizer—"

"No weapons," Blunt said.

"We can't take the risk," Mrs. Jones agreed.

"You're right." Smithers dragged himself slowly to his feet. "Just take care, Alex, old bean. You know how I worry about you. Don't you dare get yourself killed! I want to see you again."

He left, closing the door behind him.

"I'm sorry, Alex," Mrs. Jones said.

"No." Alex knew she was right. Even if he could

persuade them that he had carried out his assignment, they still wouldn't trust him. They would search him from head to toe.

"Activate the tracking device as soon as you've found the satellites," Blunt said.

"It's always possible they won't take you to them," Mrs. Jones added. "In that event, if you can't slip away, if you feel yourself to be in any danger, activate it anyway. We'll send special forces in to pull you out."

That surprised Alex. She had never shown very much concern for him in the past. It was as though his breaking into her apartment had somehow changed things between them. He glanced at her, sitting upright, neat and contained, her mouth turning slowly on the peppermint, and thought that she knew something she wasn't telling him. Well, that made two of them.

"Are you quite sure about this, Alex?" she asked.

"Yes." Alex thought for a moment. "Can you really make them believe that I escaped?"

Blunt smiled, even if it was a smile with no humor. "Oh, yes," he said. "We'll make them believe it."

It happened in the middle of London and made the six o'clock news.

A car had been driving at high speed over West Way, one of the main roads leading out of the city. The car was high up—this part of the road was suspended on huge concrete pillars. Suddenly, it lost control. Witnesses saw it swerve left and right, careering into the other traffic. At least half a dozen other cars were involved in the resulting pileup. There was a Fiat Uno crumpled up like paper. A BMW had one side torn off. A van full of flowers, unable to stop in time, crashed into the two of them. Its doors swung open and suddenly—bizarrely—the road was covered with roses and chrysanthemums. A taxi, trying to avoid the chaos, hit the crash barrier and catapulted over the edge, smashing into the bedroom window of someone's house.

It was a miracle nobody was killed, although a dozen people were rushed to nearby hospitals. The aftermath of the accident had been recorded by traffic policemen in a helicopter and there it was on television. The road was closed. Smoke was still rising from a burnt-out car. There was shattered metal and glass everywhere.

A number of witnesses were interviewed and described what they had seen. There had been a boy in the front car, they said, the one that had started it all.

They had seen him get out the moment it was all over. He had run back down the road and disappeared through the traffic. There had been a man—in a dark suit and sunglasses—who had tried to follow him. But the man had obviously been hurt. He had been limping. The boy had gotten away.

Two hours later, the road was still closed. The police said they were looking for the boy urgently, to interview him. But apart from the fact that he was about fourteen years old and dressed in black, there was no description. They didn't have a name. The traffic in west London, of course, had come to a standstill. It would take days to clear up the damage.

Sitting in a hotel room in Mayfair, Julia Rothman saw the report and her eyes narrowed. She knew who the boy was, of course. It couldn't be anyone else. She wondered what had happened. More to the point, she wondered when Alex Rider would get in touch.

In fact, it wasn't until seven o'clock that evening that Alex made the telephone call. He was in a phone booth near Marble Arch. He was already wearing the brace, giving his mouth time to get used to it. But still he found it hard to stop slurring his words.

A man answered. "Yes?"

"This is Alex Rider."

"Where are you?"

"I'm in a phone booth on the Edgware Road."

This was true. Alex was dressed once again in the black ninja outfit with which Scorpia had supplied him. The phone booth was outside a Lebanese restaurant. He had no doubt that Scorpia would be using sophisticated equipment to track the call. He wondered how long it would take them to reach him.

He thought back to the car crash. He had to admit that MI6 had stage-managed it brilliantly. No fewer than twenty cars had actually been involved and they had only had a few hours, working with a team of stuntmen, to get it right. On the one hand, not a single member of the public had been injured. But looking at the television footage and hearing the reports, Scorpia would have to admit that it looked real. That was what Blunt had said from the start. The bigger the pileup, the less reason there would be for doubt. The front page of the *Evening Standard*'s final edition carried a photograph of the taxi, embedded in the window of the house.

None of this mattered to the voice at the other end of the line.

"Is the woman dead?" it asked. The woman.

Scorpia didn't call her Mrs. Jones anymore. But then, corpses don't need names.

"Yes," Alex said.

When they came to him, they would find the Kahr P9 back in his pocket with the one bullet fired. If they examined his hands (Blunt was sure they would) there would be traces of gunpowder on his fingers. And there was a bloodstain on the sleeve of his shirt. The same blood type as Mrs. Jones. She had supplied the sample.

"What happened?"

"They caught me on the way out. They took me to Liverpool Street and they asked me questions. This afternoon they were taking me somewhere else, but I managed to get away." Alex allowed a little panic to enter his voice. He was a teenager. He had just made his first kill. And he was on the run. "Look. You said you'd bring me in once I'd done it. I'm in a phone booth. Everyone's looking for me. I want to see Nile. . . ."

A brief pause.

"All right. Make your way to Bank tube station. There's an intersection. Seven roads. Be outside the station at nine o'clock exactly and we'll come and collect you."

"Who will . . . ?" Alex began. But the phone had already gone dead.

He hung up and stepped out of the phone booth. Two police cars sped past, their lights flashing. But they weren't interested in him. He took his bearings and started off, heading east. Bank Station was on the other side of London and it would take him at least an hour to walk there. He had no money on him and couldn't risk being arrested for fare dodging on a bus. And when he got there . . . seven roads! Scorpia was being careful. They could come for him from any direction. If this was a setup and MI6 was following him, they would already have to divide themselves seven ways.

He set off down the crowded sidewalks, keeping to the shadows, trying not to think what he was letting himself in for. The night was already drawing in. He could see a hard white moon, dead in the sky. Everything would end, one way or another, the next day. There were less than twenty hours until Scorpia's deadline.

It was his deadline too.

That was the one thing he hadn't told Mrs. Jones.

He remembered what had happened on the island

of Malagosto. He had been sent to see a psychiatrist—a pleasant middle-aged man—who had put him through certain tests and then produced his medical report. What was it that Dr. Steiner had said? He was a little run-down. He needed more vitamins.

And that was when it had happened.

He felt it now. A tiny puncture in his arm.

Alex had been given an injection. . . .

17

THE CHURCH OF
FORGOTTEN SAINTS

THE SEARCH HAD already begun.

Hundreds of men and women were moving across London with hundreds more acting as backup: on the telephone, on computers, searching and cross-referencing, filing through the records. Government scientists had confirmed that the terahertz satellite dishes would have to be at least a thousand feet above the ground to be effective—and that made it easier. A search of the city's basements, cellars, and twisting alleyways would have been impossible . . . even for the entire police and army. But they were looking for something that had to be high up and in plain view. The clock was ticking, but it could be done.

Every satellite dish in London was noted, photographed, authenticated, and then eliminated from the search. Whenever necessary, the original planning application was accessed and checked against the ac-

tual dish itself. Telecommunications experts had been
called in and wherever there was any doubt, they were
taken up to the eighteenth floor, the nineteenth floor,
to see for themselves.

If people were puzzled by the sudden buzz of activity in apartment blocks and offices, nobody said
anything. The few journalists who began to ask questions were quietly pulled aside and threatened with
such ferocity that they soon decided there were other,
less dangerous stories for them to pursue. Word went
around that there was a crackdown on television li-
censes. And every hour, in every street in London,
more technicians poked and probed, examining the
dishes, making sure they had the right to be there.

And then, just after ten o'clock, six hours before
Scorpia's deadline, they found them.

There was a block of apartments on the edge of
Notting Hill Gate with amazing views over the whole
of west London. It was one of the tallest blocks in the
city—famous for both its height and its ugliness. It had
been built in the sixties by an architect who must have
been relieved he would never have to live in it.

The roof contained a number of brick structures:
the cables for the elevators, air-conditioning units,
emergency generators. It was on the side of one of

these that the inspectors found three brand-new satellite dishes facing north, south, and east.

Nobody knew what they were for. Nobody had any record of their being placed there. Within minutes, there were a dozen technicians on the roof, with more circling in helicopters. The cables were found to lead to a radio transmitting device, programmed to begin emitting high-frequency terahertz beams at exactly four o'clock.

Mark Kellner took the phone call at 10 Downing Street.

"We've done it!" he exclaimed. "A block of apartments in west London. Three satellite dishes. They're disconnecting them now."

The prime minister was with him, looking tired and pale. He managed a ghost of a smile.

"We're going to keep looking," Kellner said. "There's always a faint chance that Scorpia put other satellites in place as backup. But if there are any others, we'll find them too. I think we can say that the immediate crisis is over."

At Liverpool Street, Alan Blunt and Mrs. Jones also heard the news.

"What do you think?" Mrs. Jones asked.

Blunt shook his head. "Scorpia is more clever than

that. If these dishes have been found, it's only because they were meant to be found."

"So Kellner is wrong again."

"The man's a fool." Blunt glanced at his watch. "We don't have much time."

Mrs. Jones looked up. "All we have is Alex Rider."

Alex was on the other side of London, a long way from the satellite dishes.

He had been picked up outside Bank Station at the agreed time—but not by car. A scruffy young woman he had never seen before walked past him, whispering two words as she went.

"Follow me."

She had given him a ticket and led him into the station and onto a train. She hadn't spoken to him again, standing some distance away in the car, her eyes vacant, as though she had never met him. They had changed trains twice, waiting until the last moment as the doors slid shut and then suddenly stepping out onto the platform. If anyone had been following them, she would have seen. Finally, they emerged at King's Cross Station. She had left Alex standing in the street, signaling for him to wait. A few minutes later, a taxi had pulled up.

"Alex Rider?"

"Yes."

"Get in."

It had all been done very smoothly. As they moved off, Alex knew that it would have been impossible for any MI6 agents to have followed them. Which was, of course, exactly what Scorpia had planned.

He had been taken to a house—a different house from the one he had visited when he first arrived. This one was on the edge of Regent's Park. A man and a woman were waiting for him. He recognized them as the fake Italian parents who had accompanied him through Heathrow. They had taken him upstairs and shown him into a shabby bedroom with a bathroom attached. There was a late supper waiting for him on a tray. They left him there, locking the door behind them. There was no telephone. Alex checked the window. It was locked too.

And now it was half past one the next day and Alex was sitting on the bed, looking out of the window at the trees and Victorian railings of the park. He was feeling a little sick. He had begun to think that Scorpia simply planned to leave him here until four o'clock, that they wanted him to die with the other children in London. And that reminded him of the nanospheres that he knew were inside him, resting inside his heart. He remembered the prick of the needle, the smiling face of the doctor as he injected him with death. The thought of it made his skin crawl. Was he really doomed to spend the last hours of his life here, in this room, sitting on an unmade bed, alone?

The door opened.

Nile walked in, followed by Julia Rothman.

She was wearing an expensive coat, gray with a white fur collar, buttoned up to her neck—another designer label. Her black hair was immaculate, her makeup as much a mask as the ones that had been worn at her party at the Ca' Vedova. Her smile was a brilliant red. Her eyes seemed all the more dazzling, highlighted by a perfectly drawn line of black mascara.

"Alex," she said. She sounded genuinely delighted to see him, but Alex knew now that everything about her was fake, that nothing was to be trusted.

"I wondered if you were going to come," Alex said.

"Of course I was going to come, my dear. It's just that this is rather a busy day. How are you, Alex? I am so pleased to see you."

"Did you really kill her?" Nile asked. He was casually dressed in a loose jacket and jeans, sneakers, and a white sweatshirt.

Mrs. Rothman scowled. "Nile, do you have to be so direct and to the point?" She shrugged. "He's talking about Mrs. Jones, of course," she went on. "And I suppose we do need to know what happened. The mission was a success?"

"Yes." Alex nodded. This was the most dangerous part. He knew he couldn't talk too much. He was afraid of giving himself away. And he was horribly conscious of the brace. It fitted well, but it had to be distorting his speech, at least a bit. The wire across his teeth was white, but it was still faintly visible. Surely Mrs. Rothman would notice it was there.

"So what happened?" Nile asked.

"I broke into her apartment. It all went exactly like you said. I used the gun . . ."

"And then?"

"I took the elevator down and I was just on my way out when the two guys behind the desk grabbed me." Alex had spent half the night rehearsing this. "I don't know how they knew it was me. But before I could do anything, they had me on the floor with my hands cuffed behind my back."

"Go on." Mrs. Rothman was gazing at him. Her eyes could have been trying to suck him in.

"They took me somewhere. A cell." This part was easier—Alex was actually telling a version of the truth. "It was underneath Liverpool Street. They left me there overnight and then Blunt saw me the next day."

"What did he say?"

"Not a lot. He knew I was working for you. They'd gotten satellite photographs of me arriving at Malagosto."

Nile glanced at Mrs. Rothman. "That makes sense," he said. "I've always had a feeling we've been under surveillance."

"He didn't want to know very much," Alex went on. "He didn't really want to talk to me. He said I was going to be questioned somewhere outside of London. I hung around a bit, then a car came to collect me."

"You were handcuffed?" Mrs. Rothman asked.

"Not this time. That was their mistake. It was just an ordinary car. There was a driver in the front and an MI6 man in the back with me. I didn't know where they were taking me and I didn't want to know. I didn't really care what happened. I didn't even care if I was killed. I waited until they got a bit of speed up and then I threw myself at the driver. I got my hands over his eyes. There was nothing much he could do. He lost control and the car crashed."

"Quite a few cars crashed," Mrs. Rothman remarked.

"Yeah. But I was lucky. Everything sort of went upside-down, but the next thing I knew, we'd stopped and I was able to get out and run away. I got to a phone and I called the number you gave me—and here I am."

Nile had been watching him closely through all this. "How did it feel, Alex?" he asked. "Killing Mrs. Jones?"

"I didn't feel anything."

Nile nodded. "It was the same for me, the first time. But you have to learn to enjoy it. That'll come with time."

"You've done very well, Alex." Mrs. Rothman spoke the words, but she still sounded doubtful. "I have to say, I'm quite astonished by your daring escape. I saw it on the news and I could hardly believe it. But you've certainly passed the test. You really are one of us."

"Does that mean you'll take me back to Venice?"

"Not quite yet." Mrs. Rothman thought for a moment and he could see she was coming to a decision. "We're just at the critical point in a certain operation," she said. "It might interest you to see it. It's going to be quite spectacular. What do you think?"

Alex shrugged. He couldn't look too keen. "I don't mind," he said.

"You met Dr. Liebermann. You were there at Consanto when dear Nile dealt with him. It seems only right that you should see the fruits of his handiwork." She smiled again. "I'd like to have you with me, at the end."

So you can watch me die, Alex thought.

"I'd like to be there," he said.

Then her eyes narrowed and the smile seemed to freeze. "But I'm afraid we're going to have to search you," she said. "I do trust you, of course. But as you'll learn when you've been with Scorpia for a while, we don't leave anything to chance. You were taken prisoner by MI6. It's always possible that you were somehow contaminated even without knowing it. So before we leave here, I want you to go into the bathroom with Nile. He'll give you a thorough examination. And we're going to give you a complete change of clothes too. Everything's got to come off, Alex. We have new trousers and a shirt for you. It's all a bit embarrassing, I know, but I'm sure you'll understand."

"I've got nothing to hide," Alex said. He couldn't

help running his tongue over the brace. He was certain she'd seen it.

"Of course you haven't. I'm just being overcautious."

"Let's do it." Nile jerked a thumb in the direction of the bathroom. He seemed amused by the whole idea.

Twenty minutes later, Alex and Nile came downstairs. Alex was now dressed in loose-fitting jeans and a round neck jersey. Nile had brought the clothes with him—along with fresh socks, sneakers, and pants. Mrs. Jones had been right. If he'd had so much as a one-penny coin with him, Nile would have taken it. He had been thoroughly and comprehensively searched.

But Nile hadn't noticed the brace. Alex's mouth was the one place he hadn't looked.

"Well?" Mrs. Rothman asked. She was in a hurry to get away.

"He's clean," Nile said.

"Good. Then we can go."

There was a grandfather clock in the hall, standing in the corner on the black and white tiled floor. As Alex moved toward the front door, it struck the hour. It was two o'clock.

"Is that the time already?" Mrs. Rothman said. She reached out and touched Alex, stroking the side of his cheek. "You have just two hours left, Alex."

"Two hours until what?" Alex asked.

"In two hours' time you'll know everything."

She opened the door.

They left.

There was a car waiting for them outside, a four-wheel drive. It took them across London, heading south. They drove around the Aldwych and over Waterloo Bridge and for a moment Alex looked out on one of the most startling views of London with the Houses of Parliament, Big Ben, and the Millennium Wheel opposite. What would it look like two hours from now? Alex could imagine the ambulances and police cars screaming across London, the crowds staring in disbelief, the undersized bodies strewn over the sidewalks. It would be like another world war—but without a single shot being fired.

And then they were on the south bank of the river, making their way through Waterloo, heading east. The surrounding buildings became older and dustier. It was as though they had traveled not just a few miles but a hundred years. Alex was in the backseat, next to

Nile. Mrs. Rothman was in the front with a blank-faced driver. Nobody spoke. It was warm inside the car—the sun was shining—but Alex could feel a tension that made the air cold. He was certain they were heading for some high point where Invisible Sword must be concealed, but he had no idea what to expect. An office block? Perhaps a building under construction? He looked out of the window, his head pressed against the glass, trying to stay calm.

They stopped.

The car had pulled up in front of a strange, empty stretch of road that ran for about fifty yards before coming to a dead end. Mrs. Rothman and Nile got out of the car and Alex followed, examining his surroundings with a sinking heart. It looked as though they hadn't taken him to the satellite dishes after all. There were no tall buildings in sight, not for a mile around. The street—almost as wide as it was long—ran between two rows of dilapidated shops, the lower floors boarded up, the windows broken and discolored. The street itself was covered with rubbish; scraps of newspaper, bent cans, and old potato chip packages.

But it was the building at the end that commanded his attention. The street led to a church of some sort,

one with no steeple but with a dome and architecture
that would have been more suited to Rome or Venice
than London. It had obviously been abandoned long
ago and it had deteriorated badly, but it still struggled
to be magnificent. Two huge cracked pillars supported
a triangular roof over the main entrance. Long marble steps led up to a row of doors that were made of
solid bronze, but green rather than gold. The great
bulk of the church rose up behind, surmounted by a
dome that glinted in the afternoon sun. Statues lined
the stairs and stood, dotted across the roof. But they
had been brutalized by time and the weather. Some
were missing arms. Many had no faces. Once they
had been saints and angels. Two hundred years standing in London had turned them into cripples.

"Why are we here?" Alex asked.

Mrs. Rothman was standing next to him, looking
up at the church. "I thought you'd like to witness the
conclusion of Invisible Sword."

"I don't know anything about Invisible Sword."
Without giving himself away, Alex was searching for
any sign of the satellite dishes. But there was nothing
on the dome and, anyway, as impressive as it was, it
wasn't tall enough. The dishes had to be higher up.
"What is this place?" he asked.

Mrs. Rothman looked at him curiously. "Nile?" she asked suddenly. "Did you search him from top to bottom?"

"Yes. Just like you told me to."

"You know, Alex, I'd swear there was something different about you." She was still examining him.

Alex quietly closed his mouth, hiding the brace. He looked at her with steady eyes. "There is something different about me," he said. "I just killed someone. For Scorpia. I don't know why you wouldn't trust me after that."

"I don't trust anyone, Alex. Not even Nile." She paused. "Since you ask, this building is the Church of the Forgotten Saints. It's not actually a church. It's an oratory. It was built in the nineteenth century by a community of Catholic priests living in the area. They were rather odd. They worshipped a collection of saints who have all fallen into obscurity. You'd be amazed how many saints there are that we've completely forgotten about. Saint Fiacre, for example, is the patron saint of gardeners and taxi drivers. That must keep him busy! Saint Ambrose looks after beekeepers, and where would tailors be without Saint Homobonus? Did you know that undertakers and perfume makers both have their own saints? They were worshipped here too. I suppose it's not surprising the church fell into disuse. It was bombed in the war and it's been empty ever since. Scorpia took it over a few years ago. As you'll see, we've made one or two interesting adjustments. Do you want to come inside?"

Alex shrugged. "Whatever you say." He had no choice. For some reason, Mrs. Rothman had chosen to bring him here and presumably he would still be here when the terahertz beams were fired across London. He glanced at the dome again, wondering if the surface would be enough to protect him. He doubted it.

The three of them walked forward. The car had already driven off. Alex looked at the shops on either side. Not a single one of them was occupied. He wondered if he was being watched. It occurred to him that anyone wanting to enter the church would have to come this way and it would be easy enough to keep them under surveillance with hidden cameras. They reached the middle door, which sensed their arrival and opened electronically. That was interesting. Mrs. Rothman had spoken of adjustments and it was already clear that the oratory wasn't quite as derelict as it first appeared.

They had entered an outer chamber, a grand hall,

rectangular in shape, that served as an entrance to the main body of the church. Everything was gray: the huge flagstones, the ceiling, the stone pillars that supported it. Alex looked around him as his eyes grew accustomed to the light. There were circular windows on either side, but the glass was so thick that it seemed to exclude most of the daylight rather than allow it in. Everything was faded and dusty. Two statues—more forgotten saints?—stood on each side of a cracked and broken font. There was a faint smell of damp in the air. It was easy to believe that nobody had been here for twenty or thirty years. Alex coughed and listened to the sound travel up. The chamber was utterly silent and there seemed to be no obvious way forward. The street was behind them. A solid wall blocked the way ahead. But then Julia Rothman walked across the floor. Her stiletto heels rapped against the stone, sending echoes that flitted into the shadows.

Her movement had been some sort of signal. There was a loud buzz and overhead a series of arc lamps—concealed in the walls and ceiling—flashed on. Beams of brilliant white light crashed down from every direction. At the same time, five doors slid silently open, one after the other. They were part of the wall, built into it, disguised to look like brick. Now

Alex saw that they were in fact solid steel. More light spilled out and with it came the sound of men moving, of machinery, of frantic activity.

"Welcome to Invisible Sword," Mrs. Rothman said, and in that moment Alex knew why she had brought him here. She was proud of what she had done. She couldn't hide the pleasure in her voice. She wanted him to see.

Alex stepped through the door and into a scene he would never forget.

It was a classical church, just like the monastery on Malagosto. Scorpia seemed to enjoy cloaking itself in religion. The floor was made up of black and white tiles. There were stained-glass windows, a richly carved wooden pulpit, even a few old pews. The remains of an organ clung to one wall, but looking at the pipes, some broken, others missing, Alex knew that it would never play. The dome curved overhead, the underside painted with more saints, men and women holding the various objects with which they had once been associated: furniture, shoes, library books, and loaves of bread. All of them had been forgotten. All of them were frozen together in a single great tableau overhead.

The church had been filled with electronic equipment; computers, TV monitors, industrial lights, and a series of switches and levers that couldn't have been more out of place. Two steel gantries had been built, one on either side, with armed guards positioned at intervals. There must have been twenty or thirty people involved in the operation, at least half of them carrying automatic machine guns. As Alex took all this in, a voice rung out, amplified through speakers bolted into the walls.

"Six minutes until launch. Six minutes and counting . . ."

Alex knew that he had arrived at the center of the web and even as he stared, his tongue traveled to the roof of his mouth and pressed the switch that Smithers had built into his brace. Mark Kellner, the prime minister's director of communications, had gotten it wrong again. Scorpia hadn't attached the terahertz dishes to any tall building.

They had attached them to a hot-air balloon.

Six men dressed in dark overalls were inflating it. There was plenty of space. The floor extended in all directions and the dome was as high as a six-story building. The balloon was painted blue and white. Once released, it would blend in with the sky, barely visible. How were they going to release it? Alex wondered. The church was completely enclosed by the dome. Even so, that had to be their plan. There was a frame underneath the balloon with a single burner pointing upward, and beneath that, a platform about twenty yards square. The balloon was strangely old-fashioned, like something out of a Victorian adventure story. The platform couldn't have been more high-tech, built out of some sort of lightweight plastic with a low railing to protect the equipment it carried.

Alex recognized the equipment instantly. There were four radar dishes, one on each side, pointing in every direction of the compass. They were dull silver in color, about fifteen feet in diameter, with thin metal rods forming a triangle that protruded from their centers. Wires connected the dishes to a series of complicated-looking boxes, which took up most of the space in the center of the platform and which would also be carried up. A black pipe ran up to the burner, carrying propane gas from the tanks, which were stacked next to the other machinery. The balloon was almost inflated. It had been lying spread out on the ground, but even as Alex stood watching, more hot air was fed into the envelope by three men using a second burner device and it began to lift itself limply up.

At the same time, more men ran forward to hold

the platform steady. There were two ropes, one at each end. Alex saw that the whole thing had been tethered to a pair of iron rings set in the floor. Now he understood what Scorpia intended to do. Julia Rothman must have guessed that government scientists would work out how the soccer players at Heathrow Airport had died. She had known that they would be searching London for the radar dishes. So she had kept them hidden until the last moment. The hot-air balloon would somehow lift them up into the air. They would only need to stay there for a few minutes. By the time anyone realized what was happening, it would be too late. The golden nanospheres would have dissolved and thousands of children would be dead.

He noticed that Nile had taken off his jacket and was strapping something to his back. It was a leather harness with two lethal-looking weapons: not quite swords, not quite daggers, but something in between. Alex had seen something similar at Malagosto and knew that Nile was an expert at *iaido*, the ninja art of sword drawing. He could slice with the swords or he could throw them. Either way, he was lightning fast and Alex knew he could deliver death in an instant.

There was nothing he could do but stand and

watch. He had no gadgets, no hidden weapons. Mrs. Rothman might have bought the story of his capture and escape, but her eyes were still on him. In truth, they had never wavered. She was still suspicious. If he so much as sneezed without permission, she would give the order and he would be cut down.

How long had it been since he had activated the homing device? Sixty seconds? Maybe more. Alex felt the band running across his teeth and tried to imagine the signal being transmitted to MI6. How long would it take them to work out where it was coming from? When could he expect them to arrive?

Julia Rothman moved closer to him and laid a hand on his shoulder. Her fingers moved, caressing the side of his neck. She ran her tongue, small and moist, around the edge of her lips.

"Let me explain to you what we're doing here, Alex," she began. "As a member of Scorpia, I'm sure you'd like to know."

"Are you going for a balloon ride?" Alex asked.

"No. I'm not going anywhere." She smiled. "A few days ago, we made certain demands. These demands were directed against the American government, but we made it clear that if they did not obey, it would be the British who would suffer the consequences. The deadline runs out"—she looked at her watch—"in a little less than twenty minutes. The Americans have not done as we asked. And now it is time for the punishment to begin."

"What are you going to do?" Alex asked. He couldn't keep the horror out of his voice because, of course, he already knew.

"In a few minutes, the balloon will be completely inflated and we will raise it above this church. The ropes will keep it tethered at exactly one thousand feet, and when it reaches that point, the machinery, which you can see in the platform, will activate immediately. High-frequency radio beams will then be transmitted over London for exactly two minutes, and at that moment, I'm afraid a very large number of people will die."

"Why?" Alex could barely speak. "What do you want from the Americans? What do you want them to do?"

"As a matter of fact, we didn't want them to do anything. The demands we made were completely ridiculous. We asked them to disarm. We told them to pay us a billion dollars. We knew they'd never agree."

"Then why ask?"

"Because what our client really wants is revenge.

Revenge for the war in Iraq. Revenge against the British and the Americans who made it possible. What he wants is to ensure that the 'special friendship' between the two countries is destroyed forever. And this is how it's going to happen.

"I'm afraid that a great many people are about to die in London. The deaths are going to be sudden and totally unexpected. It'll be as though they've been struck down with an invisible sword. The whole country is going to be in shock. And then the news will come out. They died because the Americans wouldn't agree to our demands. They died because the Americans refused to help the allies who once helped them. Can you imagine what the newspapers will say? Can you imagine what people will think? By tomorrow morning, the English will hate the Americans.

"And then, Alex, in a few months' time, Invisible Sword will strike again—but next time it will be in New York. And next time our demands will be more reasonable. We'll ask for less and the Americans will give us what we want because they will have seen what happened in London and they won't want it to happen again. They'll have no choice. And that will be the end of the American-British alliance. Do you see? The Americans couldn't care less about the British. They were only concerned about themselves. That's what everyone will say and you have no idea how much hatred will have been generated. One country humiliated. The other crushed. And Scorpia will have earned twenty-five million dollars along the way."

She paused, as though waiting for him to congratulate her. Alex was meant to be a member of her organization, its newest recruit. His father would have been glad to stand at her side. But he couldn't do it. He simply couldn't find it in himself. He couldn't even pretend.

"You can't do it!" Alex whispered. "You can't kill children just to get rich."

The words were no sooner out of his mouth than he knew he had made a mistake. Julia Rothman's reaction was as fast as a snake . . . as fast as a scorpion. One moment, that soft, casual smile had been on her lips. The next, she was rigid, alert, her whole consciousness focused on Alex.

Nile looked up, sensing something wrong. Alex waited for the ax to fall. And then it came.

"Children?" Mrs. Rothman muttered. "I never said anything about children."

"But there will be children." Alex tried to backtrack. "Adults and children."

"No, Alex." Mrs. Rothman seemed almost amused. But her eyes were still as hard as black diamonds. "You know that children are the targets. I never told you that. So somebody else must have."

"I don't know what you're talking about. . . ."

She was examining him minutely. Closing in on him. And suddenly she knew. "I knew there was something different about you," she said. "What's that you've got on your teeth?"

It was too late to try to hide it. Alex opened his mouth. "I wear a brace."

"You weren't wearing a brace in Positano."

"I didn't have it in."

"Take it out now."

"It doesn't come out."

"It will—with a hammer."

Alex had no choice. He reached into his mouth and took out the piece of plastic. Nile moved closer, his eyes full of curiosity.

"Let me see it, Alex."

Like a naughty boy caught eating gum, Alex held out his hand. The brace was resting in his palm. And it was obvious it was no ordinary brace. He could see some of the circuitry leading to the switch he had already pressed.

Had he pressed it in time?

"Drop it!" Mrs. Rothman commanded.

Alex let the brace drop to the ground and she stepped forward. Her foot came down on it and Alex heard the sound of breaking plastic as she ground it into the floor. When she removed her foot, the brace was cracked in half, the wire bent. If it had been transmitting before, it certainly wasn't now.

Mrs. Rothman turned to Nile. "You're a fool, Nile. I thought I told you to search him from top to bottom."

"His mouth . . ." Nile didn't know what to say. "It was the one place I didn't look."

But she had already turned back to Alex. "You didn't do it, did you, Alex." Her voice was full of scorn. "You didn't kill her. Mrs. Jones is still alive."

Alex said nothing. Mrs. Rothman stared at him for what seemed like an eternity, then moved. She was faster and stronger than he would have guessed. Her hand slammed into the side of his face. The sound of it echoed all around. Alex fell back, dazed. His whole head was ringing and he could feel his cheek glowing red. Mrs. Rothman signaled and two guards with machine guns stepped forward so that they stood next to him, one on either side.

"We may be expecting company," she announced

in a loud, clear voice. "I want units three, four, and five to take up defensive positions."

"Units three, four, and five to the perimeter." The amplified voice relayed the command and twenty of the men ran forward, their feet stamping on the metal gantries, heading for the front of the church.

Mrs. Rothman gazed at Alex with eyes that had lost their disguise. They were utterly cruel. "Mrs. Jones may be alive," she said. "But you won't be. You have less than fifteen minutes to live, Alex. Why do you think I brought you here? It's because I want to see it for myself. I had a special reason to want to kill you and believe it or not, my dear, you're already dead."

She looked past him. The balloon was fully inflated, floating in the space between the floor and the dome. The platform with its deadly cargo was underneath it, three feet in the air. The ropes were ready. The radar dishes were set to automatic.

"Start the launch," Mrs. Rothman commanded. "It's time London saw the power of Invisible Sword."

18

HIGH RESOLUTION

"LAUNCH . . . STATUS RED. Launch . . . status red."

The disembodied voice rang out as one of the Scorpia technicians, sitting in front of a bank of machinery, reached out and pressed a button.

There was a single metallic click and then the hum of machinery, a wheel turning somewhere overhead. Alex looked up. At first glance, it seemed to him that the saints and angels were flying apart, as though they had come to life and were drifting down to the pews to pray. Then, with a gasp, he saw what was actually happening. The entire roof was moving. The dome of the oratory had been constructed with hidden hydraulic arms that were slowly pulling it open. A crack appeared and widened. He could see the sky. An inch at a time the great dome was folding back, splitting into two halves. Mrs. Rothman stared upward, her face filled with delight. Only now did Alex see how much planning had gone into this operation. The en-

tire church had been adapted—it must have cost millions—for this single moment.

And nobody would have guessed. The police and
the army had been searching across London, examining every building more than a thousand feet high.
But the radar dishes had been hidden at ground level.
Only now would the hot-air balloon carry them above
the city. Certainly someone would notice it. But by the
time they found their way across the river to this des-
olate corner, it would be too late. The radar dishes
would have done their work. Thousands of children
would have died.

And Alex would be one of them. Mrs. Rothman
hadn't killed him just now because she had no need
to. Like thousands of other children in London, he
had been injected with the nanoshells. And she had
just said it herself: He was already dead.

"Raise the balloon." Mrs. Rothman gave the order
in a soft voice. But the words were quite clear in the
great emptiness of the church.

The burner under the envelope was alight, sending a red and blue flame shooting upward. Two men
ran forward and pulled the release mechanism and at
once the platform began to rise. The entire roof had

disappeared. It was as though the oratory had been sliced open like an exotic fruit. There was more than enough room for the balloon to begin its journey, and Alex watched it float smoothly and quickly up, traveling in a straight line, as though this was something that had been rehearsed. There was no wind. Even the weather seemed to be on Scorpia's side.

Alex looked around him. His face was still smarting where Mrs. Rothman had slapped him, but he ignored the pain. He was horribly aware of the seconds ticking away, but there was still nothing he could do. Nile was watching him with as much hatred as he had ever seen in a man's face. The two samurai swords protruded just above his shoulders. Alex knew he was itching to use them. He had betrayed Scorpia and, worse, he had betrayed Nile. He had humiliated the man in front of Julia Rothman and for that Nile would dearly love to make him pay by cutting him to pieces. He only needed the tiniest excuse. The two armed guards were still close by, one on either side of him. Others watched him from the gantries and their positions at the doors. He was helpless.

And where was MI6? Alex glanced at the broken pieces of the brace. He wished now that he had activated the homing device the moment he had seen the church. But how could he have known? How could anyone have known?

"Alex, before you die, there's something I want to tell you," Mrs. Rothman said.

"I'm not interested," Alex replied.

"Oh . . . I think you will be, my dear. Because, you see, it's about your father. And your mother. There's something you ought to know."

Alex didn't want to hear it. And he had come to a decision. He was going to die—but he wouldn't just stand there. Somehow he was going to hurt Julia Rothman. She had lied to him. She had tricked him. But worse, she had almost made him betray everything he believed in. She had tried to make him part of Scorpia, like his father.

But whatever his father had been, he would never be the same.

He tensed himself, about to throw himself at her, wondering if Nile would cut him down before the guards' bullets did.

And then one of the windows shattered and something exploded inside the church, thick smoke billowing out, spreading across the black and white tiles, devouring everything. At the same time came the chatter of machine-gun fire and a second explosion, this one outside. Julia Rothman staggered and fell sideways. Nile twisted around, the white blotches on his face somehow more livid than ever, his eyes wide and staring.

Alex moved.

He lashed out at the guard on his left, swinging his elbow into the man's stomach, feeling the bone sink into soft flesh. The man doubled up. The other guard twisted around and Alex pivoted on one foot, kicking hard with the other. His heel smashed into the barrel of the man's machine gun half a second before it fired. Alex felt the bullets pass over his shoulder and heard a scream as one of the other guards was hit. Well, that made one less, anyway! He charged forward, his head down, and slammed into the guard like a charging bull. The guard cried out. Alex punched upward, his fist driving into the man's throat. The guard was thrown off his feet and sent crashing backward to the floor. Alex was free.

But everything was confused. The smoke coiled and twisted. There was more machine-gun fire, another explosion. Alex saw the balloon disappear above

the church. It hadn't been hit. It had passed through
the roof and was continuing its journey up into the
London sky. Suddenly he knew that whatever happened down here, in the balloon was where he had to
be. It carried equipment that was set to automatic.
MI6 was here. They might invade the church and capture Julia Rothman. They might even bring the balloon back down. But there could only be minutes left.
It might already be too late.

There was only one thing Alex could do. The balloon was trailing two ropes—each one a thousand
feet long. They would act as anchors when it had
reached the correct height. Alex ran forward. A man
stepped in his way and Alex automatically dropped
him with a roundhouse kick learned in karate. He
reached the nearest of the ropes and grabbed hold of
it and felt the balloon lift him off the ground.

"Stop him!" Mrs. Rothman screamed.

She had seen him, but the smoke was still obscuring him from the other guards. There was a burst of
machine-gun fire but it missed, slicing the rope a few
yards under his feet. Alex looked down and saw that
the ground was already a long way away. And then he
was pulled out of the church, up into the air, leaving
Nile, Mrs. Rothman, and the swirling chaos behind.

Half blinded by the smoke, shocked by the suddenness of the attack, Mrs. Rothman had to waste precious seconds forcing herself to calm down. She strode over to the television screens, trying to make sense of the situation. She could see soldiers in black combat dress, their faces covered by balaclava helmets, taking up positions outside the church. She could deal with them in her own time. Right now, the boy was all that mattered.

"Nile!" she snapped. "Get after him!"

Nile had been hit by the flying fragments of glass from the first explosion. For once he seemed slow to react, confused.

"Now!" she screamed.

Nile ran forward. The balloon might be out of sight, but the two ropes still hung down, shivering in front of him. He grabbed hold of one and, like Alex, was jerked into the air.

The balloon was four hundred feet above ground level. It had another six hundred to travel before the dishes would activate. The extra weight—Alex on one rope, Nile on the other—had slowed it down. But the burner was still pumping fire and hot air into the envelope. A digital display on one of the metal boxes was flickering and changing, measuring the distance. 410

. . . 420 . . . 430 . . . The machines knew nothing of what was taking place below. It didn't matter. They would do what they had been designed for. The radar dishes were waiting for the signal to start transmitting.

The balloon continued rising. There were just four minutes left.

Mrs. Jones had acted immediately. There had been five SAS teams on permanent standby in different parts of London, and as soon as Alex's signal had been received and his location verified, she had alerted the team that was closest to him with the other four moving in as backup.

Eight men had surrounded the church—all of them dressed in full combat gear, including flame-proof black overalls, beltkits, body armor, Kevlar vests, and Mk 6 combat helmets complete with throat mikes. They were carrying a variety of weapons. Most of them had a Sig 9mm pistol strapped against their thigh. One had a sawed-off, pump-action shotgun, which would be used to blast open the church doors. Others carried axes, knives, Maglites, and flashbang grenades—and each man was equipped with the same high-powered, semi-automatic machine gun, the

Heckler & Koch 9mm MP5, the favorite assault weapon of the SAS. As they spread out across the seemingly empty street, they barely looked human. They could have been radio-controlled robots sent from some future war.

They knew that the church was their target, but this operation was every soldier's nightmare. Normally, when the SAS go in, they will have been briefed by the police and regular army. They will have had access to a huge computer database giving them vital information about the building they're about to attack: the thickness of its walls, the position of windows and doors. If no information is available, they can still produce a three-dimensional computer image simply by inputting whatever details they can see outside. But this time there was nothing. The Church of the Forgotten Saints was a blank. And there were only minutes left.

Their instructions were clear. Find the radar dishes and destroy them. Find Alex Rider and get him out. But even after everything that had happened, Alan Blunt had made sure they understood their priorities. The radar dishes mattered more.

The soldiers had arrived just in time to see the

dome open and the balloon rise into the air. They were too late. If they had come equipped with Stingers— heat-seeking missiles—they would have already brought it down. But this was the middle of London. They were prepared for what was essentially a hostage situation. They hadn't expected a full-out war.

The balloon rose in front of their eyes and they were unable to stop it. They could see at once that they needed to get onto the roof of the oratory, but first they had to reach it. One of the men made a snap decision and shot a 94mm HEAT warhead rocket from a plastic firing tube. The missile looped toward the balloon but fell short, smashing through an upper window and detonating inside the church. This was the explosion that had given Alex his chance.

But now the Scorpia men showed themselves. Suddenly the SAS team found themselves under fire from both sides as a blazing torrent of bullets erupted from the abandoned shops. Somebody threw a grenade. A huge ball of flame and shattered concrete ripped through the air. One of the men was sent flying, his arms and legs limp. He crashed to the ground and lay still.

The SAS hadn't been expecting a war, but in seconds they found themselves in the middle of one.

They were outnumbered. The church was seemingly impregnable. The balloon was rising fast out of sight.

One of the soldiers had dropped to his knee and was talking furiously into his radio transmitter.

"This is Delta One Three. We have engaged the enemy and are coming under heavy fire. We need immediate backup. Urgent. Radar dishes have been located. Request immediate air strike to take them out fast. They are being carried by hot-air balloon over the target area. Repeat . . . they're in a balloon. We cannot reach them. An air strike must respond . . . condition red. Over."

The message was relayed instantly to Head Quarters Strike Command at RAF High Wycombe, forty miles outside London. It took them a few precious seconds to understand what they were being told and a few more precious seconds to believe it. But in less than a minute, two Tornado GR4 fighter jets were moving toward the main runway. Each plane was equipped with Paveway 11 general purpose bombs with built-in laser guidance systems and movable tail fins. The pilots were fully trained in low altitude precision attacks. Flying at just over seven hundred miles per hour, they would reach the church in less than eight minutes. They would blast the balloon out of the sky.

That was the plan.

Unfortunately, they didn't have eight minutes. This was the first real test for the Joint Rapid Reaction Force that had been created to tackle any major terrorist alert. But everything had happened too quickly. Scorpia had left it to the very last moment before they revealed their hand.

But by the time the planes got there, it would be too late.

Alex Rider pulled himself up the rope, one hand over the other, keeping a loop between his feet. He had done the same often enough in the school gym, but— he had no need to remind himself—this wasn't quite the same.

For a start, even when he stopped to rest, he still went up. The balloon was rising steadily. The hot air inside the envelope weighed twenty-eight grams per cubic foot. The cooler air of the London sky weighed twenty-one grams per cubic foot. This was the simple arithmetic that made the balloon fly. And that was exactly what Alex was doing. If he had looked down, he would have seen the ground four hundred feet below. But he didn't look down. That was something else that was different from a school gym. If he fell from this height, he would die.

The platform was less than thirty feet above him. He could see the great rectangle, blocking out the sky. Above it, the burner was still blazing, shooting a tongue of flame into the bulging blue-and-white envelope. Alex's shoulders and arms were aching. Worse than that, every movement sent pain shuddering through his bones. His wrists felt as though they were being torn apart. He heard another explosion and a sustained burst of machine-gun fire. He wondered if the SAS were shooting at him. If they had seen the balloon—and they must have—they would want to bring it down, no matter what the cost. What did his own life matter compared to the thousands who would die if the radar dishes reached one thousand feet?

The thought gave him new strength. If a stray bullet caught him while he was dangling from the rope, he would fall. For a whole lot of reasons, he needed to be inside the platform. He gritted his teeth and pulled himself up.

Six hundred feet. Six hundred and fifty. The balloon was unstoppable. But the distance between Alex and his goal was narrowing. There was a third explosion and he risked a glance down. Almost at once, he wished he hadn't. The ground was a very long way away. The SAS men were the size of toy soldiers. He could see them taking up their positions in the street that led to the church, trying to storm the front door. Scorpia's men were in the derelict shops on either side. The explosion that Alex had just heard must have come from a hand grenade. Alex saw a window shatter and a body pitch forward and down.

But the battle below meant nothing to him. He had seen something else that filled him with dread. A man was climbing the other rope and there could be no mistaking the black and white blotches of his face. Nile. He was moving slowly, as though he was out of breath. Alex was surprised by that. He knew how fit and strong Nile was. He could almost see the muscles rippling beneath the man's shirt as he reached up with one hand. Alex knew that he had to disable the radar dishes—permanently—before Nile arrived. Otherwise, he wouldn't stand a chance.

Something struck his hand and he cried out. Still climbing, but with his eyes fixed on Nile, Alex hadn't seen that he had at last reached the platform. He had hit his knuckles against the edge of one of the four radar dishes. For a moment he wondered if he could reach out and pull the bloody thing off. Let it fall and smash somewhere below. But he could see at once that the dishes were well fitted with metal braces. He would have to find another way.

And that meant climbing onto the platform itself. This wasn't going to be easy—and yet he had to move quickly, giving himself as much time as possible before Nile caught up with him.

He leaned backward and let go of the rope with one hand. For half a second, his stomach lurched and he thought he was going to fall. But then he lunged upward and caught hold of the edge of the railing that ran all the way around the platform. With a last effort, he pulled himself up and over, toppling down the other side. He landed awkwardly, banging his knee on the edge of a propane gas cylinder. He let the pain ripple through him as he tried to work out what to do.

He examined the balloon.

There were two cylindrical propane tanks feeding the burner just a couple of feet above his head. Thick black tubes—rubber or plastic—looped from one to the other and Alex wondered if he could unfasten them and make the flame go out. Would the balloon sink back down? Or would there be enough hot air in the envelope to keep it rising?

He examined the other metal boxes that sat, like a complicated stereo system, in the center of the platform. One box obviously controlled each radar dish. There was a tangled network of cables joining them all together. Each box had a single blinking light . . . currently yellow. The power was on. The dishes were primed. But the terahertz beams hadn't yet been activated. The fifth box was some sort of master control. This one had a window set into the surface, a digital readout. 820 . . . 830 . . . 840 . . . 850 . . . Alex watched as the altitude was measured and the balloon moved ever closer to the point of detonation.

He had to disconnect the dishes. And he had to do it before the balloon reached one thousand feet, before Nile arrived. How much time did he have? Very briefly, he considered somehow unfastening the rope that Nile was climbing. But even if it was possible, he would never be able to bring himself to do it, to kill someone in such a cold-blooded way. Mrs. Jones had been right about that. And anyway, it would take too long. No. The four twinkling lights were his targets. Somehow, he had to turn them off.

He got unsteadily to his feet and moved forward, the platform swaying slightly underneath him. For a moment he was afraid. Was the platform even designed to hold his weight? Move too fast and it might tip up and throw him off. He grimaced and edged forward. Apart from the hiss of the gas feeding the flame, the hot-air balloon was absolutely silent. Somewhere inside him, Alex wished he could simply sit back and enjoy the ride. The majestic envelope, soaring into the sky. The views of London. But he had perhaps less than a minute before Nile got there. And how long until the balloon reached the right height?

880 . . . 890 . . . 900 . . .

God. It was like being back in Murmansk again. Another digital counter, but that one had been going down, not up, and it had been attached to a nuclear bomb. Why him? Alex fell to his knees and reached out for the first of the cables.

He quickly examined it. It was thick, attached to the master control by a solid-looking socket. He tried unscrewing it, but it didn't move. He would have to tear it out, and in such a way that it would be impossible to reconnect. His hand closed around the wire and he pulled with all his strength. Nothing happened. The connections were too strong: metal screwed into metal. And the cables themselves were too thick. He needed a knife or a pair of scissors. He had nothing.

Alex leaned back and pressed his foot against the metal box. He strained backward, still gripping the cable, using his whole body weight. The balloon was still rising. The air seemed to be getting thinner. A wisp of cloud slid past—or maybe it was smoke from the fight below. Alex shouted through gritted teeth, his entire consciousness focused on the cable and its connection.

And suddenly it came free. Alex felt the cable tear. He fell backward, his head slamming into the side of the platform. Ignoring the new pain, he sat up. He could see the separate ends—the severed wires— sprouting out of his hands. There were deep welts in his palms. He had hurt his head. But when he looked around, he saw that one of the yellow lights had blinked out. One of the radar dishes was no longer functioning.

930 . . . 940 . . .

There were three left. And Alex knew he didn't have enough time to disconnect them all.

Even so, he lunged forward and grabbed hold of

the second. What else could he do? Once again, he pressed the flats of his feet against the side of the box. He took a deep breath . . .

. . . and something flashed in the corner of his eye. Instinctively, Alex threw himself sideways. The samurai sword, half a yard long, sliced the air so close to his face that he felt it. He realized that it had been aimed at his throat. But for the sun reflecting off the blade, he would have been killed.

Nile had reached the platform. He was standing in the corner, holding on to a rope. There had been two swords on his back—he had thrown only one of them. Now he reached for the other. Alex was lying flat. He couldn't move. There wasn't enough room to do anything. He was a sitting target, wedged between the metal boxes and the side of the platform. In front of him, the flame burned, carrying the balloon the last few feet.

980 . . . 990 . . . 1000.

The digital display flickered to the final figure. There was a buzzing sound inside the master control and the lights on the three remaining radar dishes changed from yellow to red. The system had activated. Terahertz signals were being beamed all over London.

Alex knew that inside him, in his very heart, the golden nanospheres had begun to break up.

Nile unsheathed the second sword.

Inside the church, Mrs. Rothman began to see that the battle was over and that she had lost. Her own men had fought well and they outnumbered the enemy— but they were simply outclassed. There had been many casualties and two more SAS units had arrived, providing backup for the first.

She could see the fighting outside. Everything was being relayed to her by a series of hidden cameras. It was right in front of her on the television monitors, one for every angle. The street had been torn apart. A wounded SAS man was being dragged away by two of his comrades, dust and debris leaping up as the surface was strafed by enemy fire. More soldiers were moving from doorway to doorway, lobbing grenades through the windows behind them. This was the sort of fighting the SAS had learned in Northern Ireland and—ironically—in Baghdad during the Iraq War.

The whole area had been cordoned off. Police cars had moved in from every direction. They couldn't be seen, but their sirens filled the air. This was London. It was the end of a working day. It was impossible to believe that something like this could really be happening here.

There was another explosion—closer this time. Thick smoke billowed over the open dome and paintwork rained down, flaking off the walls. Most of the Scorpia men had abandoned their positions, preferring to take their chances outside. A guard ran up to Mrs. Rothman, blood streaking his face.

"They're inside the church," he rasped. "We're finished. I'm leaving."

"You'll stay at your post!" Mrs. Rothman snapped.

"Forget that!" The guard spat and swore. "Everyone's gone. We're all getting out of here."

Mrs. Rothman looked nervous, afraid of being left on her own. "Then, please, let me have your gun," she said.

"Sure. Why not?" The guard handed his weapon to her.

"Thank you," she said, and shot him with a single, short burst.

She watched the man go sprawling—then went over to the television screens. The SAS were in the outer vestibule. She could see them laying plastic explosives against the fake brick wall. It was hard to be sure, but she fancied they would need rather more explosive than they were using. She had designed the wall and it was solid steel. Even so, they would get through it eventually. They wouldn't give up.

She glanced up at the balloon, now straining at the ropes, a thousand feet above London. She knew it had reached the correct height . . . the equipment inside the church had told her. In just one minute it would all be over. She thought of Alex Rider somewhere up above. All in all, it had been a mistake bringing him here. Why had she? To see him die, of course. She hadn't been there when John Rider had died and she wanted to make up for it. Miss the father, catch the son. That was why she had risked everything to bring Alex to the church and she knew the other members of the executive board of Scorpia would be less than pleased. But it didn't matter. The operation would succeed. The SAS were too late.

A huge explosion. The whole church shook. Three of the largest organ pipes keeled over and came crashing down. Brick and plaster fragments hung in the air. Half the television monitors had gone black. But the steel wall had held. She had been right about that too.

She threw the machine gun down and hurried to a door, built almost invisible into the wall of a side chapel. It was lucky that Mrs. Rothman was the sort of person who prepared for every eventuality—including the need to slip out without being seen.

The guard she had killed had been right. It was definitely time to go.

Alex lay on his back, his shoulders pressing against the wall of the platform. The first sword that Nile had thrown had sliced into the plastic floor, inches from his head, and it was still there, quivering, just beside his neck. Nile had brought out the second sword and was balancing it in his hand. He was taking his time. Alex knew that he had no need to hurry. He had nowhere to hide. One way or another, Alex was about to die. They were less than twelve feet apart. Alex had seen what Nile could do on the island of Malagosto. He knew that there was no way Nile could miss.

And yet . . .

Why was he so slow? Taking his time with the sword, still clutching the rope with the other hand . . .

Alex looked at him, examined the handsome, destroyed face, found himself searching for something in the man's eyes.

And found it.

That look. He had seen it before. He remembered Wolf, the soldier he had trained with in the SAS. And suddenly everything made sense. The secret weakness that Mrs. Rothman had mentioned. The reason why Nile had come second, not first, at Malagosto. He thought back to their meeting in the bell tower over the monastery. Nile had lingered at the door, unwilling to come forward, holding on to the frame in just the same way that he was holding on to the rope now. No wonder Nile had been so slow climbing up to the balloon.

Nile was afraid of heights.

But that wasn't going to save Alex. Fifteen seconds had passed since the lights had turned red, signaling that the dishes were now active. Already, the nanospheres with their poisonous cargo would be oscillating inside his heart. All over London, other children would be walking home, waiting for buses, pouring into tube stations, unaware of what was about to happen.

Then Nile spoke.

"This is what I promised would happen to you if you betrayed us," he said. The smile on his face might have been forced, but there could be no doubt about what he was going to do. He balanced the sword in the palm of his hand, feeling the weight before he aimed and threw. "I said I would kill you. And that's what I'm going to do, right now."

"Sure, Nile," Alex replied. "But how are you going to get back down?"

"What?" The smile faltered.

"Just look down, Nile," Alex went on. "Look how high we are." He glanced up at the flame and the envelope. "You know, I don't think this balloon is going to hold us both up."

"Shut up!" Nile hissed the words. The hand clutching the rope had gone whiter than ever. Alex could see the fingers clenching tighter and tighter.

"Look at the people! Look at the cars! See how tiny they are!"

"Stop it!"

And that was when Alex moved. He already knew what he was going to do. Nile was petrified, unable to react. All his speed and strength had become useless to him. With a gasp, Alex pulled out the first sword, freeing it from the plastic. In a single movement he swept up—slashing through the rubber pipe that fed the burner.

After that, everything happened very quickly.

The severed pipe coiled left and right like a

wounded snake. Propane gas in liquid form was still being pumped through, and as the severed end whipped past the burner, it ignited, becoming at once a huge ball of flame.

The pipe twisted back again and spat its deadly payload in the direction of Nile.

Nile had just managed to raise the second sword in the start of what would be a final throw. He was aiming at Alex's chest. Then the fireball hit him. He screamed once and disappeared. One second he was there, the next he had been blown into the air, a spinning, burning puppet of a man, falling to his death one thousand feet below.

And it looked as though Alex was about to follow him.

The entire platform was on fire, the plastic melting. There was burning liquid propane everywhere and it was dissolving everything it touched. Alex struggled to his feet as the flames licked toward him. What now? The burner had gone out, but the balloon didn't seem to be falling. The platform, however, would . . . and very soon. The four ropes holding it to the envelope were made of nylon and all four of them were on fire. One of them snapped and Alex cried out as the platform tilted, almost throwing him over the edge. His eyes darted to the machinery. The electric cables must be fireproof. The little red lights showed him that three of the dishes were still transmitting. More than a minute must have passed since Nile had appeared . . . surely! Alex pressed a hand against his chest, expecting to feel the stab of pain as the poison broke free and entered his system.

But he was still alive, and he knew he had just seconds left to get out of the burning platform. No chance of jumping down to safety. He was a thousand feet above the ground. He heard a snapping sound as a second rope began to sever. Only a few seconds remained. The fire was out of control. It was burning him. It was burning everything.

Alex jumped.

Not down—but up. He leaped first onto the control box and then up so that his hands caught the metal frame of the burner. He hauled himself up and stood. Now he could reach the circular skirt at the bottom of the envelope itself. It was incredible. Looking up, it was as though he was standing inside a huge, circular room. The walls were fabric, but they could have been solid. He was inside the balloon, imprisoned by it. He saw a nylon cord. It led all the way up to the parachute valve at the very top. Would it take his weight?

And then the remaining ropes holding the platform gave way. The platform fell, taking the burner and the radar dishes with it, disappearing from beneath Alex's feet. Alex just had time to wind the nylon cord around one hand and to grab hold of the fabric of the balloon with the other. Suddenly he was dangling. Once again his arms and wrists took the strain. He wondered if the balloon would crumple and fall. But most of the weight had gone. Only he was left. It stayed where it was.

Alex looked down. He couldn't stop himself. And he saw—in the middle of the fire and the smoke, the spinning platform, the falling ropes—that the three red lights had gone out. He was sure of it. Either the flames had destroyed the machinery or the dishes had deactivated themselves the moment they dropped below a thousand feet.

The terahertz dishes had stopped transmitting. Not one single child would die.

Nobody was sure where the bag lady had come from. Perhaps she had been sleeping in the small cemetery behind the Church of the Forgotten Saints. But now she had wandered into what, until a few minutes ago, had been a full-scale battle.

She was lucky. The SAS men had taken control of the church and the immediate area. Most of the Scorpia people were dead. The remainder had put down their weapons in surrender. A final explosion had given entrance to the church itself. SAS soldiers were already pouring in, searching for Alex.

The bag lady was obviously confused by all this activity. Possibly she was also drunk. There was a bottle of cider in one of her hands and she stopped to force the neck between her rotten teeth and drink. She had a hideous, withered face and hair that was long, knotted, and gray. She was dressed in a filthy coat, tied around her bulging waist with string. Her other hand clutched two garbage bags, which she was holding close to her, as though they contained all the treasure in the world.

One of the soldiers saw her. "Get out of here!" he yelled. "You're in danger here."

"All right, love!" The bag lady giggled. "What's the matter, then? It's like bleeding World War Three."

But she still shuffled off, out of harm's way, while the SAS men rushed past her, heading for the church.

Underneath the wig, the makeup, and the costume, Mrs. Rothman smiled to herself. It was almost incredible that these stupid SAS soldiers should let her walk away, slipping between them in plain daylight. She had a gun hidden under her coat and she would use it if anyone tried to stop her. But they were so busy rushing into the church, they had barely noticed her.

And then one of them called out.

"Stop!"

She had been seen after all. Mrs. Rothman hurried forward.

But the soldier hadn't been trying to arrest her. He had been trying to warn her. A shadow fell across her face and she looked up just in time to see a blazing rectangle with four radar dishes fall out of the sky. Julia Rothman opened her mouth to scream, but the sound never had time to reach her lips. She was crushed, driven into the sidewalk, flattened like a creature in some hideous cartoon. The SAS man who had called out the warning could only gaze at the burning wreckage in horror. Then, slowly, he looked up to see where it had come from.

But there was nothing there. The sky was clear.

Freed from the platform and the mooring ropes, the balloon had been blown north, with Alex still clinging underneath it. He was limp and exhausted. His legs and the side of his chest had been burned. It was as much as he could do simply to hang on.

But the air inside the envelope had cooled and the balloon was coming down. Alex had been lucky that, unlike the nylon ropes, the fabric of the balloon was flame-resistant.

Of course, he might still be killed. He had no control of the balloon at all and the wind might choose to steer him into a high-voltage wire. He had already crossed the river and could see Trafalgar Square with Nelson's Column looming up in front of him. It would be a sick joke to land there and end up getting run over.

Alex could only hang on and wait to find out what was going to happen. Despite the pain in his arms, he was aware of a sense of inner peace. Somehow, against all the odds, he had come through it all alive. Nile was dead. Mrs. Rothman was probably a prisoner. The nanospheres were no longer a threat.

And what about him? The wind had changed. It was carrying him to the west. Yes. There was Green Park—just two or three hundred feet below. He could see people pointing up at him and shouting. He silently urged the balloon to keep going. With a bit of luck, he might make it all the way to Chelsea, to his house, where Jack Starbright would be waiting. How much farther could it be? Did the balloon have the strength to take him there?

He hoped so, because that was all he cared about now.

He just wanted to go home.

19
DEEP COVER

It ended—inevitably, it seemed to Alex—in Alan Blunt's office on Liverpool Street.

They had left him alone for a week, but then the telephone call had come one Friday evening, asking him to come in. Asking, not telling. That was at least a change. And they had chosen a Saturday so he wouldn't have to miss school.

The balloon had dropped him on the edge of Hyde Park, lowering him to the grass as gently as an autumn leaf. It was the end of the day and by that time there were few people in the park. Alex had been able to slip away quietly, five minutes before a dozen police cars had come roaring in. It was a twenty-minute walk home and he had more or less fallen into Jack's arms before taking a hot bath, wolfing down dinner, and going to bed.

He wasn't badly hurt. There were burns on his arms and chest and his wrist was swollen where he had dangled from the balloon. Mrs. Rothman had also left her mark on his cheek. Looking at himself in the mirror, he wondered how he was going to explain the very obviously shaped bruise. In the end, he told everyone he had been mugged. In a way, he felt he had.

He had been back at Brookland for five days. Tom Harris had been one of the first people to see him crossing the school yard and had rushed over to see him. Tom had managed to get sunburned on the beach at Amalfi. His cheeks and the top of his nose were bright red.

"I knew you'd make it," he said. "I watched you do that BASE jump and it was sweet! You landed right on the roof. And then about five minutes later the whole place blew up. That was amazing. Was it you?"

"No. Not exactly."

"Jerry thought you might have been killed or captured or something, but then you phoned and you sounded a bit down, but at least you were still alive. And a couple of days later, Jerry got this humongous check to get a new parachute. Except it was about five times too much. He's in New Zealand now, thanks to you. BASE jumping off some building in Auckland. It was always his ambition." Tom took out a sheet of newspaper. "Was this you?" he demanded.

Alex looked down. It was a photograph of the hot-air balloon drifting over London. He could see a tiny figure clinging to the side. Fortunately, the picture had been taken from too far away to identify him. Nobody knew what had happened at the Church of the Forgotten Saints. And nobody knew he was involved.

"Yes," Alex said. "But Tom—you mustn't tell anyone."

"I've already told Jerry."

"No one else."

"Yeah. I know. Official secrets and all that." Tom frowned. "Maybe I should join MI6. I'm sure I'd make a great spy."

Alex thought of his friend now as he sat down opposite Alan Blunt and Mrs. Jones. He lowered himself slowly into the chair, wondering what they were going to say to him. Jack hadn't wanted him to come here at all.

"The moment they know you're capable of walking, they'll probably have you parachuting into North Korea," she had said. "They're never going to leave you alone, Alex. I don't even want to know what happened to you after Venice. But just promise me you won't let it happen again."

Alex agreed with her. He would have rather stayed at home. But he knew he had to be here. If nothing else, he owed it to Mrs. Jones.

"It's very good to see you, Alex," Blunt said. "Once again, you've done a very good job."

Very good. Very good. The highest praise Blunt knew.

"I'll just bring you up to date," Blunt went on. "I don't need to tell you that Scorpia's plot was a complete failure and I very much doubt that they'll try anything on this scale again. They lost one of their top assassins, the man called Nile, when he fell out of the balloon. How did that happen, by the way?"

"He slipped," Alex said. He didn't want to go over it again.

"I see. Well, you might like to know that Julia Rothman also died."

That was news to Alex. He had assumed she was being held by MI6.

Mrs. Jones took up the story. "The gondola from underneath the balloon fell on her as she was trying to escape," she said. "She was crushed."

"I'd have been disappointed too," Alex muttered.

Blunt sniffed. "The most important thing of all is that London's children are going to be safe. As that scientist—Dr. Stephenson—explained during COBRA, the nanoshells will slowly pass out of their bodies. I have to tell you, Alex, that the terahertz dishes were transmitting for at least seventy-five seconds. Possibly longer. God knows how close we came to a major disaster."

"I'll try to move a little faster next time," Alex said.

"Yes. Well. One other thing. You might be amused to hear that Mark Kellner resigned this morning. The prime minister's head of communications . . . remember him? He's telling the press that he wants to spend more time with his family. The funny thing is, his family can't stand him. Nobody can. Mr. Kellner made one mistake too many. Nobody could have foreseen that stunt with the hot-air balloon. But someone has to carry the can and I'm glad to say it's going to be him."

"Well, if that's all you called me in for, I'd better get home," Alex said. "I've missed two more weeks of school and I've got a lot to catch up on."

"No, Alex. I'm afraid you can't leave quite yet." Mrs. Jones sounded more serious than Alex had ever heard her and he wondered if she was going to make him pay for his attempt on her life.

"I'm sorry about what I nearly did, Mrs. Jones," he said. "But I think I've more or less made up for it. . . ."

"That's not what I want to speak to you about. As far as I'm concerned, your visit to my apartment never happened. But there's something more important. You and I have never talked about Albert Bridge."

Alex felt cold inside. "I don't want to talk about it."

"Why not?"

"Because I know what you did was right. I've seen Scorpia for myself now. I know what they were capable of. If my father was one of them, then you were right. He deserved to die."

The words hurt Alex even as he spoke them. They stung his eyes.

"There's somebody I want you to meet, Alex. He's come into the office today and he's standing outside. I know you don't want to spend any more time here than you have to, but will you let him talk with you? It will only take a few minutes."

"All right." Alex shrugged. He didn't know what Mrs. Jones wanted to prove. He had no wish to return to the circumstances of his father's death.

The door opened and a man walked in, bearded, with brown curly hair that was beginning to gray. He was casually dressed in a beaten-up leather jacket and jeans. He was about thirty years old, and although

Alex was sure he had never met him, his face seemed vaguely familiar.

"Alex Rider?" he asked. He had a soft, pleasant voice.

"Yes."

"How do you do." He held out a hand. Alex stood up and felt his hand taken in a grasp that was warm and friendly. "My name is George Adair," he said. "I think you've met my father. Sir Graham Adair."

Alex was hardly likely to forget. Sir Graham Adair was the permanent secretary to the cabinet office at 10 Downing Street. He could see the similarity in the faces of the two men. But he knew George Adair from somewhere else too. Of course. He was a lot older now. The hair color was different and he was more heavyset. But the face was the same. He had seen it on a television screen. On the bridge.

"George Adair is a senior lecturer at Imperial College here in London," Mrs. Jones explained. "But fifteen years ago he was a student. His father was already an extremely senior civil servant—"

"You were kidnapped," Alex interrupted. "You were the one Scorpia kidnapped."

"That's right. Look . . . do you mind if we all sit down? I feel very formal standing up like this."

George Adair took a seat. Alex waited for him to speak. He was puzzled and a little apprehensive. This man had been there when his father died. In a way, it was because of this man that John Rider had died. Why had Mrs. Jones brought him here now?

"I'll tell you my story and then get out of here," George Adair said. "When I was eighteen years old, I was the victim of an attempt to blackmail my father. I was snatched by an organization called Scorpia and they were going to torture me and kill me unless my dad did exactly what they said. But Scorpia made a mistake. My father could influence government policy but he couldn't actually change it. There was nothing he could do. I was told I was going to die.

"But then, at the last minute, there was a change of plan. I met a woman named Julia Rothman. She was very beautiful but a complete bitch. I think she couldn't wait to get out the red-hot pokers or whatever. Anyway, she told me that I was going to be exchanged for one of her people. He'd been captured by MI6. And they were going to swap us. On Albert Bridge.

"They drove me there very early one morning. I have to admit that I was terrified. I was certain there was going to be a double cross. I thought they might shoot me and dump me in the Thames. But everything seemed to be very straightforward. It was just like in a spy film. There was me and three men on one side of the bridge. They all had guns. And on the other side of the bridge, I could see a single figure. That was your dad. He was with some people from MI6." The lecturer glanced at Mrs. Jones. "She was one of them."

"It was my first major field operation," Mrs. Jones muttered.

"Go on," Alex said. He had been drawn in. He couldn't help himself.

"Well, somebody gave a signal and we began to walk together . . . almost as though we were going to fight a duel except that our hands were tied. I have to tell you, Alex. The bridge felt a mile long. It seemed to take forever to get across, but at last we met in the middle, your father and I, and I was sort of grateful to him because it was thanks to him that I wasn't going to be killed, and yet at the same time I knew he worked for Scorpia, so I thought he must be a bit of a scumbag.

"And then he spoke to me."

Alex held his breath. He remembered the video Mrs.

Rothman had shown him. It was true. His father and the teenager had spoken. He had been unable to hear the words and he had wondered what they had said.

"He was very calm," George Adair went on. "I hope you won't mind me saying this, Alex, but looking at you now, I can see him as he was then. He was totally in command. And this is what he said to me.

"*'There's going to be shooting. You have to move fast. Don't look around. Just run as fast as you can. You'll be safe.'*"

There was a long silence.

"My dad knew he was going to be shot?" Alex asked.

"Yes."

"But how . . . ?"

"Let me finish." George Adair ran a hand across his chin. "I took about another ten steps and suddenly there was a single shot. I know I wasn't meant to look around, but I did. Just for a second. Your father had been shot in the back. There was blood on his padded jacket. I could see a gash in the material. And then I remembered what he had told me and I began to run . . . hell for leather. I just had to get out of there."

That was another thing that Alex had noticed when he had seen the video. George Adair had reacted with amazing speed. Anyone else would surely have frozen. But he clearly knew what he was doing.

Because he had been warned.

By John Rider.

"I tore up the bridge," he went on. "Then all hell broke loose. The Scorpia people opened fire. They wanted to kill me, of course. But the MI6 lot had machine guns and they fired back. All in all, it was a miracle I wasn't hit. I managed to get to the north side of the bridge and a big car appeared out of nowhere. A door opened and I dived in. And that was just about the end of it, as far as I was concerned. I was whisked away and my own father met me a couple of minutes later. Hugely relieved. He thought he'd never see me again."

And that made sense. When Alex had met Sir Graham Adair, the civil servant had been surprisingly friendly. He had made it clear that he was in some way in Alex's debt.

"So my father . . . sacrificed himself for you," Alex said. But that didn't make sense. He still didn't understand what he was being told.

"There is one other thing I have to tell you," the man said. "It'll probably come as a shock to you. It certainly came as a shock to me. But, you see, about a month later, I went down to my father's home in Wiltshire. By then I'd been debriefed and there were a whole lot of security things I had to know about just in case Scorpia tried to have another crack at me. And . . ." He swallowed. "Your father was there."

"What?" Alex stared.

"I arrived early. And as I came in, your father was leaving. He'd been in a meeting with my dad."

"But that's—"

"I know. It's impossible. But it was definitely him. He recognized me at once. He asked me how I was. He said he was glad he'd been able to help me. And then he walked away."

"So my father . . ."

George Adair stood up. "I'm sure Mrs. Jones can explain it all to you," he said. "But my dad wanted me to tell you how very grateful we are to you. He asked me to pass that on. Your father saved my life, Alex. There's no doubt about it. I'm married now. I have two children. Funnily enough, I named the oldest one John after him. There would be no children if it hadn't been for him. My father would have no son and no grandsons. Whatever you may think of him, whatever you've been told about him, John Rider was a very brave man."

The lecturer nodded at Mrs. Jones and left the room. The door closed. There was a second long silence.

"I don't understand," Alex said.

"Your father wasn't an assassin," Mrs. Jones said. "He wasn't working for Scorpia. He was working for us."

"He was a spy?"

"A very brilliant spy," Blunt muttered. "We recruited the two brothers—Ian and John—in the same year. Ian was a good agent. But John was the better man by far."

"He worked for you!"

"Yes."

"But he killed people. Mrs. Rothman showed me. He was in prison. . . ."

"Everything Julia Rothman thought she knew about your father was wrong." Mrs. Jones sighed. "It's true that he had been in the army, that he had a distinguished career with the Parachute Regiment, and that he was decorated for his part in the Falklands

War. But the rest of it—the fight with the taxi driver, the prison sentence, and all the rest of it—we made up. It's called deep cover, Alex. We wanted John Rider to be recruited by Scorpia. He was the bait and they took him."

"Why?"

"Because Scorpia was expanding all over the world. We needed to know what it was doing, the names of the people it was employing, the size and structure of its organization. John Rider was a weapons expert. He was a brilliant fighter. And Scorpia thought he was washed up. They welcomed him with open arms."

"And all the time he was reporting to you?"

"His information saved more lives than you can imagine."

"But that's not true!" Alex's head swam. "Mrs. Rothman told me that he killed five or six people. And Yassen Gregorovich worshipped him! He showed me the scar. He said my dad saved his life."

"Your father was pretending to be a dangerous killer," Mrs. Jones said. "And so—yes, Alex—he had to kill. One of his victims was a drug dealer in the Amazon jungle. That was when he saved Yassen's life. Another of his victims was an Australian double agent.

A third was a corrupt policeman. I'm not saying that these people deserved to die. But certainly the world was able to get along very well without them and I'm afraid your father had no choice."

"What about the others?" Alex had to know.

"There were two other victims," Blunt cut in. "One was a priest working in the streets of Rio de Janeiro. The other was a woman in Sydney. They were more difficult. We couldn't let them die. And so we faked their deaths . . . in much the same way that we faked your father's."

"Albert Bridge—"

"It was faked." Mrs. Jones took up the narrative. "Your father had told us as much as we needed to know about Scorpia and we had to get him out. There were two reasons for this. The first was that your mother had just given birth to a baby boy. That was you, Alex. Your father wanted to get home. He wanted to be with you. But also it was becoming too dangerous. You see, Mrs. Rothman had fallen in love with him."

It was almost too much to take on board at once. But Alex remembered Julia Rothman talking to him at the restaurant in Positano.

"I was very attracted to him. He was a very good-looking man."

He tried to grasp at the truth through the swirling quicksand of lies and counter-lies. "She told me he was captured. In Malta . . ."

"That was faked too," Mrs. Jones said. "John Rider couldn't just walk out of Scorpia. They'd never have let him. So we had to arrange things for him. And that's what we did. He had been sent to Malta, supposedly to kill his sixth victim. He tipped us off and we were waiting for him. We staged a ferocious gun battle. You know what we're capable of, Alex. We did more or less the same thing for you with that multiple pileup on West Way. Yassen Gregorovich was there, in Malta, but we let him escape. We needed him to tell Julia Rothman what had happened. Then we 'captured' John Rider. As far as Scorpia were concerned, he would be interrogated and then either thrown back into prison or executed. They would never see him again."

"So why . . . ?" Alex still couldn't make complete sense of it. "Why Albert Bridge?"

"Albert Bridge was a bloody mess," Alan Blunt said. It was the first time Alex had ever heard him swear. "You've met Sir Graham Adair. He's a very powerful man. He also happens to be an old friend of mine. And when Scorpia took his son, I didn't think there would be anything I could do."

"It was your father's idea," Mrs. Jones went on. "He also knew the Adairs. He wanted to help. You have to understand, Alex. That's the sort of man he was. One day I want to tell you all about him—not just all this. He believed passionately in what he was doing. Serving his country. I know that sounds foolish and old-fashioned. But he was a soldier through and through. And he believed in good and evil. I don't know how else to put it. He wanted to make the world a better place."

She drew a breath.

"Your father suggested that we send him back to Scorpia as an exchange. He knew how Mrs. Rothman felt about him. He knew she would agree to anything to get him back. But at the same time, he planned to double-cross her. There was a gunman in place. But the gun was armed with blanks. John Rider had a squib in the back of his jacket. A little firework and a bottle of blood. When the shot was fired, he activated it himself. It blew a little hole in the back of his jacket. He went sprawling and pretended to be dead. It looked as though MI6 had killed him in cold blood.

But that's why I wanted you to meet George Adair just now. We never hurt your father, Alex. The idea was that now he would be safe again and he could simply disappear."

Alex buried his head in his hands. There were a hundred questions he wanted to ask. His mother, his father, Julia Rothman, the bridge . . . He was shaking and he had to force himself back under control. At last he was ready.

"I have just two questions," he said.

"Go on, Alex. We'll tell you anything you want to know."

"What was my mother's part in all this? Did she know what he was?"

"Of course she knew he was a spy. He would never have lied to her. They were very close, Alex. I never met her, I'm afraid. We don't tend to socialize very much in this business. She was a nurse before she married him. Did you know that?"

Ian Rider had told Alex that his mother had been a nurse, but he didn't want to talk about that now. He was simply building himself up, finding the strength to ask the worst question of all.

"So . . . is my dad still alive?" he asked. "And what about my mother? What happened to her?"

Mrs. Jones glanced at Alan Blunt and it was he who answered.

"After the affair on Albert Bridge, it was decided that it would be best if your father took a long vacation," he said. "Your mother went with him. We arranged a private plane to take them to the South of France. You were meant to go with them, Alex, but at the last minute you had an ear infection and they had to leave you behind with a nanny. The two of you were going to follow them out when you were better."

He paused. His eyes as ever showed nothing. But there was a little pain in his voice.

"Somehow Julia Rothman found out that she had been tricked. We don't know how. We'll never know. But Scorpia is a powerful organization. That much should be obvious to you by now. They found out that your father was still alive and that he was flying to France and they arranged for a bomb to be placed in the luggage. Your parents died together, Alex. I suppose that's something of a mercy. And it was all so quick. They wouldn't have had any idea . . ."

A plane accident.

That was what Alex had been told throughout his life.

Another lie.

Alex stood up. He wasn't sure what he was feeling. On the one hand, he was grateful. His father hadn't been an evil man. He had been the exact opposite. Everything Julia Rothman had told him and everything he had thought about himself had been wrong. But at the same time, there was an overwhelming sadness, as though he were mourning his parents for the very first time.

"Alex, we'll get a driver to take you home," Mrs. Jones said. "And we can talk more whenever you want."

"Why didn't you tell me?" Alex cried, and for the first time his voice cracked. "That's what I don't understand. I nearly killed you. But you didn't tell me the truth. You sent me back to Scorpia—just like my dad—but you never told me that it was Julia Rothman who killed him. Why not?"

"Because it would have been wrong." Mrs. Jones had also gotten to her feet. "We needed your help to find the radar dishes. There was no question about it. Everything depended on you. But I didn't want to manipulate you. I know you think that's what we always do, but if I'd told you the truth about Julia Rothman and then given you a homing device and sent you in after her, I'd have been using you in the worst possible way. You went in there, Alex, for exactly the same reason that your father went to Albert Bridge, and I wanted you to have that choice. That's what makes you such a great spy. It isn't that you were made one or trained to be one. It's just that in your heart you are one. I suppose it runs in the family."

"But I had a gun! I almost killed you . . ."

"I was never in any danger. Quite apart from the glass, you couldn't even bring yourself to aim at me, Alex. I knew you couldn't. There was no need to tell you then. And I didn't want to. The way Mrs. Rothman had tricked you was so horrible." She shrugged. "I wanted to give you the chance to work things out for yourself."

For a long moment nobody said anything.

Alex stood up. "I need to be on my own," he said.

"Of course." Mrs. Jones went over to him and touched him lightly on the arm. It was the arm that hadn't been burned. "Come back when you're ready, Alex."

"Yes—I will."

Alex moved to the door. He opened it but then seemed to have second thoughts. "Can I ask one final question, Mrs. Jones?" he asked.

"Yes. Go ahead."

"It's just something I've always wondered and I might as well ask now." He paused. "What's your first name?"

Mrs. Jones stiffened. Sitting behind his desk, Alan Blunt looked up. Then she relaxed. "It's Tulip," she said. "My parents were keen gardeners."

Alex nodded. It made sense. He wouldn't have used that name either.

He walked out, closing the door.

20

A MOTHER'S TOUCH

SCORPIA NEVER FORGOT.

Scorpia never forgave.

The sniper had been paid to take revenge and this is what he would do. His own life would be forfeited if he failed.

He knew that in a few moments, a fourteen-year-old boy would walk out of the building that pretended to be an international bank but was nothing of the sort. Did it matter to him that his target was a child? He had persuaded himself that it didn't. It's a terrible thing to kill a human being. But is it so much worse to kill a twenty-seven-year-old man who will never be twenty-eight than a fourteen-year-old boy who will never be fifteen? The sniper had decided that death is death. That didn't change. Nor did the fifty thousand dollars he would be paid for this hit.

As usual, he would aim for the heart. The target area would be smaller this time, but he would not miss. He never missed. It was time to prepare himself, to bring his breathing under control, to enter that state of calm before the kill.

He focused his attention on the gun that he was holding, the self-loading Ruger point 22 model K10/22PPF. It was a low-velocity weapon, less deadly than some he might have chosen. But the gun had two huge advantages. It was light. And it was very compact. By removing just two screws, he had been able to separate the barrel and the trigger mechanism from the stock. The stock itself folded in two. He had been able to carry the whole thing across London in an ordinary sports bag without drawing attention to himself. In his line of work, that was the critical thing.

He squared his eye against the Leupold 14x50mm Side Focus scope, adjusting the crosshairs against the door through which the boy would pass. He loved the feel of the gun in his hands, the snug fit, the perfect balance. He had had it customized to suit his needs. The stock was laminated wood with water-resistant adhesive, making it stronger and less likely to warp. The trigger mechanism had been taken apart and polished for a smoother release. Even the bullet he was using had been specially prepared. Manufactured by Eley, it was forty grains in weight and readily available

on the open market. But he had carefully drilled a
small hole in the head. The shock of air as the bullet
hit its target would cause as much damage as the bullet itself. The rifle would reload itself as fast as he
could fire it, but he would only need a single shot.

The sniper was perfectly content. When he fired,
for the blink of an eye, as the bullet began its journey
down the barrel, traveling at 1,085 feet per second, he
and the rifle would be one. The target didn't matter.
Even the payment was almost irrelevant. The act of
killing was enough in itself. It was better than anything in the world. In that moment, the sniper was
God.

He waited. He was lying on his stomach on the
roof of an office on the other side of the road. He was
a little surprised that he had been able to get access.
He knew that the building opposite him housed the
Special Operations division of MI6 and had supposed
that they would keep a careful watch on all the other
offices around. On the other hand, he had picked two
locks and dismantled a complicated security system
to get here. It hadn't been easy.

The door opened and the target appeared. If he
had wanted to, the sniper could have seen an attractive fourteen-year-old boy with fair hair, one strand

hanging down over his eyes. A boy dressed in a gray hooded sweatshirt and baggy jeans. A wooden bead necklace (he could see every bead through the scope). Brown eyes and a slightly hard, narrow mouth. The sort of face that would have attracted plenty of girls if the boy had only lived a little more.

The boy had a name, Alex Rider. But the sniper didn't think of that. He didn't even think of Alex as a boy. He was a heart, a pair of lungs, a convoluted system of veins and arteries. But very soon he would be nothing at all. That was why the sniper was here. To perform a little act of surgery—not with a scalpel but a bullet.

He licked his lips and focused all his attention through the gun. He wasn't holding the gun. The gun was part of him. His finger curled against the trigger. He relaxed, enjoying the moment, preparing to fire.

Alex Rider stepped out onto the street. It was about five o'clock and there were quite a few people around, mainly tourists arriving back in London at Liverpool Street Station. He was thinking about all the things he had been told in Alan Blunt's office. They still wouldn't quite register. It was just too much to take in. His father hadn't been an assassin. He had been a spy, working for MI6. John Rider and Ian Rider. Both spies. And now Alex Rider. At last, they were a family.

And yet . . .

Mrs. Jones had told him that she wanted him to make a choice, but he wasn't sure that the choice had ever been his. Yes, he had chosen not to belong to Scorpia. But that didn't mean he had to be a lifetime member of MI6. Alan Blunt would want to use him again. That much was certain. But maybe he would find the strength to refuse. Maybe knowing the truth at last would be enough.

All sorts of confusing thoughts were going through his mind. But he had already made one decision. He wanted to go home to Jack. He wanted to forget his homework and go out for a movie and a blowout dinner. Nothing healthy. He had said he would be home by six, but maybe he would call her and meet her at the multiplex on the Fulham Road. It was Saturday. He deserved a night out.

He took a step forward and stopped. Something had hit him in the chest. It was as though he had been punched. He looked left and right, but there was nobody close to him. How very strange.

And here was something else strange. Liverpool Street seemed to be running uphill. He knew it was

flat, but now it was definitely slanting. Even the buildings were leaning to one side. He didn't understand
what was happening. The color was rapidly draining
out of the air. As he looked, the world went from color
to black-and-white apart from a few splashes here and
there—the bright yellow of a café sign, the blue of a
car . . .

. . . and the red of blood. He looked down and was
surprised to see that his whole front had turned red.
There was an irregular shape that was spreading across
his shirt, widening by the second. At the same time, he
was aware that the sound of the traffic had faded. It
was as though something had pulled him out of the
world and he was only seeing it from a very long way
away. A few pedestrians had stopped and turned to
look at him. They were shocked. There was a woman
screaming. But she was making no sound at all.

Then the street played a trick on him, tilting so
suddenly that it almost seemed to turn upside-down.
A crowd had gathered. It was closing in on him and
Alex wished it would go away. There must have been
thirty or forty people, pointing and gesticulating. Why
were they so interested in him? And why couldn't he
move anymore? He opened his mouth to ask for help,
but no words, not even a breath, came out.

Alex was beginning to get scared. There was no pain at all, but something told him that he must have been hurt. He was lying on the sidewalk although he didn't know how he had gotten there. There was a red circle around him, widening with every second that passed. He tried to call for Mrs. Jones. He opened his mouth and did hear a voice, calling, but it was very far away.

And then he saw two people and knew that everything was going to be all right after all. They were watching him with a mixture of sadness and understanding . . . as though they had always expected this to happen but were still sorry that it had. There was a little color left in the crowd, but the two people were entirely black-and-white. The man was very handsome, dressed in military uniform, with close-cut hair and a solid, serious face. He looked very much like Alex although he appeared to be in his early thirties. The woman standing next to him was smaller and much more vulnerable. She had long, fair hair and eyes that were filled with sadness. He had seen photographs of this woman and he was astonished to see her here.

His mother.

He tried to get up, but he couldn't move. He

wanted to hold her hand, but his arms would no longer obey him. He wasn't breathing anymore, but he hadn't noticed.

The man and the woman stepped forward out of the crowd. The man said nothing. He was trying to hide his emotions. But the woman leaned down and reached out. Only now did Alex realize that he had been looking for her all his life. She reached out and touched him, her finger finding the exact spot where there was a small hole in his shirt.

No pain. Just a sense of tiredness and resignation.

Alex Rider smiled and closed his eyes.

Alex Rider Sweepstakes Official Rules and Entry Form

Official Rules for The Alex Rider Movie Sweepstakes. NO PURCHASE NECESSARY. A PURCHASE WILL NOT ENHA
YOUR CHANCE OF WINNING. Open to legal U.S. residents, ages 10 and up. How to Enter:
1. To enter The Alex Rider Movie Sweepstakes ("Sweepstakes"), please send a completed official entry form , or mail an index
in an envelope with your full name, parent's name (if a minor), mailing address, phone number and age to The Alex Rider M
Sweepstakes, Penguin Young Readers Marketing, Penguin Group (USA) Inc., 345 Hudson Street, New York, NY 10014. E
must be postmarked by May 10, 2006. No mechanically reproduced or computer generated entries allowed. Limit one ent
person. 2. Entries are void if they are in whole or in part illegible, incomplete or damaged. No responsibility is assumed fo
lost, damaged, incomplete, inaccurate, illegible, or misdirected entries. Void where prohibited by law. 3. If for any reaso
Sweepstakes is not capable of being conducted as described in these rules, Sponsor shall have the right to cancel, terminate,
ify or suspend the Sweepstakes. **Winner(s):** 1. From all eligible entries received, the winners will be chosen in a random dr
held on or about May 18, 2006 by Sponsor, whose decisions concerning all matters related to this Sweepstakes are final and
ing. 2. Winners will be notified by mail and/or e-mail. The odds of winning depend on the number of entries received. **Pri**
There will be one (1) grand prize winner, twenty-five (25) first prize winners and fifteen (15) third prize winners. 1. **Grand Prize**
Grand Prize winner will receive: • two tickets to one of the premieres of Alex Rider: Stormbreaker (Approximate Retail Value ("A
= $100) (the date and location of the premiere are tentatively set for August 2006 in New York or Los Angeles, but location and
subject to change) • two airplane tickets to the location of the premiere tentatively set for August 2006 in New York or Los Ang
but location and dates subject to change; winner must depart from a major U.S. airport hub and transportation to that hub
included in this prize (ARV = $700) • $1000 in cash to contribute toward any accommodation, transportation and meal expe
incurred during the trip. The Grand Prize winner is responsible for any expenses not expressly included in the prize descri
Airline travel must be made through Sponsor. The winner and his/her guest must travel together, and should a minor prize w
win the Grand Prize, the minor winner will be required to travel on the airplane and attend the premiere with a parent or
guardian, as well as generally be supervised by that same parent/guardian during the entirety of the trip. Winner may cho
accept the $1000 and is not obligated to travel to the premiere. (Total ARV = $1800). 2. **First Prize:** twenty-five (25) winne
receive: • An Alex Rider paperback library of books including Stormbreaker, Point Blank, Skeleton Key, Eagle Strike, and Sc
ARV: $39.95 • A signed copy of Ark Angel, the new hardcover Alex Rider book. ARV: $17.99 • Alex Rider logo patch ARV:
Second Prize: fifteen (15) winners will receive: • A signed copy of Ark Angel, the new hardcover Alex Rider book. ARV: $17
Alex Rider logo patch ARV: $5 4. In the event that there is an insufficient number of entries Sponsor reserves the right not to a
the prizes. **Eligibility:** This sweepstakes is open to legal U.S. residents, ages ten (10) or older. Employees, and their immediate
ily members living in the same household, of Sponsor its subsidiaries, affiliated and parent companies, or the agencies of a
them are not eligible for this sweepstakes. Void where prohibited by law. **General:** 1. No substitutions, transfers or assignm
of prizes allowed. In the event of unavailability, Sponsor may substitute a prize of equal or greater value. 2. All expenses, in
ing taxes on receipt and use of prize are the sole responsibility of the winners (and/or their parents or legal guardians). 3. Wi
(and/or their parents or legal guardians) may be required to execute an Affidavit of Eligibility and Release ("Affidavit"), which
be returned within fourteen (14) days of notification or another winner will be selected. Grand Prize winner's travel companion
sign and return a Release of Liability/Publicity Release prior to the issuance of travel documents. 4. By accepting the prize, w
(and/or their parents or legal guardians) grants to Sponsor the right to use his/her name, likeness, hometown and biographical
mation in advertising and promotion materials relating to the subject matter of this promotion, including posting on the Spon
websites, without further compensation or permission, except in TN and where prohibited by law. 5. By accepting a prize
ners (and/or their parents or legal guardians) release Sponsor, its subsidiaries, affiliated and parent companies or the adver
agencies of any of them from any and all liability for any loss, harm, injuries, damages, cost or expense, arising out of or relati
participation in this Sweepstakes or the acceptance, use or misuse of the prize. 6. Any dispute arising from this Sweepstake
be determined according to the laws of the State of New York, without reference to its conflict of law principles, and the en
consent to the personal jurisdiction of the State and Federal Courts located in New York County and agree that such courts
have exclusive jurisdiction over all such disputes. **Winners' List:** For the name(s) of the winner(s), send a self-addressed, sta
envelope by November 18, 2006 to: Penguin Young Readers Marketing, 345 Hudson Street, New York, NY 10014, Attn: Alex
Movie Sweepstakes Winner's List. **Sponsor:** Penguin Group (USA) Inc. 345 Hudson Street New York, NY 10014

Complete this entry form or hand print all of the
information listed below on an index card and send in an envelope t

Penguin Young Readers Group
Attn: Alex Rider Movie Sweepstakes
345 Hudson St. • New York, NY 10014

Your Name:

Your Parent's or Guardian's Name (if a minor):

Your Address:

City, State, Zip:

Phone Number: **Age:**